The Fringe Orphan

RACHEL MORRIS

THE FRINGE ORPHAN

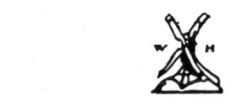

HEINEMANN : LONDON

William Heinemann Ltd
Michelin House, 81 Fulham Road, London SW3 6RB

LONDON   MELBOURNE   AUCKLAND

First published 1992
Copyright © Rachel Morris 1992

A CIP catalogue record for this book
is held by the British Library
ISBN 0 434 47914 4

Phototypeset by Intype, London
Printed in Great Britain
by Bookcraft Ltd., Midsomer Norton

DR H

· I ·

When Mattie came skating back across the black-and-white chequerboard lino it suddenly occurred to Hester where she'd seen her before. The foetus on the screen that morning, lying on its back and throwing wide its limbs, wriggling the length of its spine as it made itself comfortable. That same sense of luxury. That same buttery smoothness. That same awareness of its own good looks. 'Well, well,' the foetus had said, very pert and full of itself. Not at all like Hester. Not at all like its father. (Not that she thought much about him.)

The light in the pub was yellowy, the pews a dark brown wood like the pews of a church, Mattie black-eyed, black and white, glittering in half a dozen antique mirrors. Her hair was black and spikey, her earrings long, her smile brilliant. She wore a gold-embroidered skull cap and a black cape over some kind of pinkish dress which was draped across her bump. She put down the drinks on the table. 'What's in them?' asked Hester, picking hers up and sniffing it. 'Only a little vodka,' said Mattie. 'We're allowed to in the middle months.' And she sat down on the pew and arranged her limbs around her with more of that buttery smoothness.

Hester saw her reflection in the table top. Thin Shanks and Blue Stocking. She felt the improbable, luxurious baby turning over and over inside her. 'Pregnancy doesn't suit me,' she said sadly and Mattie didn't disagree but looked at her in silence and Hester saw in her eyes warm pity and knew that in hers Mattie saw only mirrors to reflect back her own good looks. Twenty-one, thought Hester, twenty-one if she's a day. A little warm and a little sour, thought Hester, mixing herself up like a drink – but more of the vinegar and not so much of the sugar – because I am thirty and six months pregnant and I am not happy at all.

They had been a roomful of pale women, weary and astonished at what had befallen them, so hugely pregnant that they filled the room from wall to wall. Their teacher fluttered amongst them, distributing her charts. She was a sad, plump, middle-aged woman called Judith whom they later discovered had a great faith in everything natural and the powers of mothers. They were there to learn the techniques of Natural Labour. Her children sulked and flounced their way about the house. They slammed doors and swore at her. They screamed and shouted and interrupted the classes. When the women lay quiet in relaxation they could hear the children banging and crashing above them. They wanted to know why their mother hadn't brought them this and that and the other – 'I forgot,' Judith would answer placatingly – and the women pitied her for these truculent, adolescent children, but they were not alarmed. They were kind but cool and rather ignorant and never once did they think that what had happened to Judith could ever happen to them.

'Well, well, fertility goddesses,' said Judith on that first day and she smiled at them bracingly. Hester thought this smile gave to her a rather tigerish look. The sunlight dazzled through the curtains. It turned them all to ghosts. Outside it was May, the season for high, white clouds and soft winds. The buddleias were springing forth from the city rooftops and in the gutters the rubbish which the winter rains had drenched now blew to and fro, bone dry and papery. In the garden a plum tree blossomed, round as a globe and of a

· 2 ·

pinky-white, extravagant softness. 'Now, introductions,' said Judith and one by one they gave their names: Leonie, Lindie, Caroline, Barbara and Hester, offering themselves up to the group, so transparent in the sunlight they were hardly there at all.

She asked them to lie back, to shut their eyes and empty their minds. 'I want you to feel peace spreading upwards from your toes,' she said, but when Hester shut her eyes she felt only the baby flip-flopping on top of her like a fish in a tank, and the hormones of pregnancy which were rising up as steadily as the waters of a flood. Marooned, thought Hester. Cut off from all my men and all the men in all the world and all the non-pregnant women also. And she thought of it as a kind of primaeval mud which was silting up her mind, leaving only the smallest of bright, clear channels through which the stream of her inner consciousness might still flow − commenting, questioning, perceiving − for as long as she could remember; but now, only just.

Flip-flop went the thoughts inside her, like fish in the small channel, not at all peaceful. Henry, moon-faced Henry, who was the father of her baby, a soft man; and Frank who should have been the father but was not, a thin, hollow-chested man, the heart beating loudly inside; and I, Hester, who was once such a long-legged, dangerous, bluestocking lady, such a smartarse, know-all, Oxford graduate, and thought I always would be, time without end, amen . . .

And then across her thoughts the doorbell rang and Judith got to her feet with a sigh and a minute later, through Hester's half-closed lids, Mattie on the threshold of the room, as brown and pink and red, entirely vivid, as the rest of them were pale and wan. She was prettier than them. She was all their younger sisters rolled together. 'Hallo,' she said. 'Introductions? Oh, my name's Mattie Thomas,' and she added with naive melodrama, bestowing her brilliant smile to left and right, 'I'm an unmarried mother.'

But the women all looked away.

· 3 ·

She sat down next to Hester and Hester felt how different they were, as if this girl had put her firmly back into her own body, for Hester was pale, blonde, angular and severe, with frizzed-out hair and a red gash of lipstick and a beaky nose, as if the flesh had all left her face and gone down into the stomach; but Mattie's huge belly seemed to send the flesh the other way, outwards to her extremities, to plump her face and round her arms and legs agreeably. She leant across and whispered, 'Can I share your mat? I forget everything these days. Are you the same too? I've even forgotten your name.' 'Hester,' said Hester. Mattie nodded and stared at the teacher. Her smile was so brilliant she even appeared to be smiling when her face was straight. She whispered back again, 'I intend to have all the painkillers I can get hold of.'

'Now,' said Judith, cutting across their whispers. She was settling herself down on her big bottom and smiling nervously round. 'Today I want to talk about why we became pregnant.' And then she smiled and added, 'Having babies is such a mysterious and wonderful experience,' but even as she said it Hester saw her tears begin to form (and this was to be the case in every class thereafter).

Judith believed as an article of faith that they should all express their feelings. Perhaps this was because her own were so sad and inexpressible she hoped that them expressing theirs might work a sympathetic magic and make her feel better also. And Mattie inclined towards sincerity – she was too overwhelmed by her emotions to be anything else – but the other women were English and embarrassed and drew closer to each other, feeling friendship begin to flower in mutual, shared dismay at this woman's tears and the way she would intrude.

The girl opposite Hester began to talk. She was a big girl with a face that had a kind of rubbery prettiness about it and the vestiges of an air of competence, decidedness and good sense as if she could still remember, just, that complacent belief that all things are possible if only you are sensible and

· 4 ·

work hard enough. She spoke with a fluttering of hands as if the tatters of commonsense still blew around her. She said that what with mortgages and careers and promotions and the price of houses being what they were she and Michael had simply decided that now was the right time. 'Well, you have to do it some time,' said the girl next to her. Her face had a mournful expression. She wore a trilby on her head like a last concession to style. In that hat she looked like a big, old-fashioned cowgirl.

How they lied! Only Mattie listened intently as if trying to feel her way into the conversation, her eyes going from one mouth to the next and her gaze fixed on them earnestly, as if she were reading their lips. It was as if she was trying to sort things out in her head, her brain working overtime, her mind looking backwards down through the years at everything that had ever happened.

Hester lay back on Judith's carpet. She heard the traffic in the street and Judith saying, 'Let's talk about how our lives have changed now that we're pregnant,' and the girl in the trilby saying in her light, complaining voice that once she had known hundreds of men but now it seemed she only knew women. And all at once Hester began to line them up, the hundreds of these men – Oh, how literal-minded I am, thinks Hester – and she wondered how well the girl had known them and how many she had loved and how many had loved her and whether her husband was really the one she had loved or whether that was someone else entirely . . . and then another woman whose name was Barbara said, 'It's a sign of things to come.'

Hester had met this woman on the steps just before the class began, had looked her up and down, and thought she saw in a flash what she was and in part pitied her for it and in part did not, such a big-boned, lumpish woman she was, with stringy hair and acned skin and piano legs. But Barbara had looked back, cool as a cucumber, which Hester had admired, and had said, 'Are you going to the class too? No one seems to be answering. Do you think we've got the right day?' and with a satisfying gesture because it was so cool and ironic and altogether at odds with her lumpish body, Barbara had leant forward and raised her brows and lifted the letter box and peered into its depths. 'No, I think someone's coming,' she had said and she had straightened up with aplomb and demurely settled the handbag before her in the manner of the Queen.

Which had made Hester laugh. This woman interested her because she had an air of being interesting to men. There and then Hester decided she wanted to talk with her but Barbara vanished that day just as soon as the class was over, as did a slight-looking girl whose name was Lindie; and then the girl who had talked about mortgages (whose name was Caroline) asked the girl in the trilby (whose name was Leonie) if she wanted a lift and the two of them vanished together, and that was how Mattie and Hester came to be left high and dry together on the pavement.

They sat facing each other on their wooden pews. Outside the sunshine and the light wind blew together and the men sprawled and laughed and drank and laid claim to the pavements. The darkness in the pub was brown and nicely alcoholic. Between them the lampshade swung in the wind.

'God, I'd like a cigarette,' said Mattie. 'Well, you can't,' said Hester, for the vodka was sweetening up her sournesses and sending her spirits soaring. What a slinky creature her baby had been, happy, not like herself who was prone to gloom but wriggling over and over. It had even had its thumb in its mouth and the memory of this was so sweet for Hester it was making her heart jump in her throat and the pee rush to her bladder. 'When this baby's born I shall smoke like a chimney,' said Mattie. 'Even that's not really allowed,' said Hester. 'All kinds of things are not allowed for mothers,' said Mattie sadly, but still those glittery mannerisms didn't stop, and that brilliant smile which ebbed and flowed, up to her eyes and back again.

Like Christmas presents, thought Hester. That's how the vodka was wrapping up their lives and she noticed that it made Mattie full of a hopeful vanity for she was leaning across the table as far as her huge belly would permit and, picking at the crisps, was asking, 'Do you ever imagine people talking about you, Hester, saying nice things?' 'No,' said Hester truthfully. And then Mattie said, 'Have you ever noticed how even the most terrible childhood can sometimes afterwards seem beautifully sad?' 'So did you have an unhappy childhood?' asked Hester slyly. 'Horrible,' said Mattie without irony. She was very young.

And then, which was even better, the vodka made them frank and amused and abusive towards each other. 'I suppose you think it's men who've ruined your life?' said Mattie scornfully and Hester said, 'Of course,' although the fact is any outsider would think she had ruined Henry's life and not the other way about. But Mattie scoffed and said, 'You're just being conventional. It's fashionable to blame men, that's all. Personally, I blame my family.'

And lastly it brought them to confessions. 'Where do you live, Hester?' asked Mattie – she was quizzing Hester on her life – 'I suppose you're married?' ('No.') 'Why did you become pregnant, Hester?' (Shrug.) 'Did you mean to have this baby?' (Further shrugs.) – and supplying answers to her questions as she went along. Her conversation was bumpy and precipitous, as if forever falling into sincerity. She said, 'I live with my cousins in one of those big houses at the back of Albany Street. They're designers. They're very beautiful. They're called the Oaklands. I suppose really this is their baby.' And dimly Hester perceived complaints.

She shut her eyes for a second and immediately she had one of those dreams of pregnancy to which she had become so prone (for it was as if pregnancy was dissolving the

· 7 ·

strong sinews which held her mind together and dreams kept floating off it). She dreamt it was the haunting baby who had done this to them, that it was a child glimpsed at the end of a restaurant, a child seen through a shop window, a child in his parents' arms, staring down at them, causing their flesh to prickle, entering into their dreams; a terribly pretty, large-eyed creature with rosebud mouth and curls on the nape of his fluted neck and bracelets and anklets of flesh – but then she thought, perhaps he only looks like that to me, Hester, who am so bony and so angular, because I so badly want something to come out of me which is plumper and more lovable than myself.

She dreamt they looked around for a man to be a father to their babies, that they began to nag for bigger flats and for bigger mortgages, that they asked for promotion at work because they needed more money, that they were making their preparations, the years moving in one direction, the haunting child blowing from the other corner. This was her dream, that they were bowed down to the inevitability of his coming, that it was their Common History. But in her dream the big girl with the rubbery face said, matter-of-fact, 'But that's biology, that's all you're talking about, biology.'

And then Hester heard Mattie say, 'I became pregnant because I wanted to give a present to my family,' and at this Hester opened her eyes and stared at Mattie curiously. She felt friendship begin to trickle warmly down inside her. She thought how often it is like this, a one-sided, passing, unexpressed and never-to-be-expressed admiration for something that someone else has said or done.

Because as soon as she said it Hester knew that she herself had become pregnant because she wanted to give a present to her father.

And perhaps Mattie saw the change in Hester's expression for she clutched at her huge stomach. 'My neurotic baby,' she said, scratching at its soft underside and Hester saw the shine of her eyes, her alarm and her expression which was frightened and guilty but pleased with herself.

· 8 ·

· 2 ·

When Mattie said goodbye to Hester she took a bus to Tufnell Park where she set off walking up the hill as strongly as her huge belly would permit. An old man sat on the corner selling newspapers. Beyond him the massy clouds were gathering at the top of Dartmouth Park. These clouds were dark and full-bellied and had a monumental quality which made Mattie think of depictions of the end of the world. She stopped and stared. She stood, as was her habit, with her chin in the air and as if she had her face in profile whichever way you looked at her. The cars rushed past. The old man sat and stared. Mattie just stood there and thought of disasters. Not one, nor two, nor even half a dozen, but a chain of disasters running back and forth across the world and growing hourly more terrible. The clouds were heaped up like an architectural folly. Mattie thought of tower blocks consumed by flames and chasms opening up to swallow whole cities. She thought of storms rolling and ships sinking and there being left only ashes and embers and the last thin little flames creeping amongst them, whilst overhead the clouds gathered massively in just such a blue, inhuman sky as this. An aberration, thought Mattie, that's what her girlhood had been, an aberration and a detour on her way from an angry childhood to an angry adulthood. Once when Mattie was little on the day of her spelling test she had prayed for the apocalypse. I am the Lord of Hosts, said

Mattie angrily – but her smile was as brilliant as ever – the Destroyer of Nations.

Eight sessions. Eight times she had been to see the therapist. That first time she had been early for her appointment. She had turned left down one street and right up another. Twice she had made this circuit. She had dodged across a road when the lights were amber and her fashionable winter coat flew back to show her legs. These were long and rather startling and her heels that day were very high. She hadn't looked at all pregnant. The driver of a red Allegro hooted and Mattie wished the apocalypse on him also. Goodbye to us all. That's what Mattie wanted.

'Ill wishing,' said Mattie's mother in her head. 'The worst thing that could happen to us would be to have our wishes granted.'

Oh my mama, thought Mattie. You whose wishes were rarely granted, this was exactly the kind of crap you would say. But nonetheless she looked over her shoulder to see that the Allegro was still on the road. And saw it speeding confidently away. She should have destroyed it for ever.

'You are angry,' said Dr H on that first day. 'We must find out why you are so angry.'

Dark, dark, dark, amidst the blaze of noon, thought Mattie, looking around at Dr H's study but keeping her mouth tight shut in case Dr H might think she was mad; or, worse still, ascribing too much grandeur to herself. For Dr H looked to her like a cutter-down-to-size.

What am I doing here? thought Mattie. Whose idea was it that I should go to a therapist? Not mine, certainly.

The idea of Dr H came up at Christmas after Mattie told her cousins, the Oaklands, that she was pregnant. They listened, went away and then came back – at least one of them came back on behalf of them all; it was Noah, of course, who always acted as a go-between for the Oaklands with the world. They thought that perhaps Mattie was depressed and needed to talk to someone. But what could they mean by this?

There is something very un-Oaklandish about therapy, that confession that things are amiss with the personality. Mattie supposed that Dr H had been Noah's idea – he being the most but also the least Oaklandish of them all, being less clannish and in-turned than the rest of them – and that the idea having thus been conceived would have spread in silence to the others. For an idea planted in one Oakland head always grew in them all. The telepathy between the Oaklands was quite extraordinary.

But the angrier Mattie grew the more obedient she became. And so she agreed to talk to Dr H but dressed herself in black for that first visit; black sweater, black leggings, black high heels, black overcoat, even a black beret on the back of her head. She had stepped like a professional mourner into Vanessa Oakland's kitchen early on a Thursday morning and Vanessa had looked up from the wealthy litter of her breakfast things – for the Oaklands created the prettiest, albeit the most expensive, domestic litter of anyone that Mattie had ever met – and registered, sadly, Mattie's blackness. Vanessa didn't like black, or at any rate not the dusty, rusty variety that Mattie was now wearing.

Vanessa's bosom in the mornings was very white and soft, her reddish hair falling in curls and tendrils to her shoulders. A spring crocus grew in a pot upon the breakfast table. Mattie thought that Vanessa's bosom was like a spring crocus. Vanessa's dressing gown was made from one of her own fabrics. Its colours were yellow ochre with flecks of pink and mauve. Gauguin colours. The Oaklands made things. They were architects, furniture makers, fabric designers, makers of clothes and carpets and glass, and everything they made was beautiful. What the Oaklands made was sold in Harrods and Liberty's and Sloane Street, and was collected by the V. & A. and in New York by the Museum of Modern

Art. The colours of the Oaklands were particularly extraordinary. Mattie's blackness hurt their eyes.

And nor – since she didn't really believe in anger and confusion and muddle and resentment – did Vanessa entirely understand the existence of Dr H. But nonetheless she reached across and drew a wad of notes from out of her sequinned purse. Which Mattie took in her chapped, spring hands and pocketed with guilty satisfaction. Vanessa was Mattie's cousin. Vanessa was generous as all the Oaklands were.

Dr H was obsessed by mothers. 'Listen,' said Mattie impatiently on that first day, peering short-sightedly at the therapist, 'my parents aren't relevant. I mean, obviously I know about Freud and all that and the importance of parents in general, but I don't have anything in common with my mother. I suppose if anyone's relevant it's my cousins. So why don't we talk about the Oaklands?' And in saying this she did not mean to be unhelpful, it was just that the thought had come to her quite suddenly that the Oaklands were not creators, not all their generosity and their beautiful creations withstanding. The Oaklands are thieves, says Mattie, vivid, colourful thieves.

But she thought the therapist was annoyed by her interruption. He was a small, dark-haired man, with olivey skin, full lips and round, dark eyes. He leant back in his chair and put the tips of his fingers together in what Mattie thought of as a masculine kind of way. From time to time he leant forward and wrote in a notebook with a small, gold-capped pencil. His legs were spindly and his trousers a little flared. He must have been fifty or so. Was this the stuff that saviours were made of?

'Very well,' said the therapist. 'The Oaklands, then. You say they are your cousins?'

'Yes,' said Mattie, and she added promptly, too promptly – she had been rehearsing her life as orphans will, as if it were a story, hoping she was the heroine – 'My mother and

Vanessa Oakland were first cousins, their mothers being sisters. This family of the two sisters was very arty and bohemian but Vanessa's mother married into money and my mother's mother didn't. They're all very beautiful in Vanessa's family. They have this reddish hair and lots of money. I came to live with them when I was sixteen. It was my idea. It was to do my A levels. Now I work in an art gallery.' And then Mattie fell silent.

It seemed to her that Dr H raised his brows. But he only said, 'And before that you lived with your mother?'

'Yes,' said Mattie, thinking he was obsessed by mothers.

'And your father?'

'He's dead. He died when I was six.'

'You were not going to complete strangers, of course,' observed Dr H, 'but nonetheless if your mother was all you had it must have been difficult for you to leave her.'

'Not really,' said Mattie, 'not at all.' And Dr H wrote this down also.

'And how often do you see your mother now?'

'Not often. She's mad. I mean, clinically so. It's not my imagination. She's a schizophrenic.'

'Oh, my God,' said Dr H, after a pause.

'You see,' said Mattie, 'if I tell you about my childhood you'll think I'm neurotic. I mean, what else could I be?'

To which Dr H replied, very shortly, 'I shall be the judge of that.'

His fingers were spread out upon one leg, long, squared-off fingers which between the joints grew very narrow. A junky wedding ring sat loosely on his mottled third finger. He's not at all good-looking, thought Mattie, gazing at him with her habitual air of frank and friendly superiority, and she tried to imagine what kind of woman would marry a man like him. How peculiar not to care what you look like, thought Mattie, gazing at the therapist's flared trousers which were short enough to show his bony ankles. Even in her present distress she was feeling weak tremors of com-

· 13 ·

placent pleasure at the sight of her slender fingers and her reflection in the glass of the picture on the wall.

'My mother and I aren't really alike,' said Mattie after a while on that first day, regretting the silence.

Dr H raised his brows.

'My mother's very introverted. She's not very worldly. She likes to be on her own. It's probably to do with the madness. But the Oaklands are very sociable and gregarious. And also, of course, they're rich. Whereas my mother and I were very poor. I'm really just the poor cousin,' said Mattie with a laugh.

'That can't have been very easy for you.'

Mattie was silent. How stupid understatement is, she thought.

'You've stressed to me how rich the Oaklands are,' observed Dr H.

'Only because it's part of them. It explains what they're like. The rich aren't like us.'

'As someone else once said,' said Dr H drily.

'F. Scott Fitzgerald. And it's true. At least it's true of the Oaklands. And the other thing about my cousins is that they have this thing about beauty. They like everything to look good. They're not snobs exactly. It's just that beauty gets them going, makes them laugh and smile and talk.'

Dr H looked unimpressed. Mattie tried to explain.

'My cousins are interior designers. Not the fashionable, amateur, snobbish kind but the real thing. The very real-est of real things. The Oaklands would never make anything which wasn't beautiful. Vanessa designs fabrics. Tom used to be an architect but now he makes furniture. Noah's joined the company, Aaron's making clocks now but Jonathan's still at art school. This belt I'm wearing. See. Jonathan did that.'

And Mattie wriggled her long body so that Dr H might see and admire her talented cousin's creation.

'And do you like to think of yourself as beautiful too?'

· 14 ·

asked Dr H slyly. Mattie wouldn't answer. She looked around at Dr H's study where there was nothing which was beautiful: not the walls which were beige, nor the curtains which were blue, nor the carpet which was brown. What would her friends think of her, going to a therapist? What am I doing here? thought Mattie, who could be as Oaklandish as they come.

'So why do you think you are here?' asked Dr H.

'I don't know. My cousins suggested it,' said Mattie dismissively. And at this Dr H had said, his eyes as round and dark and hard as pebbles, 'You are angry. We must find out why you are so angry.'

· 3 ·

But she couldn't keep it up.

She would have liked to have been constant. In the months when she first discovered anger she thought, well, this is it now, for the rest of my life, now I will always be angry. And this thought gave her a certain perverse pleasure, for there is a kind of grandeur in being constant, and something grown-up about having discovered anger at last. I've always been too prone to love, said Mattie to herself, but not any longer. And she eyed up the Oaklands with her new, cold, mordant eye and was pleased to see how icy-cold and clear and rinsed the world appeared when seen through the eyes of anger. But then, just when she was getting used to anger and becoming accustomed to its obsessions, how her mind would keep spinning on and on and round and round the subject of the Oaklands, those glittering, clannish, sparkling Oaklands, that Ali-Baba-and-the-forty-thieves-family-of-Oaklands – then she felt the anger slipping away – she had hardly held on to it for more than a month – and the old feelings creeping back into their places, so that sometimes she thought with sadness, and at other times with a kind of ferocious reproach, I'm not very good at anger. I am melodramatic. I can indulge in all its theatrical manifestations but the core of it I cannot maintain. Too late, Dr H, too late.

In the week preceding her third visit to the therapist she felt the change come over her. She was like a piece of meat which has started to cook and from which sadness was now rising up like steam from all its softening sinews. He had been poking about in her past, stirring up feelings which had lain dormant for many years. I only ever wanted someone to ask, thought Mattie plaintively, and she started to think more kindly of Dr H. She was aware of a soft, enfeebling sensation and a propensity towards falling in love. She began to fall in love with strangers on the underground.

On her way to Dr H she changed trains at Camden Town and stood on the platform watching a pair of twins playing. They had straight, blond hair and the alert, enquiring expressions of young animals. They were whispering to each other as they played a complex game of Push-Me-Pull-You. A young man lounged up against the wall. He was unshaven and wore a cravat around his neck. As Mattie paced up and down she gave him quick, short-sighted, surreptitious glances. When she was sure that he was staring at her she stared back at him with the full force of her contempt, which she reserved for men who looked at her uninvited. But mixed up in this contempt was also hope that he might after all turn out to be the man of her dreams, and her ambivalence gave to her short-sighted gaze a dark, dramatic, pleading look.

She ducked her head. She ran one finger – a trick she had – down her slender nose. Mattie was in pursuit of love. But the man who was a tramp was very drunk and only lounged and grinned and raised his bottle defiantly at her. For in her long, dark overcoat he mistook her for an undertaker.

The twins grew bored of their game and took to cuddling and grooming, their arms around each other's necks, their feet scuffing the ground between them. Their limbs moved in unison, with a skill they had clearly acquired together in the womb. Mattie stopped pacing and watched them. The tramp grew closer to her, thinking perhaps he had a tryst with death. The twins stopped their cuddling and gazed at the adults with rapt expressions. But Mattie moved away in

· 17 ·

distaste, not only because she saw the man was a tramp but because in any case it was a convention of Mattie's life to despise any man who might pursue her. 'Oh, so-and-so's been after me for years,' she would say in contempt, but the truth was, more humble than she seemed, she thought any man who wanted her couldn't be worth having. Mattie liked to do the pursuing. Barry Shawcross had wanted to marry her but she wouldn't marry him – during all the times she'd gone out with him she'd never stopped pursuing love at all.

When Mattie stepped out of the lift at Tufnell Park she looked down at her watch and saw to her dismay it had stopped. She shook it but nothing happened. Then the years fell away from her. She was a ten-year-old child again who fears she is late for school. She ran out of the station and came to a halt in front of an old man who sat there all day selling newspapers. A man in front of her was buying *The Times*. The newspaper vendor was very ugly but suddenly Mattie wanted to be liked by him. She hung her head. She smiled. She looked wide-eyed at this old man whom on previous occasions she had wished into oblivion. She opened her mouth but he opened his and quick as a flash said, 'I sell newspapers. I don't give directions nor tell people the time.' And he looked up at her with all the sadism which the old can sometimes muster towards the young.

Mattie hunched her shoulders. She set off up the road. When she looked in a shop window she saw in the corners of her eyes the tears poised, quivering and lustrous. They mirrored the paste diamond earrings which hung from her ears. She wiped the tears away. She didn't believe in tears. A scrawny little blonde woman hurried past with her face puckered up to the wind. Mouseface, sheepface, thought Mattie savagely. Her nerves were shot to pieces by the wails of the small child whom the blonde woman was hauling.

Dr H lived in a tall, Victorian house towards the top of Dartmouth Hill. When he opened the door Mattie greeted him by chattering loudly and inconsequentially about the weather whilst throwing off her coat with much ado, shaking her earrings and drawing off her gloves from her fingers, one by one, for all the world as if she were arriving for dinner in Knightsbridge. Mattie's affections often took the form of this feeling of cheerful superiority. Now she felt not only a small affection for the therapist, but also astonishment that Dr H's wife, whose photograph she noticed on the wall, could dress so badly. I wouldn't be seen dead . . . thought Mattie, for Mrs H was a small, square woman who dressed sensibly in a skirt and jumper. Her nose was too short and turned up wrongly, her mouth was full but not pretty, she had dark, greying hair and hands which were too large and which hung down peacefully on either side of her. As he took her coat, Mattie saw that the backs of Dr H's hands were flecked with moles and other lesions of the skin.

'Christ,' said Mattie, laughingly, in her best, social voice, 'it's so cold outside I wanted to die.' But Dr H held Mattie's coat in silence – it was longer than his own small body – and laid it across a chair, whilst evidently considering Mattie's remark in all seriousness, and Mattie's chatter faded into nothing.

Next Mattie realised that after all she liked Dr H and wanted Dr H to like her. They sat down in the study. It was on the ground floor at the back of the house and looked out onto a London garden, shadowy now that the sun had moved round to the front, and filled with the naked branches of the shrubs arching to and fro in a kind of green gloom across the loamy London clay; overhead lived Dr H's unseen family. Mattie made small talk, asking Dr H whether he had any children and wondering as she did so what they would be like. Were they good children? What was it like being a child of Dr H and what did women see in a man like him? But Dr H said, 'Let us talk about you, shall we?', his face set in implacable opposition, and Mattie felt manoeuvred back into silence.

She shut her eyes to see what she would feel, and felt the

· 19 ·

warm, sweet trickling sensation which she knew of old, starting at the top of her head and dripping downwards through her body. Once, when she'd been eighteen, she'd fallen in love – seriously in love – with three different men in the space of a month, one by one of course, and each of them aged between forty-five and sixty. She was very prone to loving older men. Down ran this sweet feeling, a languishing, obedient feeling, down through the veins of her body. I only ever wanted someone to ask, she thought.

She was feeling quite peculiar, both hot and very cold. As hot as steam, as cold as ice. Great icebergs are floating inside me, thought Mattie, and so unhappy is my gaze that it frosts up each object that it falls upon, so that even the Oaklands, those objects of desire, stand forth in all their cold splendour. But unhappiness is hot as well as cold and I am warm through the warmth of remembering my terrible childhood – although why unhappiness should be warm I do not know – as well as because of this unfashionably obedient love for older men; any older man would do. My mother was very prone to sadness. If you'd laid her out upon a table and cut her into two with a saw you would have seen inside her, in the very marrow, unhappiness like a silver thread. The tendency to unhappiness. My mother had it from the time she was a child and never got rid of it. It is inheritable, of course, like poverty, to which we are also very prone. If you cut me open what you'd see inside is anger and sadness and this sweet, obedient love for surrogate fathers. But not so much anger, thought Mattie, more unhappiness instead. And she opened her eyes.

'Too late,' she said out loud and when Dr H looked startled she went on, 'I mean, to talk about anger. You said we were going to find out why I am so angry, but the thing is that I am not any longer.' And she added to herself, but silently, I am unhappy instead. But she wouldn't say it out loud. He was a therapist. Let him find out for himself.

'I doubt that your anger has vanished altogether,' said Dr

· 20 ·

H. 'Oh, but it has,' said Mattie, 'because that's what I'm like. Changeable. I always have been. My feelings change from day to day and week to week. They always have. I'm going to make a terrible – what do you call it? – the person whom the analyst analyses? Well, whatever it is I'm going to be terrible at it because that is how I am. Changeable.' And the words sprang up unbidden in her head. *Because I'm not a real person.* But she kept her mouth tight shut. Thoughts like that were a present and a holiday all rolled into one to a therapist. But it was his job to find them out for himself, not to have them given to him upon a plate.

· 4 ·

He was poking about in her past, turning over old emotions, picking up feelings between his two fingers and holding them up to the light. It was strange being Mattie, sitting in his study. The experience was both pleasurable and painful. *Poking.* Now there's an interesting choice of words, thinks Mattie, looking straight past Dr H's shoulder and smiling to herself. It's easy, this therapist's game, she thinks. Anyone could do it.

Thus she tried to minimise the effects of the therapist's curious magic.

For this therapy was addling her brain. One minute she knew she was unhappy, the next minute she had forgotten and was amazed and astonished when the therapist put it to her. 'Listen,' Mattie said during the course of the fourth session which was in the middle of April, 'you said last week you thought I wasn't happy.' (This was true. Mattie had been astounded at the very idea.) 'Well, I've been thinking. I have been a bit depressed lately. I feel the Oaklands have become cold towards me. And I don't know why. I wanted this baby to be a present for them. I thought we could bring it up together on the kitchen floor. But after all it is my baby, they don't have to take an interest if they don't want to. A friend of theirs called Sonja, she was pregnant recently, and they were always asking after it. I suppose this baby's neurotic. Do you think I'm neurotic, having a baby like this?' And when Dr H wouldn't answer she grew irritated and said, 'I don't see why some babies are neurotic and others aren't. Isn't everyone's reasons for having a baby suspect? I think the trouble with therapists is that they don't see how bloody awful the world is. Sometimes life fails you. You don't fail. Life does. Isn't that right?'

But Dr H was silent, his black eyes brooding on her thoughtfully. He held a long, perfectly sharpened pencil between the fingers of one hand. 'I think,' he said at last, irrelevantly, 'that you have constructed for yourself a personality and a mode of life which is as far removed as possible from the traumas of your childhood.' Mattie frowned. 'If you mean that I haven't wanted to think much about my childhood,' she said untruthfully, 'then of course I haven't.'

He had said such things to her before, which made it all the more curious, the effect that Dr H's quite unremarkable words had upon her. It was a delayed effect. It was several hours before it began and then it was like a gale beginning to blow inside her. Mattie was agitated. She couldn't sit still. She left the house and walked into the park. As she struck out across the playing fields, walking very fast, she felt her mind open up, huge spaces appearing, alarmingly big, into which there instantly flowed memories of her childhood. Her agitation was increasing. At supper she couldn't sit still. She looked at her cousins from a great distance, as if through the wrong end of a telescope. Vanessa was designing as usual. There were a great many curves and curls and snakes and sinuous tendrils in her designs these days. The black cat was lying on the table, licking his limbs, bending his tongue back upon itself with a complacent tenderness, and the Snake Queen smiled at Mattie and said, mildly enough, 'I like the skirt you're wearing.' 'Thanks,' said Mattie and she excused herself and went upstairs to her room.

It was in the old extension at the end of a narrow corridor. But even here the Oaklands' beautiful things had reached, their colours and painting and glass. As she paced about the room she looked at herself in the mirror, a little bit of her

· 23 ·

disengaged, wondering at her agitation, observing herself and touching her face with her fingers. She could hear the voices of the Oaklands. They were doing what they liked best, which was telling funny stories about their friends. She thought that thus they would strengthen the ties between themselves, make themselves feel more like Oaklands. Noah came knocking at the door as she had known he would. Her action was by itself enough to announce her separateness from her cousins. Mattie thought, they're alarmed. They can't bear to see anyone slipping away. 'Mattie,' Noah called out, but she wouldn't answer. She was angry. They made her feel as if she were, after all, only sulking.

And her agitation was increasing, the gale blowing harder. Mattie leant out of the window. She was astonished that the night could be so still. The temperature had risen. A little rain was falling. It mingled with the dew in the garden, ran down the smooth trunks of the plane trees and down the high brick walls which surrounded them. As you begin so shall you end, thought Mattie. What have you done to me, Dr H? What have you done? For she felt as if all the doors to her mind had flown open simultaneously and the past had appeared before her, joining with the present, imprinting itself upon the dark, damp garden; not the past itself, but its smell and texture, its taste and feel and emotions. And it was as it had always been, both warm and cold and black and very bright.

'You're getting confused. I think we ought to go back to the beginning,' said Mattie at the end of the fifth session, when Dr H had yet again muddled up her memories of her mother and Vanessa. She had observed a frown pass over his face, so she thought with amusement, he's put out. He doesn't like it when I take control. 'And you keep interrupting me. You have no sense of narrative drive,' she complained in a humorous fashion, ever the smartarse, so that Dr H stared at her again and played with his pencil in what Mattie thought of as a positively phallic fashion. But still

· 24 ·

she liked him and didn't wish him to take offence. 'Never mind,' she actually said – 'Never mind' – and she smiled at him reassuringly.

Dr H was a pattern-maker. She would have liked to urge her story onwards, pouring out the events in sequential fashion – the march forward of time, the inevitability of events, stories with beginnings and middles and endings – but he preferred to potter amongst her past, picking up the ruined bricks and placing them one upon another, causing buildings to rise up, the potential for which she had never even seen before. Sometimes his hypotheses made her angry and she stopped and pulled them down, saying, 'It wasn't like that. You've got it all wrong,' – but at other times she stood back and wondered at his astonishing creations.

· 5 ·

As April turned to May and Mattie began her eighth session
with the therapist she fell further into her softened, weak
and wrung-out state. It was the day of her first antenatal
class. As she toiled up the hill to Dartmouth Park an old
lady addressed her and she couldn't find the words – her
head was empty – to answer. This is what comes of thinking
about my childhood, thought Mattie. She stopped in the lee
of a wall and, leaning back, felt the warmth of the bricks
through her hair. She imagined a wind blowing from behind
so that it propelled her gently forwards. The gravelly feel in
her head was gone, to be replaced by this sensation of
warmth and weakness and floating. What a peculiar person
that Hester with the beaky nose had been. Look at those
tulips, that murderous yellow. What kind of colour is yellow
anyway, thought Mattie with that mocking, ironic, uppity
voice of hers which even at moments of deepest distress was
likely to speak out. She could have wished she was more
completely tragic and not thus inclined to be uppity. A
young man walked by with a dog. Mattie tilted back her
head, opened her eyes wide, sent out urgent signals to him:
'Rescue me. Look after me. Save me from my weakness.'
Was it her imagination or did he hesitate for a moment? He
knows I fancy him, thought Mattie with satisfaction. She
straightened up and watched him down the hill. She felt too
weak to dissemble.

Dr H seemed pleased with this new phase in her condition.

And Mattie was grateful to him, really she was. Her childhood was like a burden. Is this why I feel as if I'm floating, thought Mattie, floating weakly upwards as the weight of my childhood is lifted off me? I want to confess to my childhood, she thought at the beginning of this new phase, although *confess* was a quite inappropriate word since she'd done nothing wrong. He reminded her of her old headmaster. She had a sudden, disconcerting image of herself standing naked before him, her swelling belly before her, confessing to everything. I must stop having these sexual fantasies about my therapist, thought Mattie, who had come to understand that sexiness which arises from confession, from the laying bare of one's mind because it is akin to taking off one's clothes.

She shut her eyes. 'Dear God,' she said involuntarily. This gave her an idea. 'It's all God's fault,' she said out loud. 'My mother was religious, terribly, appallingly religious.' And then she was quiet again, for her mind had gone spinning off in pursuit of confessionals and masses and that other red-haired-beautiful-Vanessa-Oakland-Catholic. Therapy as the confessional, thought Mattie. It was not something the Oaklands would ever have thought of. They were not interested in ideas, only in colours and shapes and pattern and form and that other lovely, exotic, sexual, visual world. There is something chic about Catholicism, at least of the variety that Vanessa Oakland practises. Catholic women are good and bad, sexy and intelligent, virtuous and wicked. 'And were you brought up a Catholic?' asked Dr H in that eighth session. 'What? Us? Certainly not,' she said. 'We were poor, mad, penniless, spiritual mystics. Which is to say, we were barking crazy and mad as hatters. My mother loved God and so by way of thank you he sent her mad. There was nothing chic-ly Catholic about the way we lived.'

She was pouring out everything that had ever happened to her, things she had never spoken of before, memories which had never seen the light of day. No wonder she was

feeling giddy. She was remembering her childhood angu-
ishes. She was confessing to all the people who had misused
and then abandoned her. For a while she had the illusion
that her anger was a mountain and with each bit she named
the mountain shrank a little. She found the words at last to
describe her childhood – such a naked, rootless, penniless,
spiritual childhood it had been – and now she couldn't stop
repeating them, so relieved she was at last to be able to
describe it. And at this time, so sad and so inevitable did her
story seem, speeding so rapidly and so certainly towards its
close, that before Dr H had even begun to work his serious
magic on her, she momentarily forgave her cousins.

· 6 ·

Her mother and Vanessa Oakland had been first cousins, their mothers being sisters, but Vanessa's mother married an Italian and bred into her family not only their rich, reddish-coloured hair but money also, and a quite un-English enthusiasm for the visual arts, the Italian being some kind of Milanese designer. But Mattie's grandmother on the other hand married a minor English artist – 'minor' in that he wasn't well known – people said he was really rather good – but prone to seeing religious visions – and this Mattie's mother inherited from him along with his poverty.

Her mother and Vanessa played together as children. When Mattie was young there were photographs in a bottom drawer of two little girls, chins thrown back, hands clutched to their tummies, faces frozen in hysterical, self-conscious, giggling laughter. But when the cousins reached the age of twelve or so the pictures ceased. No doubt at last the difference in their incomes made the relationship impossible.

Mattie's mother married at twenty, and one year later Mattie was born. Mattie's mother married a student but Vanessa married an architect and their reception took place in the Georgian rooms of the Architectural Association in Bloomsbury. Three years later Mattie's father and mother were separated. Mattie couldn't tell you much about this student because he died two years afterwards, too young really to have revealed who he was. He was only twenty-seven.

What slight, melancholy, unfinished lives it seemed to her her parents had. But perhaps it always seems like that in retrospect to children whose parents die too soon? Afterwards they went to live in Essex, a place of bleached skies, grey muted hills and fields of cabbages. Mattie's mother worked in the public library in Colchester but before long she began to fall ill and after that she lost her job and thereafter they lived on social security. A small – a very small – cheque came through the letter box every Thursday. 'Essex!' said Mattie with Oaklandish contempt and she described chalk pits with their abandoned Saturday diggers and farm buildings made from breeze-block walls and corrugated iron. Also, thistly fields and weedy ditches and lanes whose clay surfaces shrank and cracked each summer. And silence. How silent it was. Nothing except the sound of distant traffic on the far side of the hills and the Esso sign banging gently to and fro in its garage forecourt at the bottom of the lane. It was 1974. In London hair was long, ties were wide, shoes were platform-heeled. There was talk of sex and feminism and freedom. But none of this reached them in Dunmow End. They were marooned.

Mattie's mother passed her time in painting and having visions. Her mother was a little mad in a religious kind of way. More than a little mad. She was prone to seeing visions and in her mind she peopled the flat Essex landscape of Mattie's childhood with a rich collection of characters – God and the devil, angels, archangels and demons – and afterwards she painted them. Angels massed so densely they turned the sky to gold. Demons roosting in the trees and squabbling with the angels. Archangels perched on the primary-school roof on bright summer mornings to summon Mattie to school, and God rising like a daffodil-yellow sun over the wet, pearl-grey fields of Dunmow End. And other visions, sadder and blacker, which Mattie did not care to think about.

Once she painted Mattie at twelve, poised to fall into a

shallow valley filled with corn. Around her rose the blue, smoke-tainted mists of autumn. On her right the red sun dipped down into the milky mist. On her left a white moon floated heavenwards on its back. And there, a foot or two behind Mattie's ecstatic, childish face, was another face and a halo, for this was Mattie and her spirit, as her mother saw it, departing from her body. The sky she painted blue and misty white but golden at its zenith, the gold achieved with gold leaf inherited from Mattie's grandfather, eked out – for gold leaf is expensive – and burnished with a small, hard instrument made from obsidian.

And there is another painting in which Mattie and her mother were holding hands – they held hands quite often, as much so that Mattie might guide her mother as that her mother might guide her – and are poised again on the rim of this same valley. But now the corn is cut and the valley is striped with lines of charcoal, black and yellow ochre. Behind them are the fighting autumn clouds, black and blue, and yet the sky is also somehow golden. And the tall, dark figure of her mother, painted with surprising accuracy, bends with the storm, her classical-looking face cracked like a statue's over time. She is dreaming again, no doubt of God. Both of them are two-headed as their spirits depart from their bodies.

Her mother always depicted Mattie two-headed in her paintings. This used to upset Mattie. It was her mother who taught her the mind-out-of-body trick when she was really still quite young. Mattie used to come home from school angry and humiliated by the other girls and then her mother would say, 'Try to stand back from your own body and see it all from a distance. Remember what all this will seem like in ten thousand years, like the smallest wrinkle on the surface of time.' And she also said to her, 'Think of life as a river and you standing on the bank watching the water flow past. The mystics teach that there is nothing in human life which isn't tinged with sorrow, not love nor even pleasure; and so you should try to disengage yourself from your body and observe it all from a distance.'

But her mother frightened her. Perhaps Mattie saw where her advice would lead, for her mother's mind had left her body once too often and had scarcely returned at all. Tentatively Mattie tried the mind-out-of-body trick and was alarmed to find it worked. It was like looking through the wrong end of a telescope – the girls grew very small and distant. She didn't try it too often – she thought she was going mad – but nonetheless the advice, once given, could not be wished away. Thank you, mother.

This is what Mattie remembered: her mother tall as a pillar, carrying the shopping up from the village, bending and toiling and swaying like a woman bearing home water; her mother rolling and smoothing her white flesh into the corsets which some women still wore in the seventies; her mother sitting on the lavatory, beautiful white buttocks and thighs and the dark, green, mysterious waters of the lavatory where Mattie the child hung her head and inspected. 'Let me wear this, and this, and this,' said Mattie, turning out her mother's drawers, trying on her mother's coats and shoes. Love. But these feelings didn't last. How could they?

For then there were the wasps. Every summer her mother poured honey into the jamjars and placed them by the open window in the kitchen so that some small part of the swarming clouds of wasps who daily hovered over the sink and invaded the stinking rubbish bin might crawl into the golden liquid and be drowned. Mattie was afraid of the wasps, both alive and dead. When the sun touched the glass it turned the honey to a terrible brightness and illuminated every hair on their beautiful embalming bodies.

And then there were the naked windows. There wasn't a single pair of curtains ever that she could remember, although in her mother's bedroom there was a sheet pinned up against the glass. But from every other window they had seen the vast, white Essex sky and from every side the sun looked in on them so that Mattie in her confusion thought it was her mother's God. When she walked through the village after school on white, bright, empty afternoons and, running the gauntlet of pitying adult stares, began to climb the lane to home, then the sun dazzled in her eyes and the flints in the road grew so big they tripped her up. Once, as she walked up the path, she saw her mother on the far side of the window, not hearing Mattie's shouts. Mattie pressed her face against the glass to watch her. And she also remembered her mother in the garden, the wind tugging at her clothes, one foot raised and poised to press down on the sharp, metallic edge of the spade and the sun shining strongly on her back. Her mother drew for her a picture of the apple tree in the garden, two angels sitting amongst the blossom on the bough and the round, golden sun in one corner. God hanging in a tree like a golden apple. The eye of God was everywhere, his golden light filling the house. Mattie's mother was religious.

Mattie's mother's God was good. That's what Mattie told herself when she was little. Her mother hadn't wanted to kill the wasps, she who wouldn't willingly step upon an ant and who taught Mattie to rescue spiders stranded in the bath. Regretfully she put out the wasp traps every summer, not wanting Mattie to be stung. But nonetheless Mattie lay awake on dark summer mornings, frightened of the wasps, feeling her mother's body breathing in the bed beside her, hearing the wood pigeons cooing softly in the darkness. How long was it since she had slept with a man? Mattie didn't know. But as her mother snuggled up to her Mattie felt her need for warmth and physical affection. So there were three of them in the bed – her mother, herself and the girl who observed, an old little girl, loyal, fearful, disengaged, watching. And thinking of the wasps who all through the day to come would drown in the golden honey.

'Ah, those wasps,' said Dr H many years later. 'Clearly the business of the wasps upset you. It is hard for a child to watch her parents destroy a living creature and not be afraid that perhaps they will destroy her also.' And then he added, 'Especially hard for you who only had one parent and a rather remote one at that.' And he looked at her with such pity that Mattie bridled and shrugged and refused to say another word.

Was your childhood happy or unhappy? she thought. Well, neither. Not happy nor unhappy but just as it was. For who can ever understand the feel and texture of another person's childhood? And who, she thought angrily, peering short-sightedly at Dr H, who could ever understand the naked, rootless, penniless, spiritual world of my mother and me?

But it was unhappy of course. All through her childhood they lived on social security. This was the nature of their poverty, poverty coming in many different forms and theirs being monastic and religious. Their withdrawal from society was complete. To the green and the grey, the white and the gold of Mattie's childhood you may add again the colours of her mother's inner life, very rich and vivid but not for the sharing; and black also, because they were so poor and her father dead and her mother going mad.

One day her mother turned on the radio and said, 'Listen, it's Jacqueline du Pré.' 'Who's she?' 'A famous cellist.' Down in the village lived a plump, pretty, domesticated girl of Huguenot descent whose family had somehow been washed up in Dunmow End. Her name was Jacqueline du Pré. Whenever Mattie met her she used to stare very hard at the other girl. She couldn't see how this couldn't be the famous Jacqueline du Pré and she thought of the people she must have met in London, the places where she had been, and what it must be like to play on the radio.

Rumours reached them, even in Essex, of the success of the Oakland Design Company, and they heard also that Vanessa had produced three boys to Mattie's mother's one daughter. It was as if Vanessa were determined that her

· 34 ·

thread of life should last. On winter days Mattie's mother's fingers turned quite yellow with the cold so that Mattie thought her flesh was curdling. Mattie used to chafe her mother's fingers between her hands to make them warm. When she looked at photographs of the two little cousins, she was pleased to see that her mother looked much prettier than Vanessa. She was loyal to her mother – and later she was proud of this – but looking back she was struck by how early began her resentment against her mother's cousins.

When Mattie was eight, she developed a passion for photography. After she realised that she herself couldn't photograph the two of them together, she showed a neighbour how to use the old box camera she had inherited from the student, and thus there was a picture – she had it still – of the two of them, her mother and herself holding hands, although so strongly is the wind blowing behind them and between them that they are all but blown apart. Mattie is holding on for dear life and looking in her mother's direction but her mother's face is turned away in profile and her eyes are looking heavenwards as always.

· 7 ·

People came and went. Mattie fell in love with a pagan family.

Miranda arrived one morning in January, redolent of private education, her hair in plaits and a briefcase in one hand. She had run away from prep school and because her parents couldn't immediately find her another one, and also no doubt to punish her, they sent her down the road to Dunmow End Juniors. She only stayed two months. She shared a desk with Mattie, but her parents took her away when she started to pick up the local accent and to bring home girls from school. 'Like me,' said Mattie.

On the east coast of Essex are a handful of beautiful houses, built on low hills and looking out over the marshy beaches to the chilly morning sun and the grey English sea. The Berenses lived in one such house, a house made from yellow sandstone, imported from Wessex, standing alone on its low hill and built to the simple lines of a doll's house. A doll's house. That's what Mattie thought of when Miranda's mother stopped the car at the bottom of the hill and they looked up for one moment. Although the air was so cold the sandstone seemed very warm and yellow. From the chimney came a line of blue smoke. Behind the house were thin, high clouds in bars of pink and grey and silver. A stiff breeze was blowing. A seagull blew past. Mattie could hear the sounds of the sea and smell it through Miranda's open window.

This house with all its richness was a forerunner of the house of the Oaklands. There were tall windows, shining clean and not naked like the windows at home but lined with shutters made from natural wood. The huge bay windows on the ground floor reached out to catch the white estuary light and tossed it inwards to where smoothly polished walls and milky wooden floors – as vast as ballroom floors! – tossed the white light upwards so that all the rooms were aquiver with a violent, colourless light. There was a wide, curving staircase where they played hide-and-seek but it was impossible to tiptoe up it quietly for it was uncarpeted and of the same polished wood; and upstairs there was a painting done in the naive manner of a girl in a yellow dress, her shiny brown hair very flat upon her head, her eyes gazing down a long corridor to where at the vista's end beyond an open door a double bed was moored, as large as a boat and spread with a white counterpane.

Was there really a painting, or was it herself staring in admiration that the remembering eye remembered?

Now that it was so cold God no longer came visiting and Mattie's mother grew lonely. She turned herself outwards instead upon the world and took against Miranda's mother because the other woman chainsmoked and rode to hounds and wore dark glasses even in the depths of winter. One day when Mattie and her mother were walking home from the village they came upon the huntsmen. The horses' legs were enormously tall. The riders were dressed in scarlet and black so that they resembled soldiers. The hounds were swarming all around. Mattie and her mother stepped back upon the verge and then they saw the hunt saboteurs coming up the other way. The huntsmen spurred their horses on and Miranda's mother at the front began to curse, loudly and richly and terribly. Afterwards Mattie's mother said she was no

· 37 ·

Christian, but Mattie admired her nonetheless. For when she was young she was said to have travelled, widely and romantically, before she had married Miranda's father. Even now she kept a sailing boat down on the estuary which Miranda said she took across to France by night, bringing back cigarettes and other contraband.

At first Mattie hoped Miranda's parents might be a mother and a father to her. She observed them very carefully, the father rather short and plump – he had made a lot of money in the city – and the mother, tall and slender, dressed in slacks and practical, expensive shoes. She was forever straightening up from her weeding in the garden and stepping into the house with one hand in the pocket of her slacks and the other wrapped around a glass of gin and tonic. Mattie looked at them with ready, displaced love but in the cool manner of their class they looked right through her and didn't seem to see her at all.

They didn't take much notice of Miranda either, although one afternoon in January when it grew dark at four o'clock the two girls, moving aimlessly into the drawing room, came across Miranda's mother sitting by the fire. She began to talk. She had a story in her head which she wanted to get out. She described how one day when she had been riding on her own high up in the Himalayas she had come across a meeting of two famous English explorers, the one riding with a retinue of six, including two cameramen, the other whose name was Peregrine Clans-Derby crossing the other way in the company of one. All of them were scorched and burnt to utter blackness, their faces weeping and crumbling with fatigue, but Peregrine Clans-Derby was of the older school – he had been to Eton in 1935 – and his face was stiff as a board. 'There's no one left like Peregrine any more,' said Miranda's mother for she worshipped him, being English and inclined to fascism, to the worship of strong men. She loved men and animals. 'Men are better,' she said, 'braver and better than women.' Like mother, like daughter.

· 38 ·

All this Mattie would remember long afterwards for Miranda would grow up to be exactly like her mother. Both of them when they were little had wept for Scott's poor horses, frozen to death in the Antarctic.

Miranda was not as tall as her mother and she had the broad, confident bottom of the upper classes, but even at eight she wore her thick, blonde hair like her mother's, scraped back from her face, in which way she would later show her good cheekbones and her English rose complexion. (For Miranda would never wear make-up. She was brave. She would show her face quite naked to the world.) And she was loyal, and possessive of Mattie.

Each morning as they drove through the village she made her mother stop the big car to pick Mattie up. 'Hi, Mattie,' she would say, very proprietorial of her friend, and of this car, sliding so slinkily through the village, and of her mother who smoked a cigarette and drove with one hand on the wheel. 'Hi,' said Mattie, looking around her at the leather and the chrome, observing the icy village as it passed by through the window. Miranda liked to play with the buttons on the tape cassette. She showed them off to Mattie with a gangsterish air. Her mother braked sharply and a gaggle of children breathing smoke set off across the road. 'Mummy,' said Miranda, 'if you stop like that you'll spoil the brakes.' She was as cool in love as she would always be.

Miranda was privileged – she always was – she had no conception of any other life and Mattie both loved and hated her. There were, as always, two of Mattie: herself playing with Miranda and her alter ego, standing back and watching the two little girls playing. She was angry with this privileged world. It seemed to her that by being angry with it she could be loyal to her mother. And yet she loved Miranda, for even at eight Miranda had a brisk kindliness and a way some women have of complimenting other women on their beauty, this done quite sincerely, out of sheer, confident pleasure in another woman's looks. And so, the first time

· 39 ·

they met, Miranda slid into the chair at the desk beside Mattie and whispered in her ear, 'I like the way you've done your hair with that ribbon,' and Mattie blushed and was pleased and so the pattern was set for their later relationship.

After two months in Dunmow End her parents sent Miranda away to boarding school and thereafter in the holidays she went riding or to stay in schoolfriends' houses; and later on she holidayed on yachts or went to America with her mother or Italy or Morocco. As for Mattie, by this time she carried her childhood like a millstone round her neck and the energy which went into bearing up beneath it was such that sometimes she felt it took away her strength and made her unable to talk to other people.

And so Mattie didn't see Miranda again for a number of years, not until the summer they were sixteen when Mattie went into the drapers' shop in Great Dunmow. There amongst the rolls of fabric and buttons and thread and zips and knitting patterns Mattie saw Miranda with a young man. He was very handsome. The two of them had both shop assistants serving them. The man was smiling and laughing. It was as if he was so taken with Miranda he was trying to sell her to the shop assistants and the shop assistants to her. Mattie crept closer. She wanted to hear what they were saying. The man was trying to buy Miranda a skirt pattern; he wanted her to wear skirts, he was obviously devoted to her, he wanted to turn her into his mother. And Miranda was protesting, but cheerfully, and the two of them were putting up such a performance that the two sulky shop assistants were charmed and kept looking from Miranda to her boyfriend as if both of them were such objects of admiration.

· 8 ·

Soon the light in the house grew white, not golden. In the big upper room which Mattie's mother used for painting there were no curtains – 'You need all God's light for painting,' she used to say – but in her bedroom the sheet which hung across the window cast a shroudlike light through the narrow room, onto the unmade bed and the collection of religious books propped up upon the table. When Mattie lifted one corner of this sheet the white light entered in. It was God's own special light. It was the same terrible white light which permeated the house from end to end. It revealed everything and hid nothing, not the cheapness of the melamine furniture, nor the cracks in the linoleum floor, nor the crumbs of burnt toast on the unpolished kitchen table nor the cracks in the panes of glass. There was no point in material possessions since they only decayed and passed away and were as nothing in the eternity of God's love. Only the white light persisted, keeping her mother company all day as she painted, and following Mattie down the lane to the school, so that when she looked up from her books she saw the passage of the white sun through the Victorian glass.

Her mother wasn't a pillar after all. This had been an illusion of Mattie's six-year-old eyes. She was a tree which had broken in the middle. She was a lake which madness had frozen in the attitudes of placidity so that time passed and nothing moved or changed inside her. Madness ran across the surface of this lake in veins of malice: malice towards the world, malice towards herself, malice towards her daughter. Mattie was reaching pubescence and her mother was alarmed. 'Like a lamb amongst tigers,' she said, painting Mattie's picture with swift, sure strokes.

Mattie kept out of her way. At home she lay out in the garden to do her homework and looked up from time to time at their house with its naked windows, at its concrete facade which was cracked by the frost and pitted by the rain, at its paint which had peeled and faded through a succession of long, hot summers. In front of the house her mother had cleared the ground and laid out some plants but at the back, beyond the tiny lawn and the vegetable patch, the garden was wild and weedy and overgrown. In the summer the grass grew so high it obscured the lower branches of the apple tree. When the summer storms came, the rain beat down the grass and snapped the nettle stems, leaving them with broken necks and heads hanging down. On hot days the garden smelt of drains, of pig manure and the cesspit.

They had rented this house for ten years but had never had the money to do it up. Yet even if they had, would they have done so? Probably not, for her mother was helpless before the natural world which grew up all around them, rank and wild and ugly. Mattie began to resent the ugliness of home. Once her mother fell over as they walked down to the village and Mattie didn't step forward, not at once, to help her up. In that moment when she stood there Mattie thought, she can't even get this right.

And meanwhile God stepped in and out of their house like any other visitor. Mattie looked forward to his coming, for when her mother was in his company she grew soft and loving and mild, although she was never anything other than distant. And yet when God left her, or wouldn't come back, then she shrank in size, grew anxious and trembly, perceived slights in all directions and responded to them with anger. Mattie thought her mother didn't care for other people, not really, that there was not one person in the village whom

· 42 ·

she wholeheartedly liked. People offended her and she trembled with rage. She imagined they criticised her and she harped on about it for months. She ascribed to them passions of love and anger which Mattie knew they did not possess. Mattie thought it was as if her mother had no skin to protect herself but presented to the world the raw, bleeding, sensitive interior. Mattie dreamt she put a poultice on her mother, bandaged the raw and bleeding wound, wrapped her up like an Egyptian mummy.

The wasps were very troublesome that summer. They buzzed around the cowpats and swarmed around the litter which appeared mysteriously on the banks beside the lane. Where did this litter come from, so far from civilisation? Perhaps the farm workers dropped it? Perhaps it was blown across the countryside in the cool nights from the beaches on the coast not three miles distant?

It seemed to Mattie that by day their lane, like most of the lanes which led out from the village, had a faintly disagreeable air. Once there had been a gravel pit on the right as you first left the village, but they filled this in when Mattie was ten and thereafter she believed the lane to be haunted by the ghosts of rabbits whose burrows had been blocked by earth and who had died of suffocation. In the daytime this haunting was no more than an unpleasant pressure weighing down upon the lane. But each evening as the pressure lifted it seemed to Mattie the haunting began in earnest.

Mattie disliked the days but liked the nights. She lay in bed with the windows open and listened to the dreaming of the night, so full and loud it almost burst the silence. She opened the windows wide and tuned the transistor radio to wistful, alienated night songs, for she had heard so little music it affected her terribly. Her dreams, although very powerful to her, were also very simple – just strange men's arms around her and strange dark faces, both brutal and tender, men who threw her to the ground and thereafter did

· 43 ·

things to her she only cared to half imagine. She liked to dream these dreams at night because it was private and because she liked the darkness and the sight of the opalescent wheat fields under the pale night sky and because she associated the darkness with the litter.

Once she picked up a piece of this litter and, straightening it out, read it all before she realised it was a page ripped from a porn magazine. She recoiled in embarrassment on seeing her thoughts made manifest on paper. She screwed it up and pushed it down a drain. But thereafter when she leant out of the window she thought of this sexy litter flying like present-day witches over the silver wheat fields under the pale night sky to distribute itself in unreadable messages over the banks of the lane; and this litter became part of her nightly dreams of sex.

She was fifteen in July of that year. Each morning her mother picked up the litter and carried it into the house.

· 9 ·

Mattie went out and bought herself a pair of jeans. How proud and astonished she was that she who had emerged from poverty and madness should be so chic and glamorous. Like a light coming out of the darkness, thought Mattie, who always loved the bright, glittering surfaces of things. Her looks made her laugh, were a pleasure and a comfort to her. Where do you go to, my lovely? she sang in her sweet, rather tuneless voice, but softly so that her mother could not hear. It was nice to be romantic, astonishing to be herself. One day they would make a film about her and all kinds of people would love her because she was so beautiful.

In her mother's bedroom was a box made from pear wood, not very large and containing a number of little cupboards and drawers, intricately arranged. When Mattie was a child she used to play with this box for hours on end. Her mother said that Tom Oakland, Vanessa's husband, had made it. Whenever she said this Mattie used to make her go and fetch the photographs of herself and Vanessa. 'Why don't you get in touch with the Oaklands again?' she asked, but her mother looked vague and uninterested. She lifted her daughter's arm and stared. 'Yes,' she said and her voice was cold, 'there's a nice thatch growing under there.' It alarmed Mattie, the way her mother would let friendships slide away into nothingness. 'She was like that,' said Mattie to Dr H. 'She let go of my father and he vanished.' Mattie was afraid, of course, her mother would do the same to her.

· 45 ·

Mattie went to Colchester public library and looked up the name 'Oakland' in the London telephone directories. There were ten with addresses in the right part of London and she went through them all, ringing from a telephone box until at last, in answer to her question, 'Can I speak to Vanessa Oakland?' a boy replied, 'I'll go and fetch her,' and Mattie put the phone down hastily.

She wrote to Vanessa on two sheets of pale blue, already ruled Basildon Bond notepaper, smallest size. She wanted to use something which looked more generous and self-confident but this was all she could find in the local newsagent. In her large, childish script she wrote that she was coming to London to do her A levels – French, Drama, English – and wondered if they had any friends who might rent her out a bedsit.

As she hoped, Vanessa wrote back as follows: Dear Mattie, How lovely to hear from you. I remember you as a little girl in a picture your father sent me. As it happens, we have a spare bedroom and I'm sure it would be more fun for you to stay with us than to be with strangers. How clever of you to find a school for yourself and one which does the right O levels. I haven't heard of the school you mention but I'm sure it's excellent. Do tell your mother we would love to see her. Much love, Vanessa.

This letter was waiting for Mattie when she came home from school. She saw at once that Vanessa had the benign unworldliness of the rich. She thought Vanessa's children probably failed their exams in the blithe way the children of the wealthy so often do. But she wasn't surprised that the Oaklands would take her on unseen. She was shy but also arrogant in a teenage kind of way and it didn't occur to her the Oaklands might find her boring.

Her mother was out in the garden planting lettuce seedlings. Mattie watched her strong, yellow fingers pressing down on the black earth. She saw her lift her face to the wind and sunlight which was pouring down across the field and through a gap in the hedge. Mattie knew she was hoping that the wind would shortly lift her spirit, that the sky would grow veined and marbly, that all time would peak and out beyond the thistle fields God would appear in all his glory.

Mattie went outside and stood before her mother to block her vision. She saw that God was on his way, for her mother had grown soft and mild. She told her what her plans were but her mother only said, rather madly, 'She was the daughter of the Italian. He took me once to Brompton Oratory to see the Stations of the Cross. All that red hair in the candle-light. It's a pretty faith but they went astray in the middle ages.' Her mother was kneeling on the black earth, her face lifted upwards to the sun. Mattie was furious that she couldn't think of anything more sane to say on her daughter's imminent departure. She wanted to kick the black earth into her mother's pale, sunlit face.

· 10 ·

The summer she left home was hot and rank and often overcast. The time for blossom and flowers was long since over. Weeds filled the ditches and the dried-up ponds around the house whilst a fine dust sifted across the clayey lane, and scrubby woods on either side and fields of nettles and of thistles drowsed in the leaden August heat under a milky, cloudy sky.

Mattie went into Colchester to a men's barber shop and asked them to cut off her hair to an inch all over her head. The old man complied with a bemused expression. He seemed flabbergasted at what he was doing but Mattie was delighted. Afterwards she couldn't stop staring at herself in shop windows. She was in love with herself and her looks.

The night before she left, Mattie paid a visit to her neighbours. Ostensibly this was to say goodbye to them but actually she wished to ask if they would keep an eye on her mother. Mattie thought, she doesn't even know I'm leaving, and she was afraid, for the idea occurred to her that when she next came home she would find the house empty and deserted whilst in the tangled, weedy garden a second apple tree would have grown. She was afraid the time would come when her mother would not come back to reality, when she would speak and her mother, being in her mind no more than an apple tree, would not hear, would not answer.

But on the morning she left, her mother emerged from her dreams for an hour or two and filled a jamjar in the kitchen with wild pink campions. 'You think too much about money,' said her mother. 'The rich don't have a monopoly on happiness. Or on beauty.' She said this with her face turned away and Mattie's eyes filled with tears. She took it as a rejection, a so-go-and-live-with-the-rich-if-that's-what-you-want kind of remark. She looked about her, saw the great white sun ducking in through the windows, saw the grimy kitchen window sill – for the kitchen window sills of the poor, the ones behind the sink, are often so moistly engrained with dirt you cannot get them clean – saw the wild pink campions in the jamjar, humble little flowers on twisted stems with furry leaves, not much more than pretty weeds, living for the day.

But the Oaklands' house that summer was filled with cut flowers, vases and vases of them on the evening Mattie arrived, their blooms massed like clouds, their stems visible, floating lengthways in the water, their petals the colour of dark, white icing sugar, flowers dimly perceived and breathing silently in the summer gloom. They had been sent to commemorate the opening of an Oakland exhibition. Mattie thought they were very beautiful but her mother would have dismissed them, saying, 'Shop flowers! Wild flowers picked in the fields are so much prettier . . . ' Because that's what her mother was like.

'Consider the lilies of the field,' said her mother. 'They spin not, neither do they toil. And yet I say unto you, not Solomon in all his glory was arrayed like one of these.'

But it wasn't true. Mattie knew it then. It was the same pretty lilies-of-the-field lie her mother told in many guises. It is better to be poor than rich. There are so many things the poor have which the rich do not. The poor are rich in spirit in which the rich are lacking. And so on. Her mother believed quite positively in the virtues of poverty. She yearned to God but she believed that with every penny gained God drew away a little and his voice came less often. If she'd had any money she'd have given it away and as it was she took care never to acquire any.

But Mattie knew there were many things her mother believed which were not true and many other things she didn't know at all.

Over the years she had developed a second pair of eyes to see on behalf of her mother. She had guided her around like a small tug leading a big ship. But when the burden of this second sight grew too much that August she hardened her heart and guiltily she fled away to London.

· I I ·

She was an heiress. She was everything you might hope to grow up to be yourself. She came to meet Mattie at Victoria Coach Station and Mattie saw her leaning up against a wall, a tall and statuesque woman dressed in a pair of jeans and a shirt, and wearing a shawl around her shoulders. Her bosom was full, her thighs like pillars, her thick, reddish hair tied back with a long scarf patterned in reds and pinks. That's her, thought Mattie, as she jostled with the crowds from Colchester and Chelmsford, and as she looked in Mattie's direction Mattie looked away hastily, childishly, in case she might see her.

It was her bigness which struck Mattie first. In Dunmow End beauty had been spread very thinly. Only for an hour or two in the mornings, and in the evenings when the sun went down, had this beauty become visible and then it was no more than touches here and there, but they raised up the thin and stony landscape and for an hour or two they made it appear to be blessed. Vanessa took up so much space upon the earth! Mattie had never seen a woman before who was both fat and beautiful. She was astonished. She was rooted to the spot beside the coach. She was too embarrassed to move. She thought to herself in her stern, sixteen-year-old fashion, she shouldn't be wearing those trousers, not until she's been on a diet.

'It's Mattie, isn't it?' said Vanessa, oblivious, bending her vast, amber-eyed gaze upon her, and she held out an arm

· 51 ·

which was round and moulded like marble to take the carrier bags which Mattie held in her hands. 'Do you have any more?' she asked, looking to the boot of the coach, and Mattie blushed and shook her head.

Vanessa leant forward to kiss her. As her eyes loomed up Mattie saw the feathery irises and the blue whites around them and thought that this woman was not young, for she had lost the suppleness of youth. Instead she was stiff and yet sweet and with a yellowy look as if a yellow glaze had been poured all over her, fixing for ever the web of lines around her huge eyes, the open pores, the freckles and the tiny golden hairs on her cheeks and her cheekbones. Her physical presence was overwhelming. She had the look of having been lavished upon by life. Mattie smelt her smell of skin and flesh and perfume and shampoo. When her bosom brushed against her Mattie realised with a shock that men would find Vanessa very beautiful. Briefly Mattie hoped that she too might grow up to be so full, so opulent, to take up so much space upon the earth.

Vanessa drove the car with great vagueness, and her voice as she drove was both soft and brisk, her tone imperious but vague, the commands beginning but tailing off before they reached their end. 'Look out and see if anything's coming,' she said to Mattie with an air somehow as if she thought the car functioned by clockwork. But at other times she leant forward as if the car were a pedal car and she was pushing it with her feet. Once she turned right against the traffic so suddenly that in a car which raced towards them Mattie saw the driver lift one hand and draw a finger across his throat in a suicide gesture.

But Vanessa didn't seem to notice. She talked in fits and starts and Mattie – who was used to her mother's topics of conversation which were mostly religion, philosophy, mysticism and suchlike – couldn't understand the large part of what Vanessa was saying. But she gathered that Aaron had cleared his jewellery-making tools out of the small bed-

· 52 ·

room, that Vanessa had gone out to buy a futon – whatever that was – and they hoped she would like it. Also, they had written to her school and had been pleased to hear that Mattie had also been in touch. Next week she and Tom were going to Copenhagen – it was a business trip – but the boys would look after her and Jonathan was already hoping she could help him with his homework.

Mattie thought that everything Vanessa said was entirely conventional but it didn't matter because she said it all with great sweetness. My mother is an old stick, thought Mattie, a twig, a bone, a lump of stone; this woman's not like her at all. The shawl had slipped down onto Vanessa's knees where it slid to and fro with the movement of the car. It was a silky, blue-black creature, patterned with peacocks' eyes and imprinted with the outlines and the fine backbones of leaves. As it slipped to and fro it caught the light and Mattie thought, if I pick it up it will smell of her perfume.

They parked the car under a lime tree in a narrow lane at the side of the house. Whilst Vanessa locked the doors, Mattie looked up into the still centre of the tree and felt the dust from a long summer drift down from its dark leaves. The air was growing moist. The molecules of darkness were gathering together. They were showering down from the peak of the heavens where the sky was still bright and luminous. Mattie felt them showering down upon her. She thought of them showering down even on her mother far away in Dunmow End.

Vanessa unlocked a gate and led her into a garden. Ahead of them was the house, its garden facade made not of stucco, as was the front, but of brick to suggest privacy and domesticity. Mattie saw bushes of pale blossom, half closed against the night; creepers falling from the walls; a path beneath their feet made of narrow bricks placed on their sides and taking them to flights of shallow steps which led to higher levels. A cat appeared on the path before them, back arched in a fighting posture before he melted away. The air was moist and Mattie sensed rather than saw the canal at the bottom of the garden. After a moment a pleasure boat passed by, lit up with lights, with twinkling glasses and with laughter. In the garden the late summer twilight grew a denser, bluer grey as these lights went past.

Vanessa hurried ahead – the pink of her scarf was fading into the night as she hurried towards a glass conservatory built up against the house, its glass walls as shiningly bright as the air in the garden was dense and dark and soporific. Mattie saw through the walls of this glass palace a table laid for dinner, a party about to begin. She saw the heavy swathes of curtains, their folds as opulently stiff as the icing on a cake, covering one glass wall; and she saw the long dinner table set with shining cutlery and flowers, lined on either side with benches resembling the pews in a church, the table painted a luminous yellow ochre and the blue and white serving dishes and the red wine glittering in the bottles.

The air was like water. It was damp and subtle. It carried within it traces of distant sounds, of dogs barking, of traffic and even far-off screams, though whether of pleasure or pain she couldn't tell. After the spaces of Essex she was aware of the presence of so many houses pressing all around her, houses standing amongst their trees, windows lit up or unlit and dark in the growing darkness. She felt her senses grow soft and stretchy, affected by the beauty of everything she saw. She felt the world so thickly painted with beauty she could hardly make out its form at all. Now, she felt, she had ceased to think and for many years to come she would not think again, but would feel instead, with her skin and her head and her hair and her hands and her feet and her mind, which was all feelings, a mass of sensibilities, and no thoughts at all.

· 12 ·

A man and two boys got to their feet. The man had dark, curly hair growing well back from his high forehead and the handsome profile of a nineteenth-century French painter. His trousers were of pink plaid with narrow lines of yellow, his shirt of green plaid with narrow lines of pink, and over the shirt he wore an old brown waistcoat. All this seemed to Mattie to be quite extraordinarily stylish.

The two boys were of a smaller, slighter build. 'You never bought me any hair gel, mum,' said the older boy instantly and there was a shout of laughter from his father. 'I'm sorry,' said Vanessa benignly but also, Mattie thought, with indifference. 'You don't need hair gel,' said his father, looking at the boy's hair which waved and curled and frizzed in his mother's reddish colour. 'Yes, I do,' said the boy. 'Anyway, that's not the point,' said his younger brother jauntily, looking directly at Mattie.

The older boy was very beautiful – in the strong light of the conservatory his features were bleached to a smooth pallor in which only his huge eyes started forth – but Mattie saw at once with her old little girl's eyes that he was a middle child who fears he is unloved. She might have identified with him, being an unloved child herself, but like any underdog she wanted to be on the winning side, and so she turned and smiled at his younger brother. 'How was ma's driving?' asked this young boy. But 'Oh, puss, puss,' he cried, getting down on his knees, not waiting for an answer and she saw

· 55 ·

that the cat was pushing and twisting its way through their legs. 'Oh puss, puss, oh beautiful cat, how I love you,' cried Jonathan, all ironic affection and melodrama, as he picked the creature up, and again there was a shout of laughter from the table. Mattie was impressed by his self-confidence, that he could behave like this in front of a stranger.

'You're going to Marie Ellis school, aren't you?' he said from the floor. 'Yes,' said Mattie. 'Ma says you're good at English.' 'Yes,' said Mattie proudly. 'Actually,' he said, jumping to his feet, as bold as brass, 'I was hoping you could help me with my homework.' And there was more laughter from the table. 'You shouldn't ask her like that,' said the older boy condemningly, 'not in front of other people when she can't say no.' But still Mattie could see he would give anything to make them laugh as the other one could.

'Did she turn right against the traffic?' asked a young man who appeared in the doorway, wearing three earrings in one ear. 'Well, yes,' said Mattie. 'Did I?' asked Vanessa in surprise. 'She always does,' said the young man. 'Next time you should stop her before she gets herself killed.' 'Herself', Mattie noted, not 'you'.

He was thin and not at first sight at all remarkable to look at – certainly not as beautiful as the middle child. He was dressed in a navy zootsuit and a T-shirt and wore a cap on top of his butterscotch hair which had a streak of sea-green in it. 'Cor, Vanessa, what are these?' he asked, picking at a plate of food. 'You were meant to drive me this morning,' she said, and he looked at her with a wary rebelliousness. 'Order a taxi, mum. I told you, I charge £5 an hour.' 'You haven't said hallo properly. None of my children have,' she said and at this he drew up his thin chest proudly in his skimpy white T-shirt. 'Hallo,' he said, grinning, and they gathered round, shaking hands as if to the manner born: Noah who was twenty, Aaron who was fifteen and Jonathan who was thirteen. 'Hallo properly,' said Jonathan. Close up

· 56 ·

Mattie saw they had the square jaws and full, smooth cheeks of the well fed and cared-for.

They took her to her bedroom by way of corridors and flights of stairs and through rooms with painted floors and ceilings and narrow internal windows where stood jugs of flowers as soft and full and rounded in their massiveness as clouds. It was a large house with many floors and extensions – a roof garden and parapets, an eyrie at the top, and at the bottom a flight of steps leading up to the front door. They passed by open doors and Mattie, looking in, wondered how she was ever to distinguish between the people and the things in this layered house, where there was layer upon layer of rugs on the tables and the sofas, where the beds were piled high with blankets and shawls and Turkish carpets, the towels strewn across the rugs on the bathroom floor and trays of cups and glasses standing everywhere, whilst in Vanessa's bedroom was a wooden dressing table on which there was a litter of expensive pots and perfumes and potions.

And how to see anything at all, her head was so full of admiration and envy and anger and jealousy, thinking of herself as the poor cousin very far from home, alone in the mansions of the rich, imagining herself and her beautiful wide-eyed stare and how it must look to the observer, and thinking of Sonja in Tolstoy's *War and Peace* who was another penniless orphan – and thinking, oh my mother, how very much you would have liked that garden. Don't think she wouldn't just because she's poor, thought Mattie, trailing after them, she who was at this moment missing her mother terribly. And when they left her in her room and she sat down on the bed and looked at the chest of drawers in front of her, a rare, rich and solid piece of Oakland furniture, made to proportions which were pleasingly bourgeois and fat, she thought – and what do they know about poverty anyway? – and in her mind's eye fixed her angry stare on all her mother's beautiful cousins who were at this moment her enemies.

· 57 ·

When she came downstairs again they sat her at the kitchen table and put before her food which was very rich and strange. They were getting the house ready for a party. They were stacking up the drinks in the kitchen, polishing the glasses, laying out the food on platters, putting out ashtrays and flowers in every room. The house had taken on a festive, drunken air. There were lights switched on in every room. In her mind's eye Mattie saw the thin black cats from the poor houses across the canal scavenging already in bins which were stuffed with salmon carcasses, with paper wrappings and the cellophane from flowers. Through the windows – not one of the curtains was drawn – the guests would see the flicker of televisions and bright, soundless faces passing behind the glass, giving the illusion that the house was swaying already to noiseless music. Upstairs in the bedroom Mattie had seen bedclothes, silk and down and tapestry, tumbling to the floor in a careless splendour, whilst downstairs in the kitchen the fridges were full to overflowing and each time one of the Oakland boys went past he swung open the doors to pick and nibble and snack, and once the food came rolling out across the tiled floor, and paté and stilton and crême fraiche missed them by inches. A shower of good food. 'Waste not, want not,' as Mattie didn't say to them. She could see the Oakland boys took it all for granted.

How clannish they are, thought Mattie that night, watching them as they stood about in the reddish light of the kitchen, their eyes very large and dark, nervously waiting for the guests to arrive. Two of the guests were here already, a man and a woman with greying hair and wrinkled faces. 'Move over,' said the man to the woman – his eyes were wolfish – 'so that I can sit next to the beautiful Vanessa,' and Mattie thought Vanessa's beauty was the admiration of everyone whose eyes rested on her.

Jonathan came and sat down at the table next to Mattie. He wore a green satin smoking jacket. All his movements were still fluent because he was nearly but not quite adolescent.

'Will you write me a poem for my English homework?' he said. 'Leave her alone,' said Noah, 'not now.' 'It's a week late already,' said Jonathan. 'Tomorrow then,' said Noah. 'I won't be here tomorrow,' said Jonathan. 'I can write it now,' said Mattie proudly, and she took the pen and paper that he offered her.

As she wrote she listened to them talk. 'Did you hear about Vanessa's visit to the fortune teller?' said Noah. 'No,' said Tom and at once it was clear he wasn't at all pleased to hear this. He stared at his wife but she wouldn't look at him. She was sitting with her legs crossed, her elbows resting on her knees, staring into space. She had changed. She was wearing a pair of bright blue tights. There were yellow stars on her blue scarf. The wolfish man had his eyes fixed on her. The red wine glittered with profanity in the glasses. Vanessa smiled to herself and said, 'I went with Sonja Lefanu. She's got a new lover. He's got a title. She's been going to this fortune teller for years but she was so pleased because he laid out the cards, and guessed the name of the lover straight away.'

'Wasn't her last lover titled?' said Aaron. 'All her lovers are titled,' said Noah and everyone laughed. But Tom was staring at his wife. 'So why were you going to a fortune teller?' he asked, but still she wouldn't answer him. 'You don't believe in all that kind of thing, do you?' he said. Noah said flippantly, 'Mum's taken up with the occult,' and then Vanessa raised her head and Mattie thought she looked at her son with sudden coldness, a trapdoor seeming to open in her head, the mind falling, as Mattie had noticed mothers' minds do, from warmth to weary coldness in one second, so that Mattie knew at once it was not about Tom that Vanessa had been consulting a fortune teller but rather about Noah. And with the same prescient clarity she knew that neither of the two men knew this.

· 59 ·

'How would you like your coffee?' asked Vanessa and, not knowing what the question meant, Mattie said at last in desperation she liked it hot and strong. 'Then I shall give you only a little milk,' said Vanessa elegantly. Each time she looked away Mattie stared after her in admiration. She thought how amber, smiling and enfolding was Vanessa's gaze and how when she looked at Mattie it never faltered. We really do look quite alike, do Vanessa and me, thought Mattie – for they both had a wide mouth which only just covered their teeth, although when Mattie stopped talking her face fell back into a sad and mournful expression whilst Vanessa's was full of the reposeful awareness of her own beauty. She should have been my mother, thought Mattie. And in admiration her mind slipped out of her head, slinky-wise and cat-like, because she felt herself so much more Oaklandish on the inside than she was on the outside.

'Finished,' said Mattie, and she pushed the paper across the table. 'I thought you were good at English, Jonathan,' said Tom suddenly. 'I thought you did well in your English test.' 'I only got fifty-two per cent,' said Jonathan, 'and anyway I cheated.' 'What?' said Vanessa. 'I got William Reeves to make up six different poems and I memorised them before the exam began.' 'Wouldn't it have been easier to write them yourself?' said Noah sarcastically. But Vanessa was staring at Jonathan in amazement. 'And you still only got fifty-two per cent. Even after cheating. Oh my God,' she said, and now they were laughing because her dismay was so comical. 'Jonathan,' she said, 'how incompetent.' But Mattie was staring at him in horror and admiration.

Vanessa was telling some story about an Italian countess. 'God, ma's such a snob,' said Noah but Vanessa took no notice. She was off her sons. She was off them all. She sat there polishing glasses and growing older by the minute, the lines around her neck appearing like the strands of a necklace. She wouldn't look at them and only Jonathan was importunate. 'I like your haircut,' said Noah to Mattie and Jonathan overheard and said, 'It's a hedgehog cut. I think she's very pretty, isn't she pretty, mum?', appealing to Vanessa with the licence of the youngest child.

Vanessa turned her brooding gaze on Mattie. 'Very,' she said with sweetness. And then she added, 'You look like your mother. She was very pretty also. It would be nice to see her again. I expect she hasn't changed.' 'My mother never changes,' said Mattie with adolescent gloom, and everyone laughed so that Mattie's spirit spun away with pleasure – she saw it doing handstands and cartwheels round the room – and she ran one hand up the nape of her neck to feel its submissive slant and the soft, downy prickle, and thought triumphantly that Vanessa would not give this sweetness to anyone else, not even to her husband; but she would give it to Mattie who was the orphaned cousin. And now Mattie had that illusion which afterwards she would have again and again that because she was so pretty – and they did so like everything to be pretty – and funny as well, and because she loved them they would love her back. And she blushed and smiled and went back to drinking her coffee.

· 13 ·

The morning after the party, when the last of the guests had left and the rain had started to fall, a thief came in with the water. He let himself in by the back gate which led up from the canal. He passed the statue of the seventeenth-century lady and climbed up by the steps and crossed the lawn and climbed in through the pantry window with the aid of a Victorian bath chair which had been rotting in the kitchen garden. He crossed the kitchen floor and at some point he sat down at the table to smoke a cigarette, for he left his cigarette packet behind (and his insouciance afterwards much impressed the Oaklands: 'How stylishly we've been burg-led,' they said with shrugs of self-deprecation and amuse-ment). And then he got to his feet and crept around the house and took the oddest things.

He took the garden shears from the conservatory. He took Jonathan's new saxophone on which Jonathan had just learnt to play two notes of such extreme melancholy that he had been elated (and afterwards his loss caused him to put aside his fey madness and weep real tears of grief instead). He crept into Aaron's bedroom, where Aaron still slept under a duvet childishly streaked with Pentel pens and ink of every colour, and took one of Aaron's models. Then he went into the big bedroom where Tom and Vanessa were still asleep in the big double bed under white embroidered sheets which Katherine, the cleaning lady, weekly washed, ironed, folded and put away, and later on unfolded with a flourish to tuck

· 62 ·

across the bed, sheets with crisp, straight creases in them – very nice! He took three of Tom's jackets and all his ties and socks but discarded his pairs of trousers – 'So what's wrong with my trousers?' said Tom afterwards – and three bottles of gin (which later caused the detectives' brows to rise because they had been left for no particular reason in the wardrobe on the landing) and a hundred pounds from Vanessa's second handbag, before departing by the back door with his booty carefully stacked in the rubbish bin.

But he left the back door open so that Vanessa, coming downstairs an hour or two later, found the house curiously wide open to the world where usually it was sealed off from it by curtains and doors and central heating. She didn't like the watery morning air which wafted through the house. She felt herself invaded. She rang for the police at once and before long two detectives with crewcuts and fat faces – 'and the tiniest of eyes,' said Jonathan – came to measure the footprints and lift the fingerprints and shake their heads in disbelief over the lack of locks. They consulted their notes and found the Oaklands had been burgled twice before. They didn't think it in the least bit chic to live so carelessly and told the Oaklands that in the circumstances they were unlikely to get anything back on insurance. They stayed an hour and then they went away and the Oaklands heard no more, so that soon Tom began to say, 'Well, perhaps there never was a thief, perhaps he was a figment of our imagination,' and Jonathan said, 'Or Goldilocks, perhaps.'

But Vanessa was indignant. She took the burglary personally. She thought it was bad behaviour, on a par with not RSVPing invitations. 'There certainly was,' she said. 'I lost one hundred pounds.'

Money, beautiful money. 'I loved my cousins,' said Mattie to Dr H years later when she was twenty-one and pregnant, 'and for all kinds of reasons, but not least because they were rich. Do you understand that? The Oaklands without money were unthinkable. Mind you, it's not materialism which

· 63 ·

makes me talk like this,' she added, and he replied with a question, of course, fixing her with his sharp, black eyes: 'So what's wrong with materialism?' But Mattie was her mother's daughter and she couldn't help but disapprove of wealth and covetousness and the desire for material objects – although at the same time she wanted them, how badly she wanted them. And she looked around at Dr H's study where what colours there were – beige on the walls, blue on the curtains, brown on the floor – were being for ever bleached by the cold and silvery light; and sadly she remembered how when the Oaklands went out to dinner they always went in a gang and, wandering around their hostess's house, would pick up the objects, stroking them with their fingers to feel the texture as they asked the price. The Oaklands made the material world speak for them. It was their context. It defined them and when it spoke for them it spoke of warmth and wealth and pleasure, but also of course of love.

But he didn't understand. He was misled, she knew it, by the habitual pride with which she spoke of them, even now. Fool that he is, thought Mattie.

'I lost one hundred pounds,' said Vanessa the day the burglar came. Well, I can understand that, thought Mattie.

THE COMMON HISTORY

· 14 ·

One day Caroline, Leonie, Lindie, Barbara and Hester held their own antenatal class in the local swimming baths. Bright costumes, pink and red, white skin and blue water lapping up against them, the colour of dentists' mouthwash. The shadows of waves curling and wriggling across the tiled pool bottom, and through the water their thighs and white bosoms magnified hugely. They rode high, bobbing like ducks, pushed upwards by their bumps. How lovely it was. A little girl swam towards them, sleek and slender, neat as a fish, and they parted in admiration to let her go through, ducks bobbing all around her. They were five, not one and four, nor three and two, but five, neat and complete. For the time was coming and coming fast when they would feel more in common with each other whom they had only just met than they did with their men. They couldn't help it. 'No wonder the men are frightened,' Caroline said. It was as if pregnancy had taken hold of each romantic couple and struck them down the middle, the shattered bits regrouping themselves along the lines of the sexes, men with men and women with women. She loves her Michael, Hester thought, looking sideways on at Caroline. Blow hot, blow cold, thought Hester. Sometimes she loved the women and sometimes she did not.

After swimming they went to Lindie's flat for coffee. She was a small woman with a small mouth and straight nose and narrow blue eyes. She was inclined to sternness and always hard upon herself and plain in all her emotions and she believed that the rest of them should be as plain as she was. She had a curious profile, the forehead and nose a single line. Hester admired this profile. She thought it rather heroic. Lindie lived on the fifth floor of a council block. The day the women visited someone had just peed in the lift. It was fresh, stinking and yellow. Rubbish sacks were piled up at either end of the corridors. Caroline blenched. They were all of them appalled. They worried for Lindie's health and for that of her baby, each of them believing that their own environment was the best possible one in which to bring up a child.

Lindie's boyfriend came home that afternoon. He was a dark-haired man dressed in a Burberry which fell open to reveal trousers cinched in to a narrow, slender waist and a cigarette – a cigarette, my God! they didn't see many of those during their pregnancies – which he held sideways between the tips of all four fingers and his thumb. His name was Mario. He was very handsome. He was Hester's idea of a handsome conman (and you couldn't get much more romantic than that). Lindie sat cross-legged upon the floor, pale, stern and impassive, but Mario smiled at Hester and she looked at Lindie slyly to see if she minded and was put out to see she didn't. Hester was no threat. Lindie knew what Mario liked and it was her. She was watching the women carefully, as she always did, observing their middle-class manners, one hand placed protectively upon her belly.

Leonie was talking to Caroline. Leonie was a big, pale, fey woman who inclined as far towards coolness as Mattie inclined the other way, towards romance. Leonie affected the remoteness of her upper-class background. She spoke with disparagement of her husband, pretending to find him useless in every way. She denied all knowledge of feelings and yawned and said, 'How exotic,' when she listened to Mattie's stories, as if rage and hate and incest and jealousy were the very height of unusualness, and as if there was

· 66 ·

nothing at all unusual in being ordinary, rich but entirely ordinary, ordinary in every way. On this particular day she was describing to Caroline some extravaganza of a cot that she had seen, and Caroline was listening and so was Barbara but with her indifferent manner. But Lindie and Hester who were as poor as church mice were catching each other's eyes and Hester fancied they were both marvelling at how much money Leonie had to spend and wondering surreptitiously what her husband did and whether or not it was honourable.

'Well, we all of us have our fancies,' said Hester lightly, but she meant it. But Leonie said, 'Do we?' and looked at Hester. With her cold fish eyes, thought Hester – for she was always like this, both sad and deprecating, running Hester down, so that suddenly Hester was furious. What does she know? thought Hester, love draining through her in a twinkling, like water through a sieve; but then she thought with sadness, she knows of course we ask for bread and get given stones and it's only Mattie and me who keep on hoping.

Mattie turned up for the coffee, late as usual, and always for the coffee but never for the swimming, for she had this Oaklandish thing against physical exercise. She came knocking at the door, dressed up to the nines in frilly white Victorian underwear designed for a very large Victorian tart, with moccasins of raspberry pink and a sheepskin coat on top which she had dyed a raspberry pink to match. 'This place is like a cowshed,' said Mattie rudely – she had no time for female fertility – and she went across to the window and tried to open it. She peered into a mirror and, seeing that Hester was watching her, she asked, 'Do you feel the same on the inside as you do on the outside, Hester?' 'No,' said Hester. 'Nor do I,' said Mattie, gesturing towards her glittering reflection with a quite unconscious lack of modesty. And then she wandered round the room, staring at the photographs and picking up the magazines and all with that air

· 67 ·

she had of being talkative and discontented and struggling to understand.

Mattie liked to talk about herself and her family and the father of her baby. That day she told the women who the father was and Leonie said, a little piously, 'Babies are individuals. They shouldn't be used in their parents' quarrels.' They wanted to make much of Mattie because she was so pretty and because they admired her looks – for even in the last months of pregnancy she dressed with a certain style with which they couldn't compete – but they wanted also to cut her down to size because they felt she was a Mary to their Marthas and sometimes they felt she was too much for them, for she never told her story straight but was for ever slipping it into an invisible net or sleeve which glittered and sparkled and which imparted to her history and its sadnesses the aura of romance. Hester thought it was as if they had decided to be her mother in the way that older women, being thirty, often do.

How sly Hester was in all her observations but it was how they all were about their female friends, and towards their friends' men; sly, admiring, warm, critical, mocking, curious and sympathetic. Mattie was Hester's friend but Hester would not hesitate to criticise her behaviour to the others, and this was how they all were about each other. And so they delicately wondered if Leonie was not a little neurotic, if Caroline was not planning to go back to work too soon, if Lindie could really bring up a baby in conditions such as these, and so on. As for each other's men, well, Leonie's Christopher was a businessman, far too thin and elongated for Hester's taste and prone to wearing suits and ties. Michael and Caroline looked good together, he so sensitive and so Jewish and such an aesthete, she so gentile and so down-to-earth. Barbara's Colin was very dreary but Lindie's man, the dark-haired conman, made Hester laugh for all his charm and his fraudulent manners. When he smiled at her the first time they met and she looked at Lindie sideways to see if this offended her and was put out to see it didn't she thought, a spiv, putting him down, but all the same she liked him. She had this terrible habit of assuming other women's men were more interesting than her own.

They told each other about their symptoms, enquiring solicitously after each other's health and well-being, laughing and combing and preening and petting each other like monkeys in a zoo. And they talked. Although when Mattie was present they tended to listen, for lately she had started to talk and now she had started she found she couldn't stop. And besides, she was younger than them, more forceful and determined, and she had a story to tell.

'Why is it that Mattie's life has a story to it and mine does not?' Hester complained as soon as Mattie left – she hoped she sounded humorous but secretly she believed that she too had something to say and would say it if only Mattie would let her get a word in edgeways. But Lindie said acerbicly, 'It's because she's so full of herself,' and Hester gazed at her and said nothing because she knew it would annoy her to hear it, but she couldn't help thinking in her melancholy but romantic way that there were two kinds of people and Mattie and she were of the second kind who painted the world so thickly with their own needs and desires they could hardly make it out at all. And besides the point about Mattie also was that she didn't really belong with them, she had only stepped down for one moment from the glamorous world of Regent's Park to scrabble around with them in the poor and serious parts of Kentish Town.

· 15 ·

Hester's father was a vicar. He often preached on the subject of love. He was a small man with a narrow, bony face, dark, burning eyes and an anxious, stooped expression. He easily felt attacked and when he did would reach for malice, quick as a flash, to defend himself. He made no allowances for the fact that Hester was his daughter. In such moods they were all his enemies. She used to fear his sharp, sarcastic tongue. Her father was a clever, scholarly man and his feelings were complex and distorted, his language twisted as he tried to express himself ever more precisely. His sermons were academic discourses and this most unchristian of men, so lacking in benignness and soft charity, would preach on love not because he found it easy but because to him it seemed so difficult.

On Sunday mornings when Hester was a child she used to sit behind a pillar during sermons where he couldn't see her. There were five of them here in this congregation and one of them was an atheist. For Hester was fourteen and had ceased to believe in God in the hope that He would strike her down. But neither her father nor the Father in heaven had noticed. His words bent like light around the pillar, or rather as light does not bend, except for the light of the Lord. Her father was a good speaker. His words flew forth amongst the stone pillars, out through the embroidered windows where the light came in and stitched both sides of the church together, out across the gravestones and down to the waters of Minsmere where Tony Guilder sat fishing on a Sunday morning. And singing along ironically to their hymns. Tony Guilder was her first boyfriend.

Her father was a scholar but not a gentleman. He had a sweet smile when he was happy. He was also a clergyman and a widower – for Hester's mother died when she was six – and this gave him a certain appeal to the women around there. 'My father is all head,' says Hester, 'all head and no body and the inside of his head is black, entirely black, but still it doesn't stop the women fancying him.' Especially respectable, middle-aged women. But her father, she had observed, liked his women to be young, beautiful, a little flash and fly, with big bosoms and freckles and velvety cleavages where he liked to think these women lived. Tony Guilder lived in the very middle of his body, squatting down in his shorts to sort through his fishing tackle, his prick hanging down – Hester could see it – in front. Hester was sixteen and had just passed twelve O levels. She was like her father, long legs and big head. She was hoping to be mad, bad and dangerous to know. But if the clever men liked their women to be beautiful, what kind of man would like a clever woman? Tony Guilder, she supposed. Was her mother flash and fly? They would never tell her so how would she ever know?

Our Father who art in Heaven. 'Mattie understands this talk of God,' says Hester. She too was brought up with terrible Christianity. It is what they have in common. Hester once mentioned her father to Mattie and she said, 'Oh, so your father is a vicar, is he?' and for a moment she was no longer Mattie Oakland but Mattie Thomas, daughter of Jane Thomas, the two of them, that odd couple who lived in the farm workers' cottage at the bend of the road from Dunmow End to Arksley Cross. 'My mother went to church once,' said Mattie with an ugly droop of her mouth, 'and in the middle of the hymns she fainted. It was religious ecstasy of course. She hit her chin on the wooden pew and it poured with blood. But the vicar never stopped the hymns for one moment. They don't like religious ecstasy in the Church of England.' 'It wasn't my father,' murmured Hester confusedly, in defence of the scholar-clergyman whom she loved but did not like.

Her father was an academic. She should have been an academic too. She missed her chance of bluestockinghood by half a mark. Every month her father spent five days in London, stayed in a small hotel in Russell Square and in the British and the London and the Warburg libraries studied alchemy and necromancy; Dürer and his religious beliefs; Galileo and Copernicus; Erasmus and the printing press and Thomas Aquinas and the passions of love and the medieval mystics and many other things, all of which seemed to Hester to be hugely romantic because they were so bright and shining in the darkness and the dustiness of libraries.

When she first came to London after Oxford she went to a jazz club where an acquaintance of hers was holding her birthday party. And there she fell in love with Frank the piano player.

He was dark-haired and wore a leather jacket. His nose was heavy and his eyes deep set and his smile was as rakish and toothy as a crocodile's. He came across in the interval bringing two girls in tow with him, twins, he said – well, what do you think of that? thought Hester – with blonde ringlets and red lipstick and fur coats (for he was a man of old-fashioned tastes, as jazz men often are) which they kept drawing and re-drawing round them. But after a while they got up to powder their noses and never came back.

'Where are your friends?' asked Hester and he answered her indifferently, 'I don't know. You're clever, aren't you?' 'Very,' she said. 'Oxford?' he asked. 'Oxford,' she agreed. 'Sleep with me,' he said. 'No,' she said but he didn't seem to mind but took her instead to a pub of quite surpassing seediness, with outside toilets whose smell was a yellow stink frozen solid by the night, where broken-down-looking

· 72 ·

men sat drinking by the yellowy light with faces melted downwards round the edges by their poverty. Outside two women chatted up a man, mocking, complaining and seductive, and another woman cried and shouted out, 'I'm going to kill you, John, I'm going to kill you,' whereupon the first two fell silent – and then to his room in the basement of a squat, and the bed which was large and dirty and which stood in the middle of the room . . .

She saw him as part of a tradition, just as she saw her father as part of a tradition, although Frank's was very different and not one she knew much about. But she could dimly see where he belonged, in bars and jazz clubs, with blacks and liquor and gigs, in New Orleans and by the Mississippi and with the Mississippi and Chicago Blues. It was curious what her imagination did to these two men, romanticising them so that when she saw them in her mind's eye she saw them in profile, their lines softened, a light behind them which imparted to them a glow. It was love, she supposed.

She lived with Frank for two years. She was his intellectual mistress, his brainy and angular bluestocking and he loved it. But she soon saw why he was thirty-seven and unmarried because, although when he was good he was very, very sweet – and besides, he understood her which was even better – when he was bad he was horrible. Black moods would overwhelm him and linger for weeks and then he wouldn't talk to her except to criticise her for what she was and did and looked and said and thought and dreamed. At night he turned away from her as if her very presence offended him. His head was heavy as iron on the pillow. By day he sat over the piano playing not jazz but Mozart and Chopin sonatas, pouring out his soul and spirit into these broken-backed and broken-hearted pieces until she couldn't stand any longer the loneliness of his making love to them and not to her.

She met Henry at a party. Later on he became a friend of Frank's. He was the exact opposite of Frank, being plump

· 73 ·

and vain and soft and foppish and all this was for her at first his charm. She was distraught because she thought Frank didn't love her any more. She and Henry went to bed on Wednesday evenings when Frank was at the Bass Clef club. She thought she must be in love with Henry. Quite soon Frank began to grow suspicious. She was pleased. She was looking forward to the cathartic outpouring of all their emotions, their love and anger and rage and jealousy, to be made good at last, when they were exhausted, by sex. But what Frank did was to invite Henry for a drink, and Henry went because Henry was a man's man and because he admired Frank enormously and because he thought men ought to stick together and because even whilst making love to her he never lost his reverential admiration for everything Frank was and did.

Frank plied him with whisky from the Bass Clef cellars. Pretty soon Henry confessed. Frank was a moral man, moral and angry. He believed in his own virtue and in Hester's wickedness. His revenge was simple. He told Henry what she had told him, which was that Henry was gay, that he didn't like women, that he only liked to be screwed by men.

Imagine the scene when she got home from work that night. 'You can go,' says Frank and his black eyes are jumping out like flames. She reaches out one hand but draws it back again. For fear I might be burnt, she thinks. In her head the thoughts are popping like popcorn on a griddle. Guiltily. I wonder if he's hot to touch, she thinks. 'You can go,' he says, 'I don't want to see you again,' and she opens her mouth, then closes it, for he has packed her bags for her, has removed one entire stage in the argument, and she never thought of that. And so having nowhere else to go she went to Henry's.

· 16 ·

The other women in the group did not talk about their feelings for their men. Tied now as they were by the commitment of a baby, they preferred to keep silent and hope for the best. And so it was that only Mattie and Hester, who were semi-detached, sat one day in a fashionable patisserie in St John's Wood – it was Mattie's idea, of course, not Hester's – and talked about this and that, at length, in their female fashion, about money and material possessions and the Oaklands, but also about love and approval which were so important to them. And Mattie because she was Mattie, and because she was trying to work out everything that had ever happened to her – Mattie was putting her different loves in the order of their importance.

They had met up on the corner of St John's Wood High Street. When Hester arrived she found Mattie there already, dressed in some yellow number which she'd borrowed from Vanessa and bending her head down to an old woman who was shouting up at her. It was a white, radiant summer's day. The wind was whipping up the sunlight. Flowers were heaped up outside the florists' shops. The road was jammed with convertibles and men with bronzed forearms were driving with one hand on the wheel whilst music from their stereos, plaintive and seductive, snaked its way across the street. Even from where she stood Hester could see that Mattie wasn't listening to the old woman nor thinking of anything at all but simply was, as usual, on this brilliant summer's day, smiling with embarrassment and directing her gaze on the old woman as if she were issuing forth love, or sucking it up, so that Hester had that curious impression which she sometimes got from Mattie, that she had spread herself out in all directions in pursuit of love, until she was entirely dissolved and there was no point at which she ended and the world began.

'Hallo, Hester,' Mattie called out. They were dressed to kill. They were intending to glad-rag their way down St John's Wood High Street (for all that they were so pregnant) with the wind bowling along behind them, very light and airy and full of itself, and the two of them laughing and clutching hold of each other because they were pretending to be two of those rich creatures who live off men and pass their days in shopping.

They went into a shop selling baby things, chests of drawers and changing mats and bouncing chairs and cots which were softly padded inside the bars to protect the babies' heads. There was paper on the walls depicting old-fashioned scenes of childhood – children in smocks, with ducks and geese and rabbits. Rivers of white fabric at the windows fell from the white ceiling to the white floor; and there were white lampshades and clothes in whipped-cream mountains, jackets and leggings and vests and hats and shoes and the room was filled with the rich women and their gasps and cries of admiration, exulting in the miniatureness of everything they touched.

It was a lifestyle which made Hester feel riotous, even to witness it, but Mattie was high priest and chief worshipper on the altar of lovely things and so she had her nose in the air and was wishing, Hester could see it, she'd been born Mattie Oakland and not Mattie Thomas.

'Oh, Hester,' says Mattie as she sits at the white wickerwork table in this fashionable London patisserie. She is wearing with the yellow number a hat with a brim which gives her smooth, flattish face, her regular features and large, dark eyes, an eighteenth-century look. Mattie is all image, this image or that image; sometimes it drives Hester mad. It's as if life were just a matter of deciding what kind of person she was going to be. 'Oh, Hester,' Mattie says, 'I'm getting so fat. Perhaps it's all been a mistake,' says the pale, pregnant, tragic Mattie as if her life were only a fiction. 'It's the story of my life,' she adds, as if she were all of seventy-one, not twenty-one and the story just beginning.

But then Mattie cheers up and asks, 'Would you like a cappuccino, Hester?' in her charming fashion, and at once she looks round for the waiter, her lips parted and her eyes under the brim of her hat settling keenly here and there – for as usual Mattie is in pursuit of love, as they both are for all that they are six months pregnant, and, who knows, the waiter might be the source of it as well as of the coffee?

Who's going to pay for this coffee? thinks Hester to herself. Why, Mattie of course. She likes to pay, she always does – but where does she get her money from? Not from the art gallery, for she gave that up a month ago. So now presumably she is living off the Oaklands. Who is going to support you and your baby, Mattie? asks Hester silently, fixing her with her stare – for today she is cross with Mattie, although at the same time, in a semi-professional way (for Hester works in a museum restoring pictures and the way things look is a part of her profession) her eyes are admiring the painterly fall of the light on Mattie's face as she smiles and moves her head and each new plane and angle of her features is revealed. Mattie's smile has settled across the room upon the waiter and he, a tall, sullen Polish man, is moving towards them in a reluctant yet fascinated fashion.

Which makes Hester remember that today she is cross with Mattie because last night was Fathers' Night at the antenatal classes. (Fathers. 'Now on June 15,' said Judith, 'that's the fourth week of our course, there will be a Fathers' Night when you'll be bringing along your men.' And those of them who had one brought him along, but Mattie of course came on her own. 'Now, how many of you are single parents? Mattie, of course!' *Well, they all knew that.*) And Mattie so smiled and laughed at the men that their easy, female atmosphere was ruined.

Hester was not comfortable when there were others around to witness her relationship with Henry. Last night as each couple arrived at the front door Judith split them up, sending the men off to the left into the sitting room and the women down the corridor to where they gathered joyously in the kitchen. Hester was glad they were so divided. For these classes were theirs, their stay-at-home, daytime, female experience whilst the men went out to work, and she brought Henry along only with trepidation.

Judith asked them all to compile two lists, of the positive and negative aspects of pregnancy. From where they sat they could hear the low, serious voices of the men, hard at work. But Hester was straining to hear what they were saying and her pleasure in the company of her friends was being spoilt by her fear that in the other room Henry might be incurring the contempt of these men whom she'd never even met.

And yet at the same time another part of her mind knew that at this minute Henry would in fact be making himself likeable, appointing himself secretary, writing down the minutes, keeping track of the meeting. It was only in her mind that he failed, she knew it, but she couldn't help the way she saw him.

Mattie so smiled and laughed, thinks Hester – with her long, Oaklandish earrings and shining eyes and glittery hair – and afterwards in the car Henry began to belittle Mattie, which also made Hester angry. She knew he only did it because he fancied Mattie and yet was so unable to express his feelings generously; and she was angry also with her friend for arousing such feelings in her man when really he meant nothing to her. Today Mattie hadn't even mentioned him – he didn't interest her, Hester knew it – and yet she would rather, really she would, that his admiration were reciprocated instead of this humiliating silence, because in that way Hester might be encouraged that her choice of man was a good one. But as usual Mattie was uninterested.

Henry had a jowly face. Between the cheekbones and the ears were a series of folds and soft wrinkles. All the faces in this café today were particularly full and fleshy, the eyes large, rather prominent and shining, the mouths very pink, the hair full and luxuriant. There was something unreal about these faces – they resembled the faces in a nineteenth-century French café painting – and their unreality was confusing Hester. The waiter had taken their order. He was weaving his way between the tables and chairs, his head bowed, his back expressive of all the distaste and reluctance he had for this job. And Mattie's eyes were following after him, flaring and flaming and settling upon him until, with a flash of knowledge, Hester saw what it was that had so attracted her, for his apron had pulled down his shirt collar and the spot where the neck met the shoulder was on him particularly soft and tender.

And then Mattie's mind flipped over into another thought. 'Do you love Henry?' she asked, staring at Hester and licking the cappuccino froth from the back of her spoon. Curious, inquisitive, impertinent Mattie, so that Hester replied, 'Oh yes,' but with such sarcasm and evident insincerity that Mattie stared at Hester in wonder, spoon poised, undecided. 'I wish I loved a man like that,' she said at last. 'Like how?' 'I mean, I wish I loved the father of my baby properly, in the right way, so that we could live together,' and at this a bleak, mournful inturned look settled upon Mattie's face, such as Hester would one day see on her daughter's face when she shouted at her, and Hester relented and thought, poor Mattie, who loves but doesn't find it easy, the love inextricably muddled up with anger and resentment.

· 79 ·

'Do you think more about your father or your mother, Hester?' said Mattie in her blithe, careless way as if to hide the importance of what she was saying.

'My father,' said Hester, thinking of the scholar-clergyman whom she hadn't seen since the weekend she took Henry down there, which was of course the weekend she fell out of interest in him altogether and completely.

'I think more about my mother,' said Mattie. 'I used to think about my father a lot, dream about him and wonder what he was like, when I was young and first started being interested in going out with boys. It was as if I had to know my father first before I could know other men. But now I think about my mother. Even before I became pregnant I was thinking about her all the time. Isn't that funny? Why should that be?' And she began to fiddle with the buttons on her jacket. She had dropped twenty years from her age. She was looking round the room as if she were looking for a mother at this very minute.

Hester thought, her childhood is like a baby who will not lie decently down to sleep. And she answered her wearily because sometimes she grew tired of this intense, naive, egocentric girl. 'Perhaps because the mother is more primal,' said Hester. 'Perhaps because we are daughters and therefore our mothers are a part of us. I don't know. But what I do think is this, that although there are so many different loves and they are all so various, at the same time they are all part and parcel of the same one, so that to call them by different names is entirely stupid, because it is not mothers but both parents who are the problem, and all the love affairs which come afterwards are simply versions of the love affairs with our parents and all life is an endless seeking to go back into them. And then sometimes I think the problem is the other way round and that there is only one word, "love", and we need more than one because that word has been appropriated to describe the relationship between men and women. And what about those other powerful feelings, that pursuit of

· 80 ·

other people to be our mothers and fathers and brothers and sisters which doesn't stop all through our lives until we die; so that to talk about "incest" is also stupid because nearly all love is incestuous by definition, because it is informed by those early feelings . . .'

And then Hester stopped because she saw that Mattie hadn't heard a word of what she was saying but was staring with her large eyes which were so blind, both actually and metaphorically, at the waiter as he cleared away the cappuccino cups. At the table next to her a little boy sat on his mother's lap, holding a spoon to his mouth and pushing out his lips in thoughtful contemplation as he watched them. Mattie took no notice. She hadn't even seen him. You would never have thought that any day now she was going to give birth to just such a two-armed, two-legged, one-headed creature as this. But then Mattie was afraid – it was the bottom line for her as for the rest of them – afraid that she would not, could not, love this creature whom she knew would cling to her like the Old Man of the Sea, making her lopsided, never letting her go.

Your mother loved you. No she didn't. My mother loved me. No she didn't. But I never thought I might not love my child.

The waiter is coming back with fresh cappuccinos. He puts the cups down carefully on the table, watches his hands as slowly they move the sugar, the salt and the pepper to make room. And then he looks up quickly, sideways, slyly, straight into Mattie's face with a look in his eyes of shining tenderness but with pride and contempt settling round his mouth. And Mattie blushes. She has seen the tenderness, Hester knows it, but not the pride. Sometimes she is so transparent you can see right through her. She smiles, retreats embarrassed at the directness of his look, but nonetheless is pleased. And nor has she seen the look which the woman at the counter is giving them, a blonde, stocky woman who is clearly the waiter's wife, and who will come over in ten minutes or so to clear away the cups and take a closer look at this girl whom her husband is smiling at. And once again Mattie will see in her eyes not a dislike but a motherliness and will smile at her. Because that's what Mattie's like.

And then Mattie said, 'Have you ever seen an Oakland fabric, Hester?' and all of a sudden she's up and paying the bill and leading Hester out and across a road and into a shop with pale, polished, wooden floors and a barrel-vaulted ceiling of the same, and not one item of furniture or anything else that anyone might be selling. But Mattie has been here before and she dives through into the back where in a sudden radiance swathes of fabric fall twenty feet or more to the yellow-glazed stone flooring and through a glass wall at the back a dark green, bosomy, evergreen tree is puffing out its darkness and a black-haired, young-old girl, polished up like a stone, is sitting and turning the pages of a magazine and looking them up and down. 'Can I help you?' she asks, and Mattie turns her head and gives her a Mattie-ish look: eyes wide open, mouth clamped tight shut, a curious, affronted look as if fearful that she might not be liked and yet hopeful that she might.

'Look,' says Mattie, 'Oakland fabrics,' and she smiles and reaches up to stroke them in that narcissistic way that pretty women often have, as if it were themselves that they were stroking. The colours are astonishing. She is holding up a fabric which is predominantly of reds and blues: Paris blue with its coppery sheen, mountain blue and cerulean blue, a light, bright, greeny-blue much favoured by the Oaklands for its atmospheric and celestial effects; and madder lake, a beautiful, transparent red, and carmine which the ancients said surpassed even madder lake in beauty, and fiery, glazing burnt sienna. 'Oh, the colours of the Oaklands are wonder-

· 82 ·

ful,' says Mattie with a nonchalant pride, and she draws forth other fabrics so that Hester can also see Naples yellow (dark), an old, mysterious yellow and raw sienna, and green cinnabar and malachite green, and Egyptian blue (named after the blue the ancients used) and Venetian red and vermilion and sinope, a light red ochre from Asia Minor, and of course a hundred thousand combinations and deviations and variations of them all, for all the critics agreed that what characterised the products of the Oaklands was a simplicity of form combined with a richness of colour.

We are all of us lured onwards by our dreams, thinks Hester. (She wished she were her father's dream.) Leonie's was the Dream of the Good Wife and Good Mother, for all that she would deprecate it. And Mario was Lindie's dream, just as the Oaklands were Mattie's objects of desire. They were wrapped in romance for her and always would be and so she conceived her baby as a present for them, just as Hester conceived her baby in order to give a present to her father. But it was her bad luck and her baby's and Henry's also, who was the father of her baby, that she couldn't see him as anything more than a fat, vain man.

LOVE AND APPROVAL

· 17 ·

The Oaklands were most peculiar towards their friends. It was one of the first things that Mattie noticed as she began to emerge at last from her long Oakland babyhood.

Every summer they rented a cottage in the town of Southwold, a pretty, undeveloped place of whitewashed cottages and green, open spaces, sited upon a low cliff so that the eye is drawn always upwards to the bright, blue air. It is a town much frequented in July and August by the upper middle classes – 'Camden sur mer', as Noah described it scornfully. But still he came each summer to visit and this year was staying in a cottage on the other side of town with his girlfriend Sylvie.

And the Oaklands also rented a beach hut down upon the promenade, at that point where it begins to disappear beneath the sand and the landscape takes on the wild and duney look of Maine or New England. Here there were gathered one August morning Vanessa and Mattie and a friend of Vanessa's called Sonja Lefanu, the three of them waiting for the arrival of Vanessa's menfolk: Tom from the London train which will drop him at Darsham, eight miles distant; Noah and Sylvie from across the dunes at Walberswick, where they went early this morning to buy fresh fish and from where they are coming, squabbling and bickering as they walk across the tussocky sand (or rather Noah squabbles and Sylvie struggles with her shoes and parries him defensively because she loves him too much to bear to quar-

· 85 ·

rel – 'What do they quarrel about?' asks Sonja. 'Oh, you know, whether or not Sylvie's hungry, that kind of thing,' Vanessa answers) – and Aaron and Jonathan down the cliff path from the town where they have been chatting up the waitress in a local café.

Vanessa has pinned up the washing on the verandah and a vivid, multicoloured collection of skirts and swimsuits and sweaters and towels all blow and crack in the wind so that the hut begins to resemble the tent of a medieval courtly knight with all its flags and pennants flying. There are jamjars full of sea lavender and pinks upon the timber flooring and cups half full of coffee strewn about in a painterly fashion. The two women sit on deckchairs and raise their faces to the pale and silvery sun.

Sonja is just back from a holiday in Istanbul with her husband Philip. Now she is bending Vanessa's ear on the subject of his behaviour. She says he is a wimp. She says she can hardly bear this. And Vanessa listens with half an ear and her sweet and absentminded smile. A book of Paul Klee's paintings is lying open on the ground beside her. The wind is whipping its pages over violently. Out to sea on this bright morning the same wind is beating up the water into sculptured waves. The sun is still low in the sky. It glitters on the sea and a yacht beats past upon a sea of diamonds. But the wind! It is threatening to whip down your throat as soon as you open your mouth.

Not that this stops Sonja. Mattie, who is sitting on the steps very close to Vanessa, thinks she knows what Vanessa is really thinking about. She is thinking about her sons, of course, but especially about Aaron, for Aaron this summer – when he is just nineteen and Mattie twenty – Aaron has been offered a place to read History of Art at Oxford and the Oaklands, whom you might have thought would be delighted by this upturn in his fortunes, have fallen into a terrible tizzy of doubt, anxiety and disapproval. It is not very Oaklandish to go to Oxford and Aaron has turned

· 86 ·

down his place at art school, which is very un-Oaklandish indeed. What Aaron *ought* to be doing with his life is a great topic of conversation amongst them during these months of July and August, which they spend, as they always do, commuting distractedly between London and the coast of Suffolk.

And Vanessa is also thinking about Paul Klee's paintings, which she has only just rediscovered. She is luxuriating in their colours, and the feel of them, and is wondering if one might transfer this feel – which is of a lovely, literate rhythm – onto fabric and what one would do with the fabric if one did. This is what Vanessa is thinking and Mattie knows it but Sonja doesn't. Poor Sonja, thinks Mattie, poor Sonja who doesn't live in the heart of the Oaklands, whose words on this bright morning are being whipped away absurdly from out her mouth, who looks at the beautiful Vanessa who is transparent like a vase – all beautiful line and form and a centre which is quite transparent – but Sonja doesn't see right through her. Poor Sonja, thinks Mattie, who cannot imagine how one would ever reach this state of videos and nannies and Range Rovers and burglar alarms and thinning hair and too much make-up and an inadequate husband. Why doesn't she leave him? thinks Mattie, whose affections these days when she is so happy often take this form of a feeling of friendly superiority.

And at this very moment Vanessa looks up and fixes Sonja with her large-eyed gaze, both sweet and acerbic as if she were thinking the very same thing as Mattie. For these days Vanessa often communes with Mattie by means of a sympathetic telepathy. 'He does pay your bills, Sonja,' Vanessa protests mildly, 'and he's very handsome, really quite painterly, in a dinner jacket.' And both women giggle.

Sonja and Vanessa have had another of their rows and are now in a state of post-row forgiveness, or at any rate Sonja is forgiving Vanessa, both loudly and graciously, and Vanessa is being enigmatic, as she always is. Sonja is a big,

· 87 ·

smartly-dressed woman with a smart, fashionable mind, a barrister by profession, who took up with the Oaklands because they are a little bit famous, because she is stirred by Tom's good looks, by his peachy lips and his way of looking at her which is rather too direct, and because she is moved in a way quite unfamiliar to herself by Vanessa's sweetness. She counts herself the very closest of Vanessa's friends and rings her up with information on where to get things cheap.

Vanessa won't let anyone else laugh at Sonja except herself. 'She's been very good to me,' she says, not apparently considering it at all disloyal that she herself should tell funny stories about Sonja all round London. But Sonja did and once, when hearing one of these stories at fourth hand, she confronted Vanessa, who hung her head like a child and said nothing. But afterwards Vanessa was cross because she was proud and hated to be wrong-footed, and especially in public, and so she didn't apologise – she never did – but a month or two later Sonja received an invitation to an Oakland party. She turned up very hurt and angry and dressed in brilliant yellow but the Oakland boys were more than usually attentive and Tom poured her a glass of wine with an air of sympathy only mildly spiced with Oakland irony and Vanessa sat at the kitchen table looking distraught and very pretty. Someone had been in the night before and had taken her necklace of seed pearls. 'But how did they get in?' asked Sonja and Vanessa said, 'I left the window open,' and Sonja felt better and forgave her.

But Sonja is not at all perceptive. On the morning that the three women are sitting down beside the beach hut, Sonja is gazing vaguely into the distance when she sees Noah and Sylvie come into view across the sand dunes.

Noah has shed his city zootsuits and two-tone correspondents' shoes and is dressed, instead, colonial style in shorts and socks and shoes. How small and thin and black and white he is compared with his adoring mother, but elegant nonetheless. And struggling along behind him is Sylvie, who

· 88 ·

wears Doc Martins and black wool tights and a grey wool mini skirt – very short – and a black sweater on top with a hole in it. Camden Town clothing. 'Sylvie's very nice,' murmurs Sonja before they are yet in earshot and Mattie through her closed eyes sees Vanessa smile her even more abstracted smile and reflects without even having to reflect that she herself would never say such a thing to Vanessa.

For Vanessa was famous for loving her three sons to distraction. She liked to try to make them do what she wanted them to do. She indulged them in all directions, but at the back of her mind, way back beyond the softness and malleability, was a small, hard, round entity which was her will and determination. And whilst as babies they bored her, when they reached the age of four or so and began to squirm away from her kisses, to arch their backs in protest in her arms and say, 'No,' and 'No, no, no, no, no,' then her interest and her will were engaged.

And when they grew older, if Tom were away for the night on business, she would sit with them in the conservatory, listening to their records and eating fish and chips with them. And Mattie, coming home through the garden, would see the four of them together, Vanessa wearing a dress of iridescent velvet, her reddish hair heaped up loosely on her head and her face very white in the bright light of the conservatory, whilst Aaron sat in the shadows but Jonathan sat in the light and beat his hands on the table in time to the music. Behind them the dishes would be piling up in a satisfying kind of way and at their elbows the cat would be eating a lump of fishy batter guiltily. And they would have the air, the four of them, of faintly incestuous complicity, as if Vanessa had become for the moment a girlfriend to her sons, as mothers sometimes will in their husband's absence.

But Sonja never saw this, nor how powerful Vanessa was, which Mattie had known from the very moment she had arrived by the way her menfolk mocked her, teasing her as employees will sometimes tease their employer, or servants

· 89 ·

their master, dogging her footsteps, chipping away at her power, hoping to take a bit of it on to themselves. And so Noah used to tell funny stories about his mother; how Vanessa will talk to anyone, absolutely anyone, even to beggars in the street, and give incredibly generously to them of course – although never in a million years could you call Ma a socialist – quite the reverse; she's deeply feudalistic and a great believer in private charity. 'It's true, Ma,' he says, when Vanessa smiles and shakes her head. 'Vanessa's a libertarian,' says Tom admiringly. 'What's a libertarian?' asks Vanessa. 'It means you believe that everyone should do what they like and no one should interfere in other people's lives.' 'Certainly I am,' says Vanessa.

But Jonathan says, mournfully, 'That's not how she treats us.'

'Hello, Sonja,' says Noah now, very urbane, and he leans forward to kiss her on her painted cheek. 'Hello, darling,' says Sonja with real feeling. She is very fond of Noah. 'What's that you're carrying?' 'Sprats.' 'Spats?' *Sprats.* Little fish.' 'Are they nice?' asks Sonja. 'Don't ask him!' cries Sylvie, shaking around her long, dark, tangled hair. Her eyes are bold and enthusiastic but submissive nonetheless. Sprats are clearly what they have been arguing about this time.

There is a kind of Oaklandish acerbity which it takes a while to get the feel of, takes a while indeed to get the feel of the Oaklands altogether, with their tartness and their sweetness – which comes in a subtle and unpredictable mixture – and their mocking affections, for Sonja is really one of Vanessa's oldest friends. The Oaklands rate friendship very highly, in the way that the privileged often do. It is important for them to be loving and loyal and to forgive their friends for their sins and errors towards other people. And yet at the same time they are the most fiendish of gossips and will say the most terrible things when their friends have turned their backs.

· 90 ·

Or indeed have not yet turned them, for now Noah is describing how Brangwen Lefanu, who is something of a favourite of theirs because of her sassy, four-year-oldish behaviour, has eaten her mother's wedding ring. 'Well, that says it all,' says Noah, for Sonja is well known for the terribleness of her marriage. (He is laughing at her but she doesn't seem to mind.) Sonja and Philip went to great lengths to get it back. 'Well, that's a good sign,' Vanessa calls out in her sweet, vague way. Is she laughing at Sonja also?

It is easy to get the Oaklands wrong, to adopt the wrong tone with them, to be too loud or too soft, too enthusiastic or not enthusiastic enough. 'Sonja looks well,' says Noah after she has departed. 'She's been to Istanbul,' says Vanessa. 'What was she doing there?' asks Noah and Vanessa answers, mild as ever, 'Oh, haggling for carpets and stopping Philip breathing.'

· 18 ·

In Southwold twilight began at seven o'clock. It gathered in
the corners of the rooms. It crept out of the old stone walls
of the cottage. It washed to and fro through the open windows until there was no longer any distinction between
inside and out, and all the world was a flowing, darkening
ocean in which there swam the disembodied redness of night
stocks and geraniums, the whitewashed walls of the neigh-
bouring cottages, the scent of petrol and flowers, and the
sounds of holidaymakers in the pub across the street, scents
and sounds like traces in the dark ocean and beyond all this
the low, cushioning roar of the distant sea.

The cottage was in darkness. The back door was open and
the night slugs were coming in from the yard. Down at the
beach hut Tom and Noah and Jonathan were cooking the
supper, and quarrelling no doubt, and drinking and talking
and laughing. Sonja Lefanu was with them but Aaron was
in the front room working and Mattie was in the kitchen.
She was making coffee for herself and Vanessa. She had
knocked on Aaron's door but he hadn't answered. Now she
hesitated. She wrapped her dressing gown very tightly round
herself. She exulted momentarily in the slenderness of her
waist. She felt her eyes grow large and pale in the twilight,
her open mouth gulping in the night air, her stomach floating
away in the gathering darkness until there was as much night
air inside her as out. Then she picked up the coffees and
crept upstairs to the bedroom.

Vanessa was working. She was sitting up between the satin sheets, her red hair rumpled and disordered and all around her samples and swatches of fabric, sheets of paper and the childrens' crayons she used to sketch out her designs. She wore a small pair of gold-rimmed spectacles. She was wrapped in that silk dressing gown whose colours were yellow ochre with flecks of pink and mauve. The fabric was one of her own designs. All around her was a scene of pleasant domestic confusion: the paintings brought from London of beds and baths and dressings and undressings; the jewellery box left open on the bed and spilling out jewellery; the silk dresses strewn across the chairs; and at the end of her bed two clothing rails from which there hung the dresses and blouses and skirts she had brought from London.

Mattie watched. She held a cup of coffee in either hand. She thought that at any moment now Vanessa would turn to her and wash her over with her nonchalant charm, which never lay in anything she actually said but rather in the sweetness with which she said to Mattie, 'Oh, how lovely,' (of the coffee) and 'What do you think of this?' (holding up a sample against Mattie's skin) and 'Oh yes, the tones are lovely, especially in a pinkish light,' (dimming the light in the shade with a piece of fabric and smiling her sweet, intent smile). For Vanessa is not clever (although she is shrewd in business, very shrewd indeed). There is a kind of idleness and indifference in the way in which she turns away from the world. She never reads a newspaper and turns over the book in Mattie's hands, saying, 'What are you reading, Mattie?' in her mocking, affectionate way. Once, not long after Mattie came to live with them, she came and sat beside Mattie on the bed and, peering at the television, she asked, 'Who's that?' pointing to the Prime Minister, so that Mattie marvelled because Vanessa who was an heiress was neither thin nor wicked as heiresses tended to be, and although she was beautiful she wasn't clever, which gave her beauty a certain kind of poignancy and made Mattie's love for her all

· 93 ·

the more remarkable, because Mattie at this time in her life was full of disdain for people who were not clever.

'Vanessa?' said Mattie tentatively as she stepped forward. Vanessa looked up. Mattie sat down on the bed. 'That's pretty,' she said, picking up a sample, but Vanessa said nothing. You could never tell with Vanessa whether your comments were intelligent or entirely stupid. Her eyes were cloudy, tender and exhausted by the effort of creativity. 'Slender waist,' she said, touching Mattie, and Mattie looked away and smiled in the manner of a child smiling away from the source of her own pleasure; and in so doing met her reflection in the mirror, her cross, blushing, spiky, smiling reflection, the darkish skin and dark hair which lent themselves to the wearing of colours, and which Vanessa so admired and because Vanessa admired them so did Mattie – Mattie saw her own reflection and was pleased. 'The others are down at the beach hut making supper,' she said, 'but Aaron's downstairs. He's working.'

Mattie liked to sit on Vanessa's bed and paint her toenails. She liked to watch Vanessa work. She liked to try on Vanessa's clothes and she liked to tell Vanessa everything, to lay her feelings at Vanessa's feet and subject them to Vanessa's satiny gaze and her inconsequential observations.

Vanessa's clothes were extraordinary. There were black, cropped silk trousers and spotted harem pants. There were overshirts patterned in bronze and cream and jackets made from some kind of skin and so finely pleated that they resembled Fortuny silk, and others made from cashmere lined with silk. There were scarves of Mediterranean colours which Mattie liked to wind around her head and pots of cream with which to wipe away imaginary wrinkles. There was perfume and jewellery, rings and earrings and heavy necklaces which Mattie placed about her neck, so that she could pace about the room and feel the weight of wealth upon her shoulders and kneel down on the floor and bow forwards and touch the ground with her forehead like a slave girl in a harem. (It's the rich who go clothed, thinks Mattie, and the poor who go naked.) And sometimes on a Sunday morning when the Oaklands were out she liked to sit in Vanessa's bedroom in the London house and paint her face with clown's colours, pink and yellow and green, so that there might look back from the mirror a pretty, startled, outlandish face with which she was enormously taken. And then she would sit back on her haunches, in her turban, her silk pants and painted toenails and gaze up at the ceiling where Tom had painted for Vanessa, in the manner of a loving husband, the Oaklands' factory and all its employees at work, in blues and pinks, figures both solid and airy.

Now she ran one finger down the side of the clothing rail. She pushed out her chin and smiled to herself and admired the silky ripple. How beautiful is the word 'mothering', thought Mattie, the most beautiful word in the language, and she felt a frustrated sweetness, the more sweet and frustrated because she didn't recognise it, but it made her feel giddy, this need to put her head on Vanessa's lap, this woman who was her mother.

She was thinking of Barry Shawcross, a sober and legal-istic friend of Vanessa's who took Mattie out from time to time. Only last week he had taken her to an exhibition and to walk in St James's Park, where the ornamental birds rose up in clouds from the surface of the lake and the blind and shuttered windows of government looked down on them. Mattie had been dressed to kill that day in white jodhpurs and a white shirt of Vanessa's. The white light of the park had lain upon her gratefully. It was a place for spies, for assignations and dead-letter drops but Barry Shawcross's scarf was too long and his trousers too short and he wasn't a spy – no such luck, thought Mattie – for in his company her mind would run onwards in two streams, one cold because he was so taken with her he would keep asking her out, and the other warm because after all she liked him. And she had looked around restlessly, romantically, thinking with panic and sadness that we are debased by the company we keep, and that to be seen in the company of Barry Shawcross – when she should have been with that group, or with that, or with that – all this suggested a certain fear and uncertainty on her part which she didn't like at all. Young boys skimmed past on skateboards and she looked after them with longing. 'I wish I could skateboard,' she said out loud.

Now she was hanging round Vanessa's bedroom, seeking Vanessa's approval on the subject of going out with him. 'Barry Shawcross is coming down tonight. He's asked me out to tea in Norwich,' said Mattie, fingering a slip of polka-dotted chiffon. Vanessa put down her work. She took off her glasses. 'So what will you wear?' she asked. 'Noah says I should wear something classy, respectable and discreet,' said Mattie and she blushed to offer up such malice whilst looking at Vanessa sideways on to see how she would take it. For once long ago Mattie had noticed that the Oaklands took a great interest in her boyfriends, a delighted and scandalous interest in the ups and downs and ins and outs of her relationships, and that they were especially delighted when she was running two or three at the same time or when she was particularly tough or high-handed with them. Now Vanessa smiled. She looked down at her work and smiled with resignation and pleasure because she liked her childrens' malice – she couldn't help herself – it was so lively and so spirited against the world.

And Mattie saw the smile and thus, having consulted the spirit of her cousins, and having found it ironic and amused but not noticeably for Barry, not for Barry at all, Mattie withdrew the affection which tentatively, momentarily she had considered placing in his hands. For it simply was not possible to love except with her cousins' approval.

'Can I try this on?' asked Mattie. It was some kind of wool jacket which smelt of Vanessa's smell. How beautiful are thy feet with shoes, O Prince's daughter, thought Mattie,

· 96 ·

the joints of thy thighs are like jewels, the
work of the hands of a cunning workman.
Thy navel is like a round goblet
which wanteth not liquor; thy belly
is like a heap of wheat set about
with lilies.
Thy two breasts are like two young
roes that are twins.
Thy neck is as a tower of ivory;
thine eyes like the fishpools of Heshbon . . .

for Mattie knew her bible back to front. She had learnt it
from her mother. She knew all kinds of poetry.

And when she opened her eyes again and saw Vanessa's
huge, amber-eyed gaze bent upon her, the helpless gaze with
its feathery irises and the blue whites around them, and also
her arms like marble with which she could scarcely manage
the world and her smell of skin and flesh and perfume and
shampoo then Mattie thought, I love her.

She knelt down on the floor. She laid out the jacket flat,
did up the buttons, turned over the sleeves, folded it up like
a baby. And as she did so she enumerated the different
aspects of her love for Vanessa, measuring its length, its
breadth and its height, for tonight was the very peak, the
acme of her love for the Oaklands. She felt loyal and generous towards Vanessa and would defend her from every
critic. (For the Oaklands, being famous, had their critics. It
was inevitable.) She admired Vanessa's beauty with a pure,
uncompetitive admiration such as daughters sometimes feel
towards their mothers. She liked to sit and watch Vanessa
talking, reading, working, and to admire the tilt of her head,
her reddish curls and her amber, enfolding, smiling gaze.
She liked to go shopping with Vanessa and to let her buy
her clothes and to admire her own, Mattie's, long white
fingers and her twenty-year-old figure. She took a great
pleasure in Vanessa's clothes and when Vanessa went away

· 97 ·

she packed her bags for her. She liked to carry her clothes from the wardrobe to the suitcase, and she liked how they lay across her arm in a heavy, silky, slipping and slithering weight. And she liked the way in which, when she patted these clothes down into the squashy leather bags, they puffed up again as if with the sense of their own beauty. And later on she even liked to bring her boyfriends home for Vanessa's approval.

'Would you like that?' asked Vanessa, looking at Mattie through her gold spectacles. Mattie stroked the jacket. It was gathering up the light with the tips of its long hair so that it seemed to have a halo. 'Don't you want it?' asked Mattie. She was poised on the brink, not wishing to be seen to be jumping in too greedily. Vanessa said nothing and Mattie understood Vanessa's silence. She meant she wouldn't have offered it if she hadn't wanted to. Vanessa used silences. They were like all her weapons, simple but subtle. They ushered people in the direction she wanted them to go. 'Put it on,' said Vanessa, 'Turn round.' It was as if Mattie's looks belonged to her, but if that were true then Mattie gave them freely. 'Oh yes,' said Vanessa. 'Oh yes, it's lovely.'

· 19 ·

Aaron was measuring the duration of the twilights. He was scholarly and literal-minded. He made not only furniture like his father but also clocks. He liked to know the length and breadth of things and was the only one of the Oaklands, that medieval family, those pre-Galileo and earlier-than-Copernicus Oaklands, who really understood that the earth goes round the sun and not the sun around the earth. Aaron never ceased to wonder at the ignorance of his family.

He was sitting in the front room with his head bent down to the light of the lamp. He was planning a model of the effect of the moon upon the tides. He imagined a round, wooden moon attached by a wooden rod to a painted, paper ocean. When the moon moved round in an ellipse it pulled the ocean first this way, then that. He was a big, well-built boy of eighteen. When he bent his head you could see the groove running down the back of his neck.

He heard the two women talking in the room upstairs. He got to his feet, treading heavily up the narrow stairs, and loomed through the doorway of his mother's bedroom. She was sitting up in bed and working. On the bed beside her sat his pretty cousin, Mattie, the cuckoo, painting her toenails in her usual narcissistic way. A scarf of Vanessa's was wound around her head. She was wearing one of Vanessa's jackets. The nail polish was Vanessa's best, bought at Harrods. Aaron stared. He was six foot, straight, curly-haired and flame-and-peaches. He had been embarked for some years

· 99 ·

now on a full-scale and unrequited love affair with his mother, was Hamleting it up, a disregarded prince, in a loving, angry, righteous fashion.

'Mum,' he said, and she looked up at him sombrely, seemingly neither pleased nor displeased but simply waiting. Once when Sonja Lefanu had rung up Vanessa – well, she would, wouldn't she? – to tell her that the *Independent* had written something unkind about her and Tom, Aaron had been angry on his mother's behalf but Vanessa had laughed it off. She would have none of his anger. She wouldn't even be angry with Sonja, so that the love in Aaron's outstretched hands, wrapped up like a present, ticked away like a bomb and Vanessa sheered away from it.

Perhaps she didn't even see it. It was remarkable how blind Vanessa could be; not about the world, which she understood pretty well, but about her relationship with the world. Or perhaps again she didn't want his love because he was so intense and intensity of feeling always alarmed the Oaklands. They preferred their emotions light, funny and ironic. And, besides, he got it wrong. Ever prone to virtue he became more and more self-righteous when what the Oaklands liked of course was the fizz of malice, of boldness and mild wickedness.

'Mum,' he said again, and he sat down on the bed. He was subdued. The angry thoughts were still running behind his eyes, but quietly now. He and Jonathan had had a row today and such a startlingly bitter row had it been that Aaron now felt childlike and exhausted.

Jonathan, jaunty Jonathan, failed his O levels that summer but passed with flying colours the first stages of the Oakland examination. For the Oaklands are great setters of examinations. They believe they are not, of course. They believe you would be hard put to find another family so laid back, liberal and tolerant, so little inclined to nag their children about their homework, so much inclined to forgive them for failing their exams. But the truth is that the Oaklands simply set their own exams, make their own demands, and perhaps at eight it is easier to pass your spelling test than it is to fail it in the way the Oaklands so admire – with wit and verve and knowingness and a kind of Oakland irony. (They are not fair, thinks Aaron, they are not fair at all.)

Slender, jaunty Jonathan has sprinkled blue-green sparkle on his coppery hair, has borrowed his brother's tapestry waistcoat and his mother's best lipstick and eyeshadow bought from Harrods. Jonathan was the family's secretary, the organiser of appointments, the keeper of his mother's diary. 'Oh look,' he said the first time he met Mattie, 'she's got the Oakland nose,' for, being the youngest, he was anxious to keep up and was thus already turning the Oaklands into a living myth. Jonathan was not above cheating in his exams but was inclined to heroism as well as to wickedness – he nursed his girlfriends when they fell ill and punched their ex-boyfriends in the face for them – and the Oaklands loved it. Vanessa would not hear a word said against him. Noah was her man but Jonathan was her baby and if he wished to camp it up around the house like some blue-green coppery sprite, borrowing money without asking from her handbag or her dressing table – what's mine is yours, mother, and what's yours is mine – with a horde of baby-doll Lolitas following after him, and he raising mayhem because he couldn't find the cat's flea powder and he loved the black cat to distraction and had brought her all the way from London, well, then he could do whatever he liked and with his mother's blessing. And Vanessa even permitted him to sit in her bedroom whilst she worked and then he scoffed and mocked in his possessive way and tried to teach her poker and she put down the cards any old how with her left hand and he said, 'Jesus, mum, not like that,' and she did it again just like that in order that he might say it twice: '*Jesus, mum, not like that.*' For she was a soft-eyed and emollient woman, to be pushed and pulled and tugged at by her son. And Aaron was jealous, terribly jealous, but

Vanessa didn't care, not even when Jonathan failed his exams after having cheated at them.

Aaron failed the Oakland examination but Jonathan passed. Jonathan always got Oaklandism right. In another family Aaron would have been honoured.

The two boys had come scrambling down the cliff path that morning, limbs flying loose as their tempers rose, so that Aaron half tripped and fell before they reached the bottom. They had been chatting up the same waitress in the café. Now they were striking sparks off each other. Aaron was as white as a sheet beneath his summer tan. They flopped down on the ground outside the hut but Jonathan jumped up again and tripped over Aaron's outstretched foot. 'You cunt,' shouted Aaron, starting up, and then the Oaklands stared in alarm and astonishment at the bitterness of his tone. 'You fucking cunt yourself,' screamed Jonathan, starting up in his turn, and Aaron swung out a fist – his eyes were full of tears, huge tears were brimming over and twisting down his face – but his fist fell short of Jonathan, who had crumpled slowly to the ground at his mother's feet. 'I feel terrible,' said Jonathan in amazement, staring up at her. And then Noah's Sylvie had said in her high, naive voice, 'Oh, Jonathan, you're covered in spots,' and the Oaklands had stared and seen that it was true. He was blotchy as a baby. He had quite indubitably caught the measles.

After that it became a party. First the spots came and then they went, so one minute he was bright scarlet and the next as white as snow. He was feeling terribly well, pleased to have so much attention. Vanessa wanted him to see a doctor, but he sat up on the promenade and said how well he felt, albeit a little light-headed, the sun very bright and strong, the sky a dizzy blue. In the afternoon he slept for a while beneath an old curtain on the camp bed in the hut but when the night came on and the air was so pleasantly cool on his spots he got to his feet and helped Tom and Noah barbecue the quails. He had decided to give up vegetarianism, his latest fad, in honour of the quails which Tom had brought from London and of measles.

'They're waiting for us in the beach hut,' said Aaron now to his mother, picking at the counterpane, admiring his cousin's pretty foot, wishing she would go away. 'You look like Mrs Tiggy-Winkle in those glasses,' he added, looking sideways on at Vanessa. Vanessa took them off.

'Tom says there's no point in me getting contact lenses. I'd step on them or swallow them or something stupid,' she remarked.

'Dad's a bully,' said Aaron.

'He can't help it. It's his Jewish background.'

'He's only a bit Jewish,' said Aaron petulantly. 'He uses it as an excuse. Jonathan's given up vegetarianism. That only lasted a week.'

'That's good.' How brisk she was. 'He's human so he'd better eat meat like the rest of us. Can I go down to the hut dressed like this, Mattie?'

Mattie considered. 'I don't see why not,' she said.

'But how can I go round an English seaside town dressed in harem pants?'

'Easy,' said Mattie smartly. 'We're Londoners so we can wear what we like,' and Vanessa and even Aaron laughed because her pride in being an Oakland was so transparent.

His mother was putting on her make-up in front of the mirror. Her broad, speckled back was the colour of a brown egg, the strong hands in the mirror plaiting the strands of her necklace and repairing her beauty. She was being very cool and brisk. She was admiring her statuesque head. That's because she's still cross with me, thought Aaron.

It was Oxford which had caused so much trouble for them this summer. Aaron knew they talked about it behind his back, that they had taken against the idea in just the way they would, which was both irrationally and yet extremely strongly, had become in fact quite happily united in their worries on the subject: which were that really he was an

· 103 ·

artist and all that academic stuff would make him unhappy and deflect him from his purpose. But at other times he thought they said, 'Poor Aaron, he's not really creative, he's too much of an academic.' Because first they invented and then they re-invented him, he knew they did it, and their many inventions of himself oppressed him because he didn't know what he was and their power over him was to seem to understand him far better than he knew himself. And simply knowing that they were saying this made him angry, in fact made him absolutely furious, both because of the extreme caring and the extreme indifference of his family towards him. They made him want to tremble and shout and shriek and faint and hit out against them. And yet this also he had noticed about his mild, humorous yet wilful mother, that if you became angry with her, even if you were angry because she didn't love you enough, then by being angry you could make her angry, very coldly so, because she thought that anger was disloyal and she didn't understand how much you needed her to love you.

That had been another quarrel the night before. They had been talking over supper of a family friend. 'Did you know that Juliet's cross with mum?' Noah had called out. 'She said if my shoulders got any wider I'd start to look like an Irish navvy,' said Vanessa with a kind of comic mournfulness. But Tom said, 'Vanessa's been gossiping about her,' his tone of voice suggesting that he might or might not be passing judgement on her himself, so that Vanessa looked at him sharply. 'That's not what it felt like,' she protested. 'She doesn't understand the tone in which things are said. Oh dear,' she added in a comic, despairing, laugh-at-me-with-me shrug.

'Did you know Juliet's pregnant?' asked one of the guests. 'Oh my God, poor baby,' said another one, with such vehemence that everyone laughed. 'Who's the father?' asked Aaron in the manner of a callow youth. 'Oh, I don't think that's at issue,' said Vanessa gently. 'But you were gossiping,' Aaron went on, staring at Vanessa angrily. 'What?' she said, doing a double-take. Then she stared back at him coldly. 'Not at all. It's the tone in which things are said that counts.' How very cold she was. Tom leant forward. 'That's very painterly,' he said, and he squared off his hands to look through them at the picture of Vanessa, her face half-turned into the shadows, her heavy head and spilling hair and full bosom. 'There, like that,' he said. 'You look like a nineteenth-century madam in a fashionable brothel.' And at this Vanessa knew not to be insulted but to be complimented, as she was meant to be, and which she understood in her Oaklandish fashion; and she relented and smiled at him.

Now she was rummaging around on the bed, looking for the bits which went inside her handbag. 'The clock's broken,' Aaron said, picking it up off the floor. He had made it for her only last Christmas. 'So it has,' she said, taking it from his hands. Then she gave it back. 'Tom threw it at my head and missed,' she said, looking into his eyes and smiling a small smile. He stared back at her. Slowly he decided she was being amusing and reluctantly smiled back. How sweet her smile was. It made him want to faint.

That summer something terrible happened to Aaron. He and Jonathan were in the habit of drinking in the evenings in the Sole Bay Arms. There they grew quite friendly with a group of local boys and one evening Aaron found himself recounting funny stories about what had happened when Jonathan's girlfriend's mother had displayed their dope plant in the parlour window because she felt sorry for it, tucked away in the dark as it was, and because she didn't see how a plant by itself could be as wicked as they said it was. Afterwards he could not claim in all honesty that he had not known that the father of one of the boys was a policeman, but he had noticed in himself before this nervous inability to stop talking, as if the desire to express himself, so long repressed, would flow forth sweetly and unstoppably as soon as he opened his mouth. And he was gratified to have an audience. He spoke very rapidly for fear of being interrupted by his wittier brother. He felt helpless before the spate of his own words. And yet the story was wasted on the local boys because they hadn't seen its humorous angles and afterwards Aaron felt that nothing could ever be more shaming in his life than thus to be found out in the inability to keep a secret.

For the boy's father came himself with a uniformed colleague. Tom and Vanessa let them in because they too, like the girlfriend's mother, could not believe that society could really take it all so seriously. The policeman found a small bag containing a twist of silver paper in which was a lump of Jonathan's best Lebanese. Jonathan departed in the police car. He was heroic as he always was in extremis. He looked pale and awestruck but he didn't murmur a word of reproach. And watching them go all Aaron could think was that his family would never confide in him again, that he had now blown all chance of being loved by them for at least a couple of years.

· 20 ·

The Oaklands liked to stick together. For all that they were so gregarious, they believed – they couldn't help themselves – that the rest of the world was irrational, unpredictable and dangerous. And so they stuck together like children holding hands in a strange and dangerous place and in this Vanessa was the worst, the ringleader and the captain. Sometimes the phone would ring and Vanessa would pick it up and then gently lay it down upon the table and go about her business, but looking at it sideways, apprehensively, from time to time. And they were all of them always peculiar about outsiders, so that if a friend – even an old friend – rang up and said he was coming to see them, they were invariably astonished and alarmed. And after he had departed they always began to agitate in a guilty, comic fashion that they might have said the wrong thing, and that so-and-so, who had been a friend for years, might now be offended. 'You shouldn't have said that,' they would say to each other, but with such relish at the prospect of being disapproved of and at the same time drawing together in a collective, humorous tizz. Because at bottom they were not at ease with outsiders, not really, not in the way they were at ease with each other.

That night beside the beach hut Tom and Noah brought out the barbecue to roast the quails. It was a light, bright, rarified night as if the molecules of darkness, spread too thinly, were springing apart. Down beside the water's edge the waves were visible, curling sideways up the beach to break with infinite laziness whilst the white foam frilled along the waves from end to end. Jonathan fetched the tape cassette. He put on jazz and other music from the fifties and sixties, which the Oakland boys played in deference to their parents' antiquated tastes. When the Oakland men began to sing along and Vanessa, who liked to play at being bourgeois, said, 'Shush. What will the neighbours think?' and the men grinned as if to say 'Sod the neighbours', then all the Oaklands remembered simultaneously in their telepathic way that Barry Shawcross was intending to drive down from London this very evening to stay in the cottage for a day or two. At once they began to work themselves up into a state about his imminent arrival. They speculated upon the motives for his visit. They wondered whether he had really forgiven them for a remark which Tom thought he might have made – but he couldn't remember – a month or two ago. They thought he probably disapproved of them for their raffish and bohemian behaviour. Poor Barry, they kept saying, poor Barry. And so when at length, at ten o'clock or so, he came loping down the cliff path, a tall, awkward man with a balding head, both conventional and eccentric, and as solitary and individualistic as the Oaklands were gregarious and liked to stick together – when he came towards them along the promenade, his face very intent as it always was with his secret purposes, then you couldn't have said whether he wasn't out to ambush them or whether they, with their bright, disembodied faces lifted to the lamp light, caught as if by a camera flash, weren't lying in wait for him.

He was a lawyer by profession and although he was by no means old – he was not yet even forty – he very early on in his life had taken up the pleasures of the old, and now he was growing stern as he found these pleasures inadequate to ward off his desires. With his long jaw and soft mouth and brown eyes and high, prematurely balding forehead, he resembled a handsome, preppy, North American academic;

· 108 ·

but his mind was altogether sterner, more melancholy and European than such a comparison would suggest.

He was not at all like the Oaklands. He had decided to pass his life as an observer. He had thought that by means of small and contemplative pleasures he could be happy. The Oaklands had known him for years. It was he who had introduced them to Southwold, where they now went every summer but which he had frequented for many years past because he liked its air of old-fashioned gentility. He liked the green, open spaces and the bright blue air and the blue-and-white wind which blew in off the sea and the luminous white light in which the town was bathed and which gave the people of the town the sharp clarity of figures in a painting. His father had been a signal man in Lincolnshire, a fact of which he was not ashamed but proud, for he thought there was a quiet glory to be had from belonging to that England in which everyone had had their place. He liked towns which had an air of civic pride about them. He thought the life of a small town was the height of English civilisation. He liked the bunting in the streets of Southwold and the flowers in the window boxes and the striped and painted beach huts along the promenade. He liked the clean-looking children who played cricket on the common and the Scripture Missionaries in their sandals singing hymns on the beach as they tried to convert the little children. Above all, he liked to sit out on the dunes beside the sign which said 'Jim's Café' and have his tea brought to him in stout white china cups and saucers whilst the high wind blew the sand in drifts around the metal table legs and bird-like yachts skimmed across the water to beach themselves upon the sand.

He was attached to everything that lasted, to the Queen and to history, to the delivering of the daily newspapers, and to his making of his own breakfast in the mornings; first a cup of tea and then a cup of coffee, and always in that order. By temperament he was inclined to vote Tory but he

· 109 ·

disapproved of the modern habit of voting governments in
and out in quick succession and so if a Labour government
were in power he would always vote for them to give them
one more chance. He was both very intelligent and very
simple, and he organised his emotional life in such a way
that his emotions were few, simple, overt and very correct.
And thus, thought Mattie, who went out with Barry Shawcross from time to time, he had settled down in his melancholy but contented way to live a life in which you might
have thought that all the strong colours and bold patterns
had been washed away until it resembled nothing more than
the view from his father's signal box in flat, rural, dreaming
Lincolnshire.

But although he had supposed that eventually his age
would catch up with his inclinations, he very soon discovered he couldn't cheat upon himself in this way, that he
was not as old as he had thought. And then he grew alarmed,
because hitherto his fragile pleasures had been sufficient for
him and he felt stubbornly unwilling to give up what he
thought he had discovered, which was the secret of being
happy. And besides, he didn't know how else to live and
felt quite unable to copy the vain, careless, happy lives of
his contemporaries. And so instead he tried to make himself
strong and to fend off his desires and this was why he had
grown stern and remote and inclined to blame other people
for not showing the same control which he showed towards
himself.

The Oakland men didn't know what to make of him, for
he had always been first and foremost a friend of Vanessa's
and thus it was generally agreed amongst them that he must
be in love with her – and this was a thought which they
didn't like at all, and which caused them to treat him with
a kind of bemused irony which lapsed sometimes into malice
because they couldn't help themselves, they did so resent the
special favour which Vanessa showed him. 'How's the office,
Barry?' they would ask, and then they would blush and

shake their heads bemusedly at the irony they heard in their own voices.

They smiled at his foppish ways and at his unfamiliarity with the modern world. They were puzzled by the pleasures he derived from life, these being so small and rather contemplative and old-manly. They were fond enough of him in their lordly fashion but they found his slow speech quite painful to listen to – they didn't understand that he had studied Classics at Cambridge and that this had given him a taste for, as well as the means to express, the precise and absolute truth in every matter – and Jonathan, who was the youngest and the least controlled of them all, found his long sentences and his so-many-clauses and the verb always at the end so difficult that he spilled his glass of wine whenever Barry began to speak. In this way he stopped Barry murdering the conversation, for the uproar was enormous as everyone scrambled about to save Barry's trousers; but the Oaklands did so like an uproar, and then Noah could finish Barry's sentence for him, and sometimes even his words if his speech had slowed down nearly to a halt.

The night he came to Southwold there were kissing couples – he saw them – spread out along the cliff top from the Sole Bay Inn as far as South Common. They were laughing and embracing in the stillness of the night. Barry stopped and listened. Down below him on the shore the waves were creeping idly inwards and yet in the stillness they were making a sound like a hundred diesel engines roaring. He listened for the presence of the Oaklands. He descended by donkey steps through air which sparkled like black granite. He saw them sitting out upon the promenade. They were bundled up against the cold. They were dipping their lumps of bread into what remained of their supper. Behind them out to sea floated a copper moon, its circle so absurdly large that Barry thought all the Oaklands might have dined inside it. Sonja Lefanu was there. Vanessa had her weary face turned towards him. Beside her sat her cousin Mattie, the fringe orphan, her face halfway in shadow and the line of darkness running down the centre of her face so that one beautiful eye was visible in the bright darkness and the other eye was hidden. She made him think of the dark-eyed ladies at the Picasso exhibition where recently he had taken her. Next to her, he noticed, sat Noah Oakland. The other men had their backs turned towards him.

'Those vagabonds,' he thought, and was surprised by his own vehemence, 'those lying, charming vagabonds.' For he had no idea how little he liked Vanessa's menfolk, and their raffish, unreliable conversation; nor how little they liked him.

They had become aware of his presence. 'Hello, Barry,' they chorused and they turned round, oddly shy, and moved up to make room for him, whilst Tom poured a glass of wine. 'Have you driven all the way from London?' asked Vanessa, doing her charming thing, which was to make her mind entirely transparent so you could see the astonished thoughts swimming around inside it, such as 'How brave of you!' and 'But where are your driving goggles, and the dust from such a long journey?' 'It's not that far, Ma,' Jonathan protested. 'I've got the measles,' he added and he swung his strained and staring face on Barry so that the other man was startled out of the nonchalance he took care always to adopt in the Oaklands' presence. 'My God, so you have,' he said, and shuddered. 'I feel terrible, Ma,' said Jonathan, and he sank back into her arms as if into a lover's.

Barry thought the one-eyed, beautiful fringe orphan was smiling at him distantly. There were two aspects to Barry. There was one which was clear-headed and appraising, and another which was soft and blushing and formless. The clear-headed Barry knew that he was good enough to go out with Mattie, but the second Barry blushed and dripped olive oil down his new white shirt. His passions were breaking up her face, turning her into a Picasso lady with the

· 112 ·

black eyes so skewwhiff and the nose twisted by desire to sit in profile with the full mouth.

'So how are you, Barry?' Noah shouted jovially, and Barry blushed again.

'I'm fine, Noah,' he replied.

'Have you been to the Sailors' Reading Room at the top of the cliff?'

'Of course,' said Barry.

'There were three old fishermen in there today,' said Noah. 'I overheard them. They were playing poker and the one who won got to sleep with the other ones' wives.'

'Liar,' said Jonathan instantly.

'It's true,' said Noah.

'Southwold is far too respectable for that kind of thing,' said Vanessa.

'It's nothing to do with respectability,' said Noah. 'It's an old English habit. Gambling on your wife. That's why the old people still do it.'

'I saw a dog pee on South Green the other day,' said Tom. 'Old ladies stood around and shuddered when they saw it.'

'Did you know that this is the only town in England where you can't get a tabloid newspaper and where they stare at you if you run in the street?' said Aaron.

'Sonja lets her dog pee on South Green,' said Vanessa with mild amusement.

'I certainly do,' said Sonja. 'This place is far too respectable. I shall let her pee there every day.'

'Saw you!' shouted Barry, banging on the table. 'Are you all listening out there? Her dog pees on South Green!' and then he stopped, embarrassed by the hysteria he heard in his own voice. They had wrong-footed him again. The Oaklands and his own repressed desires had leapt up and taken him hysterically by the throat.

'I've just remembered my news,' he said more soberly, recalling the purpose of his visit, which he had forgotten the moment he turned the corner and saw them sitting out upon

· 113 ·

the promenade. 'Your question about the copyright laws,' he said, and at this the Oaklands grew suddenly serious, for this was work and no longer a laughing matter. They had wanted to know if Barry could make out a case for them in law against a company who had been producing designs very similar to their own. 'It's a task for you,' Noah had said, small, impertinent Noah, looking Barry straight in the eye – for some reason the Oaklands were always putting tasks before their friends.

'The law isn't entirely clear,' said Barry now, speaking more rapidly than before, for the law was what he understood. 'You might win but you might not. Very few judges understand how the process of creativity works, and you would have to convince a judge that the theft of a design had actually taken place.'

'So what are you saying?' asked Noah.

'I'm saying that I couldn't guarantee you would win. Not even fifty-fifty.'

'But you're a barrister,' said Noah. 'Can't you just go into court and put forward arguments which will convince the judge?'

'The law's not like that,' said Barry, and now he was looking at Noah very coolly, for Noah was disappointed and he was making no effort to hide it and his disappointment was a hard and unforgiving thing. He doesn't like us, thought Noah, staring into the other man's eyes. Why does he come and eat our food if he doesn't like us? And he thought his worst suspicions of Barry Shawcross were confirmed: that the man was neither bold nor loyal. But Barry was staring back. His long love for Vanessa was reviving itself. Her menfolk were brigands and thieves and if he had been another kind of man he would have taken her away from them.

The waves came roaring up the beach. The moon glimmered upon the wet shingle. A dog barked hysterically as he slipped sideways across the shining wetness. Mattie stared

· 114 ·

at the two men in alarm. She took the Oaklands' side, of course. She thought there was nothing more important in this world than to be bold and brave and positive. Doesn't he understand, she thought, what the Oaklands want from him? The two men stared at each other until Noah looked away. Noah was like all the Oaklands but more so. He was like all the Oaklands put together. Poor Barry, he thought suddenly, poor Barry, it's not his fault he's not an Oakland.

· 21 ·

Barry Shawcross stayed two nights and then went to a con-
cert in Aldeburgh and from there drove straight to London.
The Oaklands were both pleased and sorry to see him go.
That left only Sylvie, Noah's girlfriend, the outsider in their
midst.

Noah is the chef this Saturday night. He is making paella
and clam soup with the help of two gas rings, a cauldron
and a frying pan. He has set his younger brother to clean
and beard the clams, but Jonathan is drifting away from the
task just as soon as he is able. For these are the days when
Jonathan is frightened of Noah, who all this summer has
been upbraiding him for frittering away their mother's
money and failing his exams. Once, long ago, the younger
ones stole his mother's love from him and now Noah can't
believe that her affections can be directed on to more than
one person. So he does them down in her eyes in order to
raise himself up.

Each of the Oakland boys is different. The younger ones
went to private schools and are respectively dreamy and
resentful (Aaron) and jaunty and flamboyant (Jonathan). But
Noah went down the road to the local comprehensive and
added to his arty, Oakland nature a slightly nasal accent, a
deadpan sense of humour and a kind of street sharpness.
And he also learnt from his comprehensive education the art
of making friends, of whom he has hundreds, far more than
the other Oaklands, those gregarious people, have. They

· 116 ·

used to say that Noah's idea of an intimate party was to post a notice in the underground at Camden Town. Noah is small and thin with pale, not very healthy skin, high cheekbones and reddish hair so dark it is almost black. Noah is not beautiful as the rest of the Oaklands are but his ascendancy amongst them is enormous.

Noah is hard and soft and sweet and sour. He is a mafioso, a paterfamilias, a capo di tutti. Or so says Jonathan, and it is true that there is no end to the pride which Noah takes in his family, nor to the shame that he feels when one of the younger ones does something to drag them down. He carps and criticises and bullies and nags them. He quizzes them as to their ambitions and intentions. He stands over them with a clock, making them finish their homework, Noah who has scarcely three O levels to his name! 'Noah is a bully,' says Jonathan, who is awestruck, admiring and angry with his older brother because in all his twenty-five years Noah has never done anything in the slightest bit naff.

A wind has started to blow. Inside the beach hut Noah is stirring the yellow rice with cumin and coriander and adding white wine so that the rice plumps up into a yellow cushion. One by one he tosses in the prawns, the blue-black mussels and the scarlet crayfish, his face narrow, saturnine and intent upon the food. From time to time he takes out another bottle to his family who are crouched down behind the shelter of the railings on the verandah, playing a game of cards by torchlight. Each time he steps out through the swing doors he brings out the yellow light in tatters behind him. The meal will be late as usual – they will be lucky to eat before midnight – for his meals are amazing confections but as he works he drinks and dreams and fantasises.

He is full of the dreams and delusions of this Walter Mitty decade. He has read the magazines, he knows about the Man for the Eighties, for the Nineties, and for the new millennium. He knows that life is all image and nothing else, that it is simply a matter of getting the style right. His own achievements are real enough. When he finished at art school he went into the family business and now, apart from working on the fabrics with Vanessa, he is also managing the company's financial affairs. He is as organised in his business life, in his getting to the factory at eight in the morning and his getting home at eight at night, as he is disorganised in his personal life. It is remarkable the things that Noah knows (and the things that he does not).It is Noah who has put the Oakland finances on to a sounder footing, making Tom and Vanessa sit down with their accountant, encouraging them to buy the shop they rented and to rent the factory they set out to buy. Before this, Vanesssa and Tom just reached into their pockets and pulled out the notes by the handful. And apart from his art and the business Noah also always knows the whereabouts of a party on a Saturday night; he knows where to get hold of drugs, both legal and illegal, and fake MOTs and cheap holiday deals; he knows of rooms to let and extraordinary jobs on offer, reading aloud to millionaires and tending their fax machines; he knows how to rent a market stall by Camden Lock and how to buy a houseboat and moor it by Regent's Park; and he knows how to get a discount on a meal at the Jamaican Restaurant and also the bars where the off-duty policemen drink, and the Irish and the blacks; and once he was drinking in a pub when they closed the doors at midnight to lock them in and transformed the place into a private party and drew out the dice and the gambling tables.

All this Noah knows and yet in his mind he is something far greater than any of this. Wild horses could not lead him to confess to all his dreams and fantasies. He is the Artist with the Artist's temperament. He is the Showman and the Great Provider. He is the Designer, the Photographer of the Decade. And he is the King, the Paterfamilias, the Capo di Capi di Tutti.

Noah believes that through image all things are possible. Like all his generation, he worships style, the making of the right choice between the face shaven or unshaven, the hair cropped short or in a pigtail, the clothes stark white or entirely black. Style is for Noah his talisman, his lucky charm, and he believes, he cannot help himself, that it is his style, his huge style, along with his boundless energy and will, which marks him out as something exceptional and which will fulfil his powerful ambitions.

And yet at the same time at bottom Noah is also afraid, afraid that this ambition may be based upon only flimsy foundations, for Noah, like his mild mother and so many of his generation, is almost illiterate, has read scarcely a dozen books in all his life to date. Instead he has been watching television, and now his head is stuffed with images; he has a painter's imagination but no capacity at all for constructing arguments or for working out ideas, and so the world rushes him forward in its vivid, meaningless way. And he knows it. 'Yeah?' he says, when Vanessa tells him that Mattie has passed her exams again. 'That's good, Mattie,' he says with ever more lordly kindness. But to Jonathan he says, 'Jesus Christ, Jonathan, when the fuck are you ever intending to do any work?' And Jonathan skedaddles away like a frightened cat.

They are playing cards out on the verandah. Vanessa is winning. She is not as mild as she first seems – she is not mild at all – she plays with the absolute and unwavering determination that she will win. Sylvie and Mattie are lagging behind. They are both of them dreaming, but separately, of the Oaklands, those objects of desire. 'There you go, ladies,' says Noah, putting another bottle of wine before them. He doesn't look at Sylvie, only at his mother. He is thinking to himself, my mum is a Catholic girl and Catholic girls sin and then repent and that's what makes them so interesting. And Catholic girls are powerful, very powerful, but they submit their power to God and other men, and that's what makes them interesting also. 'Is Ma winning again?' he asks. 'She is,' says Tom. 'Watch she doesn't cheat,'

· 119 ·

says Noah. And Vanessa says complacently, 'I don't have to cheat. I'm winning anyway,' and she smiles up at him.

For he is her favourite son, her first-born, her best beloved, and she loves him to distraction for his energy, his style and his sociability. She thinks to herself with pride that he is one of those people whose presence, for some indefinable reason, seems to make a party complete. Sometimes in London, if the Oaklands are not working late, they will gather together and cast around in a restless, dissatisfied way, for something to do. And then at length someone will say, 'I know, let's try the new Indonesian restaurant at Euston,' and then half of them will begin to squabble about this plan and the other half to search around for the restaurant number until they all begin to quarrel about what they should order and then someone always says, 'Where's Noah?' 'Oh yes, find Noah,' says Vanessa or Tom or Aaron or Jonathan. 'Yes, Noah must come.' 'Ring him at the factory,' they say to each other, or 'Ring him at home.' ('And ask . . . ' they would add as an afterthought in years to come in the days of his wife, remembering her belatedly. And sometimes she would accompany him but often she would not, so that you might have wondered what privately she was thinking. But the part with the wife would come later . . .)

Small, thin Noah. He is the pillar of strength which holds up the family, the one to whom they turn, the one on whom they all rely. Small, thin Noah, they think to themselves, how satisfying is this discrepancy between his size and status.

· 22 ·

But tall Sylvie sits alone in the darkness. Her long, pre-Raphaelite hair is streaming across her shoulders, her neck has its customary crick in it, her head being bent forward in a submissive pose. Her feet are bare and she looks like an artist's model. She and Noah quarrelled this afternoon – he said some terrible things to her – and not only did he not apologise but now he is behaving as if nothing had happened and this re-writing of history is confusing her.

She had been taking photographs of him. She aspired to be a photographer, as they all did. She had wanted to photograph him earlier, he who was her absurd but sexy dandy, as he was making himself beautiful, as he always did on a Saturday night – going to and fro from the bathroom to the bedroom in the cottage; reaching up for his sunglasses which are hooked around the corner of the mirror; fingering the suits which are hanging from the door and which are far too big for his small frame; and buttoning up the shirt of fine, creamy lawn with its ivory buttons which he bought once in a second-hand shop in Camden Town which Sylvie's sister ran – how jealous Sylvie had been! – and which he always wore on a Saturday night and threw on the floor on a Sunday morning, where it lay in a rumpled heap, its fabric falling naturally into dips and dimples and valleys of shadows (and Sylvie used to pick it up and take it home and wash but never iron it because she lived in a squat and had no iron).

He had been lying on the floor in the bedroom. She had been leaning over him, taking pictures. 'It's a pity you don't have any cleavage,' he remarked, looking up at her, and he was quite glittery with malice. He needed rescuing. He was caught up and trapped by his own malice. But could she rescue him? She could not.

She had taken a set of photographs once – they were her favourites, she was thinking of them now as she sat out on the verandah playing cards – of Noah standing amongst the fruits and flowers in Berwick Street market down in Soho which was just round the corner from the block of flats where she lived. She had dressed him up like a doll, Noah, who in real life was so very undressable-up, because he wouldn't listen to her, he went his own way regardless, although Sylvie was rather sensible, not all her pre-Raphael-ite hair withstanding, and often she knew better than him, and she knew it. But on this occasion he had let her dress him up in his black Italian suit and his white T-shirt which was torn around the neck and more than a little grubby, and she had put him down amongst the street traders and the strip joints and the mountains of glowing, luminous fruits and flowers at just that time of day when the blue evening air begins to thicken and the electric lights are flashing in every colour and the city seems to quicken and to move towards bed and sex and love. And there he had stood, poised on the balls of his feet, allowing himself to be photo-graphed, his hair slicked back – for he was growing it long – and a brooch in his lapel in the manner of Oscar Wilde. He was gazing off to the right, his face palely reposed and one finger creeping up to stroke his upper lip and its shadow of designer stubble.

'You could have transplants,' he said as she leant over him, 'like Dolly Parton. I've heard they're rather good these days.'

Pity Noah, and Sylvie also, for his hard-soft, sweet-sour-ness. Pity them both for his overwhelming desire to *be* someone, and because he is so nervously poised between his hopes of success and his fears of failure, this nervousness giving him an air of jaunty arrogance. And pity them also because he who is so confident in the outside world is so fearful of the bedroom world, of his clinging love for his mother, and of his girlfriend Sylvie who is so soft and formless and clinging and loving. He is like all those twenty-five-year-old men who stand on street corners watching the cars go by, jangling the coins in their pockets, glad to be out of the house and away from the women; alive now, alert and relaxed.

'You're not very soft,' he complained from the floor – but what he meant was, *You're too soft* – 'all chest and no bosom. What kind of mother are you going to make?'

And yet he is as kind to her as his nature will permit. To Mattie he is often very sweet, but then the relationship of cousinhood is so easy, it being close but not too close. Once he said to Mattie, 'So, did you have a very unhappy childhood?' and she sat bolt upright in her chair and stared at him, the smile on her face both scornful and impressed. She thought this was perhaps the nicest thing that anyone had ever said. But then Noah was like that. For it had to be admitted that the rest of the Oaklands were not much interested in childhoods and parents and psychologising and the past, and only Noah had ever sat down beside her and asked her about her mother and the home in Dunmow End.

Noah was perceptive when he cared to be – it was his power – and he understood the link between past and future, although contrarily he also understood that what people are now they will not always be, and this knowledge perhaps, but mostly because he was, in his hard-soft, sweet-sour, thin, cockney, lordly fashion, really rather good-natured, this was the reason he was charming to waitresses and secretaries. (And he also knew – although from where Mattie couldn't have said – how therapeutic it was to talk about the past, how soothing it was to acknowledge how terrible the past had been.)

But to Sylvie he can scarcely bring himself to be kind at all. She drives him mad with her soft clingingness and the way she is so unreliable. He need only turn his back for an instant and she will be talking to another man. He thinks maybe he needs another woman, a stronger, bolder, more sassy kind of woman, but it isn't true of course. Such a woman would simply prolong the struggle to subdue her and make it that much more satisfying, but struggle they would without a doubt. He and Sylvie are always parting with a cataclysmic row and then Noah abandons the business altogether and goes to bed for the day, taking with him for company the black cat whom he loves, not as Jonathan loves it, in a fey and charming fashion, but with a hard-edged and febrile intensity. For Noah is a boy abroad in the world, panic-struck, distraught and aggressive.

They will eat late tonight. They will eat in that warm interlude brought on by drink and sleepiness, the best of the conversation passed and gone two hours ago, the body asleep, the mind limping on until sleepiness ambushes it also. It is a warm and comforting time to eat although conducive to indigestion. And it is perhaps indigestion which will cause Noah and Sylvie to argue again tonight, and to argue again tomorrow morning, about the shape of the sky when seen through the flaps of the curtains, and Sylvie will get up in tears and disarray and return on her own to London.

· 124 ·

· 23 ·

All that summer the Oaklands treated Mattie with a great and particular kindness which Mattie felt and luxuriated in, saying to herself, I am the youngest, the much loved, the anointed one, the only daughter, oh how lovely. They took her to the local theatre in Southwold to see *A Midsummer Night's Dream* and Mattie walked amongst them but in front of them as if she were their lucky mascot. And all through the evening they giggled and rustled their programmes and Vanessa kept whispering, 'Ask Mattie, Mattie understands these things, Mattie will know what it means.' For Mattie, they all agreed, Mattie who always passed her exams, was surely a child prodigy.

Mattie went paddling in the sea the next morning – a white and hazy morning when the wind blew out of the sky in its pure and elemental fashion. She thought it was her mother's kind of sky, her mother's kind of day, a day for seeing God, when the wind blew truths at you. The Oaklands sat outside the beach hut but Noah sat upon the sand. Since he and Sylvie had quarrelled the night before he had been making sand pies for Brangwen, Sonja Lefanu's little girl, who was telling him what to do in her sassy, four-year-old way, and this was making him laugh but also inclining him to cry. 'Ooh, er, it's the James Bond lady,' he called out to Mattie, and she looked down and saw through the water the bones of her nice feet like chicken bones and on the sand her best, most battered, once expensive leather handbag, in which were the novels she was currently reading; and she thought to herself how little she owned, but how little she needed to own, except for her pretty body, her clear mind which saw and understood everything, and the Oaklands, her beloved family, who were of inestimable value to her.

She was just twenty now and considered she understood the Oaklands pretty well, in all their charming faults and virtues. She looked back towards the beach where the flat, white light of the sea surface lapped the shore and when she saw the Oaklands spilling out of the beach hut, they and all their belongings, she thought, how careless they are with possessions – trying out her hand now at a touch of Oakland criticism – for she had the pleasant illusion that although she loved her cousins very dearly she was also loving them very lightly and could withdraw from this love in an instant if she had to. And besides she had long ago noticed that it didn't do to be too kind to the Oaklands, that it was better to treat them a little briskly. How vain they are, thought Mattie, indulgent of everything she couldn't do – she couldn't draw or paint or design, for instance – but equally indulgent of everything at which she excelled. That she was effortlessly good at school work was something they responded to with a slightly mocking wonder. (Although she used to hear them boasting about her results at dinner parties.) And Mattie laughed and thought how Oaklandish it was, to rate only the things you do best.

Noah was staring up at her and grinning as if he had never seen her before. The corners of his heart-shaped face were hard as diamonds. The white sun shone in his narrow black eyes. His body was small and slender as a boy's. His freckled face was scoured like the sand, brown and orange and silver and white. 'Sleep with me, Matt,' he said, and the wind blew out of the bleached bone sky at him. He only meant to say, 'How pretty you are and how much I admire you,' but it came out like this, 'Sleep with me, Matt,' and Mattie

· 126 ·

thought, I am their lucky mascot, the heart of the Oaklands, and to sleep with me would be to sleep with themselves, and what more could the narcissistic Oaklands want? And she held out her arms and stood on one leg and fell into several pert poses as she thought, how droll and funny I am and how lightly I tread between the different loves of the Oaklands and how easily I understand them.

'Certainly not,' she said, delighted he had asked, delighted to say no. How small he was, he made her laugh; if they were to sleep together his feet would hardly come down to her calves.

'Certainly not,' she said again with blissful elegance and delight. 'It would be incest.'

INCEST

· 24 ·

Hester's father was a mountain peak. On the one hand, going up, was her love for Henry and on the other, going down, was her indifference to him. Sometimes in her dreams she held up her hands into a steeple and thought, that is my father.

Mattie and she were lying out one evening, end to end, on a long park bench on Primrose Hill. This hill was a benign and soothing spot. It rose up like a green breast into the sky. On this evening dogs barked, the sky was flawless, the evening languished, the streets below them were white and stuccoed. They had climbed up until they could see Regent's Park and the zoo and Snowdon's Aviary, and then they went on climbing – the two of them who were seven months pregnant and could scarcely believe it – because no doubt a part of them would have liked to destroy the babies but also because it was a benign and soothing spot and they liked to feel its airs were good for these babies that they didn't really believe in and would also have liked to get rid of – until the baby inside Hester was spinning on top of her lungs, her heart was racing, her breath was flapping and struggling, and then they lay down on a long bench, feet to feet, Hester at one end and Mattie at the other.

Their hands were clasped over their tummies. They were like carved figures on a tombstone, dead as doornails. They were talking about fatherly love by which Mattie meant the father of her baby; but Hester meant her father, the vicar, and her love for him, which was weighing upon her so heavily that evening since she had quarrelled with Henry only an hour before.

They had quarrelled as it happens over whether or not Mattie was unhappy – Hester said she was and he said she wasn't – which was also a quarrel about which of them, Henry or her, had had the worst childhood. They were in competition on this subject although Henry didn't know it – 'Henry knows nothing,' said Hester – and how sad Hester was because her mother was dead. But it was also a quarrel over Hester's father because he was such a lousy father and yet such a brilliant quarreller, far better than Henry who was confused by quarrels and who dragged along behind her and got in the way and put his feet in the wrong places and generally behaved like a man at a dance who doesn't understand rhythm.

Hester didn't feel well that night. Her ankles were swollen and her chest was scalded with heartburn and wouldn't stop burning. When she first conceived this baby she had wanted to guard it with her life. She had felt that malice, ill will and hostility could destroy it and so she had folded her clothes about it, she had wrapped her arms around it, she had cradled it in her mind. But as the weeks passed – twenty-four, twenty-five, twenty-six – and the baby acquired arms and legs and began to kick with them, and ears and eyes, and a feeling, sentient mind (she fancied she could feel it thinking inside her), then it also occurred to her that this baby meant to survive, and possibly at her expense. She saw that those mothers with the brightest and prettiest and most responsive children were themselves the thinnest and palest and tiredest. Babies are parasites. As babies grow mothers die – very slowly, of course – but die they do nonetheless. How frightened Hester was.

'You exaggerate the fear,' said Henry. 'What about the glow of motherhood? What about the pride in carrying the baby? Not everyone is afraid. Other mothers have a glow

· 130 ·

about them. It's only you who are afraid, and you are projecting.'

But she didn't believe him. She felt her mind fur up like an old kettle.

Now, stretched out on Primrose Hill, she played the game of images. Her father was a mountain peak. Her father was a statue stretched out upon a tombstone. Her father was the waves rolling shorewards and in the troughs between the waves were her lovers and then the next wave came rolling inwards and her lovers vanished.

Only Frank rode out the waves. During the time she was in love with him she looked at her father with soft pity and saw him for what he was, so small and bad-tempered and cantankerous.

She had met Henry at a party where she'd gone on her own since Frank had left her for a gig in Glasgow. She was looking for someone to love. Henry came into the kitchen looking for an aspirin. When he saw her standing there he demanded she massage his neck and shoulders. After a while he stood up and she saw that he was a small, egg-shaped man with neat features and a soft mouth which stayed open and which fell downwards at the corners in discontent. He drew her to him. He sat her on his knee and asked her what she'd done that day. 'I've had a driving lesson,' she replied and then he said with the air of a man who thinks himself very witty, 'Remind me not to drive round here on a Saturday afternoon.' Ha, ha.

She made up her mind there and then not to sleep with him and, that decided, she was able to look at him and unwillingly to admire him. He had been drinking as alcoholics do, slowly and steadily, and the wine had all but hidden his tired eyes and his paunch, and had heightened his urbanity. She watched him swan around the room from

woman to woman and she watched how they, too, unwillingly admired him because he was so little and so importunate, drinking from their glasses and patting at their bottoms.

After the party finished – and he stayed nearly to the end
as if he didn't want to miss a moment – they went home
arm in arm, he in the middle and a woman on either side.
Of course he was hedging his bets. But when this other
woman departed, as finally she did – she's fatter and plainer
than me, thinks Hester, and her hair is not so pretty – then
Henry went into the kitchen and produced a dish of quite
surpassing richness, all meat and fruit and nuts and she felt
slayed by its creamy tenderness. He took her and her full
stomach off to bed and she made no protest. He screwed
her in a soft and buttery way and then he fell asleep and she
put her arms around him and rested her hands on his fat
waist and felt all the good food they had eaten, all that good,
fat living which he carried like a lifebelt round his waist.
And she was surprised at what a comfort it was to her.

She didn't sleep with him only to annoy Frank and nor
did she mean it only as a slander when she told Frank he
was gay. She really did think he might be a little bit homo-
sexual and besides she didn't intend it as an insult but that's
how they took it, both of them, and Frank threw her out as
if she were his enemy, and Henry took her in as if she were
the same, and never afterwards quite trusted her, although
he never said a word about it. She simply became another
millimetre in the discontented drooping of his mouth – and
for a while the affair went forwards in its fat and buttery
way.

Morning and evening they lay in bed with the curtains
drawn in a haze of full, fat living. During the day she went
to work but Henry lounged at home in a dressing gown he
had bought – 'A man must have a dressing gown,' he said
– drinking coffee and looking at the jobs pages and thinking
of what they would eat. In the afternoons he went to the

market and in the evenings he cooked and when all that good food had reduced her to her knees they went to bed again.

He was generous with his money – he had some kind of private income – and he was kind to her and took an interest in her career and because she wished to love him, so she did, and thus they might have gone on indefinitely except that Henry was sociable. He liked to go to parties and he liked to give them – dinner parties, drinks parties, breakfast parties, parties at Christmas and on his birthday – and every time they went out or someone came in she thought she saw Henry with their eyes and her love for him faltered. She saw his discontent, how he believed the world should have given him so much more by way of an income and yet how languorous and lazy he was when it came to earning it. She saw his petty snobberies, how his interest in a guest would be revived if you told him they were famous. She saw how he knew nothing about feelings, and how full he was of vanity, patting women's bottoms as if he were so sexy; and how he was importunate and tactless, and blind, never seeing how her love for him faltered, but coming home and taking her to bed, and resurrecting her love for him – but only by a whisker – and he never even saw it.

And yet time and again he did resurrect her love, until one night at one of these parties she met a man who knew her father.

He lived in the same part of Suffolk, maybe even in her father's parish, where her father had that reputation which single men often have when they are also impossibly high-minded and principled and angry. 'Croxthorpe?' said this man. 'Are you related to David Croxthorpe?' And when she said she was he launched into the story, as if it would be news to her, of the time her father officiated at a wedding and wandered for a moment from the marriage service into the burial for the dead because he preferred the language, it being so much sadder, more sonorous and moving. 'Ashes to ashes, dust to dust,' said her father to the astonished bride and groom, because that was her father.

She saw this man was impressed by the strength of her father's passions, and she saw also that Henry was listening and admiring her because her father was famous, if only to this small extent – Henry, who knows nothing about passion – but as for her she felt such a pang of twisted, thwarted love at the memory of her father that when Henry said, 'Let's go and visit him,' she agreed at once.

They set off on a Saturday morning. They went by way of various back roads. They made detours to visit breweries and restaurants and delicatessens since Henry had got it into his head he was going to be a food critic. They stopped and ate lunch at three o'clock and so came to her father's village just as it was growing dark, a bright, cold, fiery winter evening when the sky had all the light and the earth had nothing. And yet as they went past Minsmere she saw its waters were still shining, those waters which are old, they are very old, they are as old as the Flood itself, and there was her father's church thrown up above them like a great whale beached upon a mountain.

Henry wore a sweater and a sheepskin jacket on top. He had tied a scarf in a foppish fashion round his neck. He drove in his usual, slapdash, vain and dangerous way and she was afraid that in these narrow lanes they would kill one of her father's parishioners. But they arrived at last in safety at the big house and went in and found it all in darkness and cold, very cold, and no food upon the table. Henry drew a bottle out of his bag and began to poke around for a bottle opener. Hester looked at his back and his plump bottom and then she turned and saw her father in the doorway.

She had only two ways of behaving towards her father. When he was unhappy she skirted round him, feeling how he kept her at a distance and what ambivalence and malice he felt towards her because she was a woman, so that she became more bony, more angular and less female by the

· 134 ·

minute. But when he was happy then she zoomed round him and delighted in his approval. Now she saw he was happy, that his eyes had that dazed, sweet look which they always had when he emerged from a period of unhappy malice, as if he were wondering what could have led him to be so cruel. 'Dad,' said Hester and she stepped forward and at that Henry turned round. 'Ah, Mr Croxthorpe,' he said – and he was a small, fat man facing a small, thin one – 'we brought a bottle with us. Mustn't drink the communion wine, must we?' Ha, ha.

Hester saw her father look at him and in that look she fell out of love with Henry instantly and irretrievably. From this moment forth his languor became in her mind mere laziness, his mild sweetness weakness, his love of food and wine greediness. From this moment forth she knew that he was mostly unemployable, that since he had been up to Cambridge ten years ago he had come away with pretensions to the good life, to good food and wine and holidays, and now wouldn't work for anyone for less than £30,000 a year; that he had charm but was quite unperceptive and would often walk all over her feelings, not even knowing that she had them; that he was a man's man and the women he liked were the women he fancied, because everyone was always judged by looks and sex.

But still they slept together one more time, that night – Henry wanted it and she didn't but because she was no longer in love with him she thought it didn't matter whether they did or they didn't. But as it happened it did matter because the durex broke and in her father's house that night they conceived a baby. Seven months ago. Last November. For a long time she didn't believe it. She was sure her indifference to him would have been her contraceptive. And now of course she believed it was her father's baby, in spirit if not in fact, that she was carrying.

Her father didn't approve of Henry. What chance did Henry have? She was stuck way back in her childhood. But then so was Mattie. It was what they had in common, why they were good friends, because they were both of them fixed way back in the past. Of all the women in the group – Leonie, Lindie, Barbara, Caroline, Mattie and Hester – only Mattie and Hester would admit to incestuous babies.

· 25 ·

Tonight Mattie was exuberant. Sometimes Hester thought there was no onward march of the personality, no endless development towards truth but only a repeated return to what they once were, the endless beginning again of exuberance and the forgetting of sad knowledge. So Mattie that night was exuberant.

She walked in just as their quarrel was beginning, when Henry was saying in an irritated voice, because he was made impatient by all these female claims to sadness, 'Why do you always talk about Mattie as if she's unhappy? You make her sound so sad. She's not sad at all,' and Hester was answering sharply – because she felt got at, because sometimes she thought she muddled up Mattie and herself in her head – 'So how would you know? You've only met her a couple of times, and besides you didn't even like her. You only ever like women if they fancy you,' she added, which although irrelevant was true, and Henry blushed with mortification to be so put down, his short nose growing even shorter, his small, sensitive mouth turning down even further.

Hester was consumed with irritation that he couldn't see Mattie's charms, consumed by outrage that perhaps he could. 'And besides,' she said, and now she was self-pitying, 'she was unhappy. She lost her mother and that's something children never recover from.' Her own mother had died when she was six but Henry didn't seem to notice the reference. 'Mattie's mother isn't dead,' he said, literal-minded as

· 137 ·

ever, which meant that she could answer smartly, 'No, but she went mad and it amounts to the same thing . . . '

And then the door bell rang and Henry went and there was Mattie, standing there looking Mattie-ish as ever, and not sad at all, her bright, dark eyes both lively and disdainful, her black hair glittering with coppery-bronze highlights. She was wearing pink and red. Her head was hung with heavy jewellery. She was dressed up like an African queen and she carried the bump before her as if it were a separate thing, the individual not yet erased, the mind still spinning off in pursuit of love in the old world. Round her head was a length of Oakland fabric.

'Hey, it's Hester,' Mattie said, and Hester thought that tonight Mattie was feeling delighted but also rather grand because her beauty was making her feel superior. Hester saw her look around at the domestic set-up – the cramped basement flat, the supper on the table – with her usual artless mixture of scorn and curiosity. 'Hallo, Mattie,' said Hester, heaving herself to her feet. 'That's pretty,' said Mattie, reaching out to touch Hester's necklace, relieved at last to be able to find something to praise in her appearance. Mattie loved nice things. She couldn't understand how Hester could be so uninterested.

Hester saw her look nervously at Henry. She and Henry didn't get on. The first time they had met was at the Fathers' Night four weeks before when Mattie had been holding forth on female friendship, the pleasures of which she had only just discovered. 'I think babies are women's business,' she had been saying, 'they're women's creations and nothing to do with men.' 'Men do have something to do with it,' Henry had said. 'Like fifty per cent.' And then Mattie had looked at him with such a mulish expression she had made Hester laugh. It was as if Mattie would claim that black was white and babies came by parthenogenesis if that was what she cared to.

'Have you walked here?' asked Hester curiously. 'Only

· 138 ·

from the bus stop,' said Mattie. 'I can't walk that far these days. Have you noticed that too?' 'It is normal at this stage,' said Henry. 'You are going to have a baby,' and Mattie started at his tone as if she had been pricked.

Hester saw Mattie sensed a quarrel in the air and that quarrels between parents frightened her. Perhaps she remembered her parents quarrelling in Eden? 'Let's go out,' said Hester – she felt so trapped, so bloody trapped – and without a word and with scarcely a backward glance at Henry they went out into the streets.

Tonight Mattie was exuberant, very full of the blithe awareness of her own good looks, so pleased with this arrangement of being alive on such a flawless London evening.

'Where are we going,' asked Hester. 'To Primrose Hill,' said Mattie. 'Because it's so pretty?' asked Hester. 'Because it's so pretty,' Mattie agreed, not minding at all that Hester was teasing her. Mattie liked not only nice clothes but leafy London streets where men and women sat out at cafés and, made leisurely by money, were able to turn their minds to art. She was a natural £40,000-a-year person (Hester being about £15,000); such pleasures don't come any cheaper. And now though the world was rushing by them Hester saw that Mattie was hanging on to the male images as they flashed past: the man with the handsome boxer's profile standing with one foot forward in a statuesque way surveying the world, and another man who ran from the house to the car, tossing his keys into the air and snatching them back as he went. Mattie liked maleness. She saw it all. But Hester, who never felt such pure pleasure in the present moment as Mattie then was feeling – she was jealous and admiring.

Mattie was glancing to all sides of her and picking up men, left, right and centre, seven months pregnant as she was. They picked up a man before they reached the end of the street, a white-faced man with a straggly beard who habitually sat on the wall outside the newsagents reciting

· 139 ·

poetry. When she saw what she had done Mattie looked alarmed and the man looked annoyed to see them hurrying away from him so hastily.

Mattie was racing along on a river of admiration. She was throwing out sops of consolation to Hester who was her not-so-pretty friend. She was singing to herself, 'One year, two year, three year, more, How can I deny what went before? Five year, six year, seven year, eight, Turn my love to deepest hate? Do you like living in London, Hester?' she asked. 'Yes, I suppose so. I don't know where else I would live.' 'I love it. I love everything about it. I want to live here for ever. Oh, Hester, look at your ankles. They're so swollen. Do they hurt?' 'No, but they make me feel very tired. And I feel ugly because I've never had such thick ankles before.' 'I wonder if I shall get them,' Mattie said, glancing as she did so – she couldn't help herself – at her own slender ankles. 'I shouldn't think so,' said Hester, 'You seem immune to things like this.'

But Mattie couldn't stop thinking about Hester's ankles. She was still standing and staring at them. She was as solicitous as a child but really her mind was on other things and besides there was not a lot to say when racing along on a river of admiration except to admire the landscape as it shot past. And so they were stopping to look in shop windows, to hanker after jewellery and shoes and knickers, all the way down Regent's Park Road, Hester and Mattie and Mattie's alter ego who was walking three steps behind and singing and dancing and praising Mattie's lovely appearance, until they came to a shop which was selling Oaklandish-looking knick-knacks.

They stopped and stared and Hester knew Mattie was also thinking how Oaklandish they were because after a while she said – and her voice was gloomy, 'My problem was always the Oaklands,' in the way she had which was to love them, praise them and blame them all at the same time. But tonight she only spoke with the habit of theatrical sadness,

· 140 ·

she didn't really mean it, for after a while she said, 'Have you ever thought what it would be like to be born in some situation from which you couldn't escape, like some remote village in the Pyrenees, for instance?' – by which she meant, of course, how lucky I am to be here and how wonderful are my cousins. She was by nature blithe. Tonight she couldn't quite hang on to the fact that they had wronged her.

They picked up another man on Primrose Hill.

When they had climbed up as far as they could they lay down and Hester shut her eyes and felt her stomach a dead weight on top of her. She was afraid she might have killed the baby. She folded her hands, and thus stretched out she was like a carved figure on a tombstone, dead as doornails. But when she opened her eyes she saw that Mattie wasn't dead at all. She looked like an eighteenth-century lady reclining in her boudoir. She was casting her eyes in all directions, the queen of this green hillside and all this limpid and polluted air, and with her eyes she had picked up a man in a T-shirt and jeans. He had a pink complexion, pink and brown, and brown curly hair. He didn't dare come any closer but nor could he bring himself to go away, and so he hovered on the grass at a fixed distance, smiling, as if kept there by a magnet. Hester saw that Mattie had noticed him but so long as he kept his distance she quite liked him to exist.

'I'm hungry,' Mattie said. 'I fancy an ice cream.' 'It would be nice. Why don't you go down the hill and get one?' 'It would be nice if someone went down the hill and got one for us,' said Mattie, and they looked at the brown-and-pink man who was still hovering and staring. 'He looks rather sweet,' said Hester. 'He's all right if you like that kind of thing.' 'All right if it suits?' 'All right if it suits,' said Mattie, agreeing. Hester thought he looked rather simple. 'Poor thing,' said Mattie who believed – she couldn't help herself

· 141 ·

– that her own beauty would make everyone, even this man, feel better.

Hester wanted to talk to someone about her father. She said to Mattie, 'What did your father do?' and Mattie was quiet so that Hester felt Mattie's mind come to the edge of that great chasm which is the hole left in our heads when one of our parents die. (Of course she is unhappy, thought Hester, not Henry and all that exuberance withstanding.)

'He was a student,' said Mattie at last. 'They didn't have any money, my mother and him, but they got married because it was romantic. They were both students but she had a grant and he didn't so he had to work as well, and he worked and he painted and he never slept and he was hungry so then he caught bronchitis and it turned into pneumonia.'

It was a mythological death, of course, like the death of all those parents who die young, and yet it was Mattie's daily tipple, her little piece of buttered cake and pleasure, the idea that her father died for art. 'And he didn't have any family,' she went on, 'or at least none my mother had ever heard of. I think he was quite a solitary person, both him and my mother. Do you think the father of my baby is going to be interested in him, Hester?'

'I don't know,' said Hester. 'Perhaps, perhaps not. But how do you know it's going to be a him anyway?'

'Oh, all that family runs to boys. I hope he's born a Leo. I shall have his horoscope read at once. I want him to be beautiful. He's going to be a present to my family and we'll bring him up together on the kitchen floor. But I don't understand about fathers, Hester. I mean, I don't understand the nature of fatherly love. I understand about mother love.'

'Do you? How does mother love work?'

'Well, I suppose it's innate. You have a baby and then you feel it. Love.'

'I don't know anything about mothers,' said Hester.

'Well, nor do I really,' said Mattie.

· 142 ·

'And nor about fathers,' said Hester (wondering as she said this why she hadn't thought of it before).

'Neither do I,' said Mattie and she added, 'Isn't it funny how alike we are in that way?'

And at that they lay back with their eyes shut and contemplated their sad and orphaned states.

Then Hester had an idea. She heard exuberance filling Mattie up again with a sigh and she said quickly, before Mattie's exuberance could overwhelm her, 'The terrible thing about not having a parent is that you have no one to compare yourself with, no one to look at and say, Oh, that is what I'm like too. It makes it harder for me to understand myself.'

'I've no idea who I am,' said Mattie truthfully, 'sometimes I'm one person and sometimes I'm another. Actually, the person I most look like is Vanessa. Perhaps there's been some mistake. Perhaps she's my mother.' And at that Mattie's exuberance overcame her and she said, 'How many times have you been in love, Hester?'

'Dozens of times,' (drily). 'Nature abhors a vacuum. It's the way my mind's arranged. I'm always in pursuit of love.'

'Oh, so am I,' said Mattie. 'Every day of my adult life. Not that I'm complaining,' she added smugly, 'only commenting.'

'But that was in the old world,' said Hester with her hands on her bump but Mattie didn't hear. She was rehearsing her life, Hester could hear her doing it, as orphans will, as if it were a story, remembering her heydays and salad days and pyjama days.

'Noah. Noah Oakland,' Mattie was saying dreamily, 'He was such a smartarse,' she was saying, as if this were today's favourite phrase, as if she were in love with it, 'He was such a smartarse, he was king of all the smartarses.'

· 26 ·

In Southwold each bleached and silvery day had been succeeded by another until the Oaklands could no longer remember what it felt like to be cold and boldly began to think that they would like to wear their winter clothes once more and to run to and fro from the taxi to the house and back again through the pouring rain. But when they returned to London it did begin to rain and then it wouldn't stop – except for once when the skies cleared for a day or two and the sun appeared, surprisingly low upon the horizon, a more mellow and orangey sun than they had remembered which cast a speckled light upon the grass and through the increasingly naked branches of the trees – and Vanessa went to a Vivienne Westwood sale and brought home a tartan mohair cape and Mattie came in from out of the rain, stamping and spraying water sideways from out of her cropped and sparkling hair, and saying that if the rain went on much longer her feet would start to rot. Rain impinges more upon the poor than on the rich. Mattie noticed changes in the weather but Vanessa said this must be because of her country childhood. 'Jay-sus, Mattie, like a dog,' said Jonathan when she stamped her soaking feet upon the mat, but Noah snapped her with his camera, caught the droplets flying like sparks in all directions.

She wouldn't sleep with him and so, instead, he photographed her. 'Lovely copper-bronze highlights and scarlet toenails,' he said, and he photographed her slipping upside down from a couch which he had draped with the counter-pane he had once designed for his mother. This was a won-derfully exotic creature which he had dyed in every shade of pink and red. Usually it lay heavily asleep across Vanessa's bed but today Noah had dragged it out and placed it on the couch and placed Mattie upon it in order that he might photograph her on a bed of flaming reds and pinks. He was an Oakland. He loved colours. He wanted to see if he could create in colour that same sense of grainy significance you find in black and whites.

First of all he photographed her with his polaroid. He worked in silence, hardly seeming to look at her at all. After a while she got up and came round and looked over his shoulder. She saw he had caused her to spin forwards, help-lessly, bobbing upside down like a flower in a river of pinks and reds – it was Mattie all right, springing outwards, upside down and bold-and-soft-as-butter-looking-for-her-Eden Mattie – and she was pleased and thought, how sad I am, and was touched and moved by her own image, how sad and young and beautiful. 'Do I look like that?' she asked, but he wouldn't pander to her vanity. His indifference was wonderful. 'You moved,' said her thin, small cousin in his lordly, cockney way, not taking his eyes from the pictures. But since he hadn't been looking how could he know?

He had created a reddish light over her eyelids. 'That's the colour you should always use,' he said, still not looking at her, eyes on the pictures, mind on her mouth, and he added, 'You're very beautiful, Matt, but your lipstick is all wrong, it should be carmine,' and she was impressed; she couldn't help herself.

The more still she tried to keep her body the more her mind would wander.

'What would Sylvie say?' she asked him.

'What about?' He was abrupt. It was as if he had no idea to what she was referring.

'If we slept together. It would be two-timing her.'

· 145 ·

'Sylvie and I have split up,' he said.

'Since when?'

'Since last week.'

'Why did you leave her?'

'I didn't leave her. She left me. So, you see,' he said. End of conversation.

'But why?' she persisted, but he wouldn't answer. He left the question hanging in mid-air, although after ten minutes or so had passed he said, 'She told me once she fancied a big, butch rugby player.' And Mattie stared at him, and tried to work out if he was meaning to be funny. Poor Noah.

How hard he worked. He was like this in the factory, sitting there hour after hour, thinking and designing, not saying a word, whilst all the old women whom his parents employed brought him cups of tea and fussed and clucked and cuddled after his comforts. (For there was no one like the Oaklands for bringing out the feudal side of other people's natures.) Mattie liked people who were intent and full of concentration. She thought you could gather up this concentration in both hands to admire it. But why isn't he looking at me? she thought, trying out her hand now at pique to see what that felt like, and she stared at his downturned face very hard and willed him to look up at her. Which at length he did. 'How are you, Matt?' he asked, really quite tenderly. 'All right,' she said. And I'm not going to make love to you, she added, but under her breath because it was a secret. He hasn't asked me to sleep with him again, she thought, but the next minute, when he was arranging the fall of the light on her limbs, he did just that, so Mattie could answer him joyfully, smartly, a second time, 'Certainly not, it would be incest.'

This answer seemed to cheer him up. 'No, it wouldn't,' he said.

'How do you know?'

'I looked it up in the dictionary. Love between cousins,

· 146 ·

especially second cousins, is okay. You have beautiful feet, Mattie. I've noticed them before. Beautiful feet are very rare.'

'I know.'

'Why haven't you painted those toes?'

'Because I only do the first two on each foot. Do you like them?'

'Very much.'

'Anyway,' said Mattie after a pause, 'it would *feel* like incest.'

'What kind of incest would it feel like?'

'Brother-sister incest.'

'Oh my beautiful sister-cousin, Mattie,' said Noah, grinning now all over his face.

'Don't laugh at me,' said Mattie, whilst her mind went spinning irrelevantly away: I am the daughter of the house and Noah, Aaron and Jonathan are my three brothers. I am the youngest, the much loved, the best beloved, the anointed one, the only daughter. Oh how lovely.

It seemed there was no end to the women who rang up Noah until he pulled the extension out of the wall so that he could work in peace. Mattie liked to try to figure out which of the women were friends and which of them were lovers, or might become so. Someone came knocking at the front door. Noah took no notice. They knocked again. 'Noah?' said Mattie tentatively. 'What?' he said. So she got to her feet and went across and opened the window wide. A woman turned her face skywards and asked for Noah in a high, breathless voice. Not a girlfriend, thought Mattie; he would never go out with anyone whose voice was shrill like that. 'Noah,' she said, and he looked up from the camera. 'You've moved again,' he said. 'There's someone at the door,' she said. 'What?' He leant out of the window and Mattie saw the hairs rise on the white nape of his neck. 'Yeah. Yeah.' He listened for a while. 'Hang on a second,' he said, and turned back into the room. 'Mattie, cover your-

· 147 ·

self up. You'll get cold.' Obediently she did so. Noah was leaning out again. 'No,' he said. 'Not Mattie. Hattie. With an "h". No, no,' he said, grinning, '*Fattie*. F-A-T-T-I-E . . . Yeah . . . No. I'm working,' he said. And then after a pause, in his easy, comfortable, peremptory tones he added, 'You do that.'

And at these words something curious happened. A tree moved outside and a feathery shadow passed dimly across the floor. A bird sang in the street. A car revved up. A cat cried out. All these sounds she heard, both separate and blended together, very clear and yet also distant and defining the circle of silence where she stood with Noah. Silence rose in a roar. She saw the dark hairs rise on the white nape of his neck, and she saw the coarse weave of his grubby, off-white T-shirt. He was so small she thought she could swallow him up. She thought, I love him. I love my cousin Noah. And then the moment passed and the sounds of the street came pressing in on them and Noah turned and said, 'Have you had enough, Matt?' but as if he was hoping she had not, and she felt a warm feeling, a feeling she rarely had – oh, very rarely indeed – of great contentment.

She nodded. She turned over luxuriously. She yawned. She pretended to be bored. 'I've had enough,' she said, because she wanted him out of the room. She had the idea that this feeling of love was not yet focused, that it might yet fix itself on anyone. 'I fancy a drink,' said Noah and he sauntered towards the door, small, thin, ordinary Noah. Ordinary and yet extraordinary. 'Do you fancy one too?'

· 27 ·

He took her first to Camden Town where the crowds were so dense they stopped the traffic and fat from the hamburger stalls singed the air and ran across the street. Noah led the way and Mattie followed. She wore a sequinned cap pulled far down on her head. She was dressed in black. She looked like Death, a pretty Death but the crowd was full of Deaths like her, for black was in this year. The blue air was full of the oily smell of burning chestnuts. Mattie didn't wear a coat. She thought coats were for people who were frightened, who wanted to shut out the world. She was so elated she was making eyes at everyone she passed, both men and women. It seemed to her that everyone in this crowd knew each other and loved each other and were chatting and talking away like the oldest and bestest of friends.

A young man sold T-shirts at a stall. His limbs were long, his face thin, his nose pointy and he wore a baker's hat on his head. He was not at all good-looking but his bow-like mouth in the light of the shop curved upwards enigmatically, and he drew the looks of the crowd and tossed them back and drew them back to him again. 'Miff,' said Noah, pushing towards him, 'what kind of crap are you selling today?' and they clasped hands for a moment so that a small package was exchanged which Mattie took to be drugs, for Noah dabbled a bit, not dealing but smoking and shooting and sniffing and snorting and buying on behalf of his friends.

'Come on,' said Noah, and they moved on to a café in the back streets near the park. It was this year's fashionable café. There were so many models and photographers sitting in the window that there was not one person there who wasn't both inhabiting himself and languidly, pleasurably observing his looks from the outside. Mattie saw their vanity and forgave them for it, for she recognised the same thing in herself. These days she didn't go anywhere without carrying in her head a subliminal impression of herself, herself seen as it were from the corner of one eye, and her slender figure and Vogue-y looks never failed to make herself laugh. The crush was enormous. Noah and Mattie squeezed between the tables. Faces pressed up against her, huge, black-rimmed eyes and leather jackets and long legs in lurex tights. 'I like your hat,' said a girl as they passed. Mattie thought if you counted all their alter egos the numbers in the café would be doubled, from perhaps fifty to one hundred. Oh, how funny I am, thought Mattie.

They sat down at a table with two men and a girl and Noah at once began to talk. Mattie couldn't work out if he knew them already. He didn't introduce her but she didn't care. She opened a newspaper but very soon he said, 'It's time to go. She's probably still at work.' It's time for bed, said Zebedee, thought Mattie jumping after him. She saw through the crowded café her image blurred and softened in a mirror, her eyes huge, her cheeks glowing, the mouth as soft as fruit. Oh, Ms Charming Face, thought Mattie, swooning.

He led the way to the door and took her to a bus stop and insisted on sitting in the front seat at the top where he said you could see better. He liked to look at the people in the streets and what they were wearing, the lights and the makes of the cars, the blocks of flats which were being refurbished and what was displayed in the shops. He pointed out these things to Mattie. He noticed everything, down to the smallest detail. He was interested in image and style and design. He was the kind of person who if he went out to buy a stereo could only buy the best, the most fashionable and designery one available. 'Does image matter that much?' Mattie asked him, but he didn't like to be thus interrogated. He turned his bored, guileless, masculine eyes upon her. 'What do you mean?' he said.

Wardour Street was full of people hurrying to and fro. There were lights on behind Venetian blinds and intermittently the blue-white flash of a camera shooting. Noah spoke into an intercom and they were admitted to an office which was carpeted in grey, and furnished in chrome and matt black. A plump girl sat on a desk. She had long strawberry blonde hair. She wore a mini skirt and had the prettiest of piano legs. 'Noah,' she said, swinging these legs down from the desk.

'Hello, Katie,' he said and he kissed her. He introduced her to Mattie. The girl smiled with the frank and charming admiration of her age so that Mattie's spirit contracted to a speck with embarrassment and then swelled up again even as she was noting this smile and wondering how to do it. 'Are you a model?' asked Katie. 'Don't be stupid,' said Noah. 'Katie's father is a vicar,' he added, apropos of nothing. 'Shut up, Noah,' said Katie. 'And she sleeps with her brother,' said Noah. 'Only when he's nowhere else to go,' said Katie, blushing. But when Mattie came to think of it, this was exactly what she would have expected, for she thought Katie would be both kind and entirely ignorant of conventional morality. She had just decided how much she admired this girl and was wondering whether they meant the bit about the brother literally when Noah said, 'Time to go.' 'Just like the White Rabbit,' said Katie, which reference Mattie understood but Noah did not. Which was pleasing.

He was sweet-natured. He was suprisingly sweet-natured. He was far more sweet-natured than she had supposed. His eyes rested with pity – she saw it – on bag ladies and beggars and he gave money to the blind man who played the accor-

· 151 ·

dion beside Hungerford Bridge. He was a believer in private charity like his mother. He gave with his eyes half shut and a look of private, Catholic reverence on his face, as did Vanessa, whom he admired so enormously. Mattie followed after him. She was proud of him but she could hardly bear to look at the beggar she was so full of pity for his life. She thought, once I was poor like that but now I am rich. How extraordinary to be lucky, to be singled out by fate.

It was growing dark. They stopped outside the National Theatre to listen to a samba band. One man played a saxophone and another man and a woman danced beneath a tree, the underside of whose leaves were illuminated by the yellow light of a street lamp. The men wore bowler hats and the woman the smallest and skinniest of green lurex dresses. On her feet were white sling-back shoes and with these she rapped out an intricate pattern on the pavement. The river flowed behind them. They danced in a curiously inverted world, the leaves of the trees rustling and blowing, lit up upside down. In the interval the woman came round jangling a hat for money. She stopped to say a few words to Noah so that Mattie, who had thought they were there by chance, now thought perhaps it had been an assignation. He slipped a small package into her hat and thus having delivered his assignment he said, 'Let's go to Centrepoint.'

'Why?' asked Mattie. 'Why not?' he said. 'Do you want to walk or catch a bus?' 'Walk,' said Mattie in order to see what would happen next. So they crossed back over the river and went through Trafalgar Square and up into Charing Cross Road. The tower block rose up before them. It was ablaze with lights. It was rearing up into the sky like a festive ocean liner.

'The lights are on tonight,' said Noah. 'It's empty,' said Mattie. 'No, it's not,' he said. 'Did you know it's on a ley line? Like Primrose Hill and Glastonbury and Stonehenge and Milton Keynes.' 'Milton Keynes?' 'Yeah,' said Noah. 'The railway station. That's why the hippies gather there at the solstice.' He looked at the tower block in an appraising kind of way as if he were a buyer.

Mattie was looking in the shop windows. She let her eyes run idly over the posters in Athena. There was a poster of a poem by William Blake, illustrated by one of his own paintings. 'Do you like William Blake?' she asked. 'No,' said Noah, who was king of all the smartarses, staring at the tower block as if he were trying to suck the essence of its meaning from it; which he was, for he thought of it as the power at the heart of the city and like all his generation he was hugely taken with power. 'Barbarian,' said Mattie. *I have no name*, said the poem. *I am but two days old. What shall I call thee? I happy am. Joy is my name – Sweet joy befall thee.* A naked child played with a sheep. Within a flower a baby floated, halfway between heaven and earth. My mother was a William Blake-ish sort of character, thought Mattie, what with her visions and her madness, and then Noah leant over and kissed her and said, 'Let's go home, Mattie,' in tones of gratitude as if he knew already she was going to sleep with him. Which knowledge at this moment struck her as very surprising. How does he know? she thought.

'Mattie,' he said again with such serious gratitude she wanted to laugh, and he hailed a taxi and pushed her inside and at the other end led her out again and into the house and up to his bedroom where the curtains were drawn but the lights from the street shone through and the darkness seemed pale and granular to the touch, the air somehow thick with tangled bedclothes and dirty washing. He sat her on the bed. He slid into bed beside her. He began to kiss and cuddle her. He set about her, little boyish Noah whose feet only came down to her calves so that she looked down on him as well as up and wanted to laugh at him. In the darkness his face was picked out with pointillist dots fading away at the feet into the grey twilight. But he was weighty, he was surprisingly weighty on top of her and then he drew up her skirt and put his prick inside her and so sudden a sense of completeness did this give her that she stopped wanting to laugh and wanted to cry out instead. He took away her centre – he centred her elsewhere, away from her head and her feelings – filled her centre with sharp strokes of honey. And then he took away her pleasure, took it to himself, and came, and in the moment he did so he hung above her like a fish impaled upon a hook. And Mattie stared at him and thought she had never seen this expression on a man's face before and thought delightedly it must be her power had done this, that it was in response to her, Mattie, specifically, that he died like this above her for a moment.

How pleased she was. She began to smile. It was lovely to be so powerful, lovely to have the upper hand, lovely to give pleasure so generously where she chose. She was very languid. But just as she was feeling all this, he put his finger between her legs and made her come – her small, thin cousin! – she was astonished: it had never happened to her before. It is difficult for anxious, observing people ever to lose themselves. She saw greenness and grass and laughter, and Oakland patterns and shapes and colours. She began to laugh breathlessly. She lay back on the unfamiliar sheets and didn't want to laugh at him any longer. On the contrary, she wanted to weep in a pleasurable kind of way for everything that had ever happened.

He gave her visions. He carried his life behind him in tatters – when she shut her eyes she saw it – the parties and the crowds and the freeways and the blue-black darkness which was adazzle with the white lights of street lamps and the red and yellow lights of cars and the beat of the blue-black kingdom from eight at night when the nervy rhythm begins to five in the morning. He was so thin he twisted and turned in her arms and she held him tight to save him

· 154 ·

but he slipped away and she shut her eyes and followed him. He gave her visions. Of how small he was and how enormous was her love for him, and how thin he was and how deep was his layered world, and how bony he was but how soft was her love for him. And he showed her his London, from Camden Town in the north, south by way of Covent Garden and Soho down to where the river twists and turns and blackly rolls over and over whilst up above on Hungerford Bridge the trains come rolling in, the rolling stock all lit up in the darkness, crossing the bridge into Charing Cross Station. ('You could make an amazing film about this bridge,' said Noah.) And he showed her his beautiful mother and how beautiful was Mattie's love for her so that the darkness was filled with Oakland colours and shapes spinning and falling. And he showed her how beautiful even was her past, sad but beautiful, because it had happened and everything that had happened was beautiful. So she shut her eyes again and saw:

herself and her mother at home walking across the cornfields in the evening after the corn had been cut. The sky was in their faces, God was in her mother's eyes as she floated three inches above the ground and, as they reached each shallow, yellow hilltop they saw another and another one before them. And there was Mattie as a small child, running away and back again over the prickly stubble, leaping and jumping each wave of shaven corn; and there was Mattie as an older child, trailing in her mother's wake; her mother trailing clouds of God behind her, God overflowing her head and touching Mattie, so that wide-eyed and open-mouthed Mattie floated across the stubble buoyed up by this borrowed glory.

Mattie smiled. She had never had such a beautiful vision of her mother before. She had thought of her living alone year after year, but now this image, which normally depressed her, struck Mattie with great poignancy. She had been wrong. The past was not unhappy after all. It was there

· 155 ·

and pursuing its own happiness and she shut her eyes again and saw her mother floating away above the cornfields, attached only by a string around one ankle to the earth, and Mattie the child waving her goodbye as you might wave goodbye to a balloon voyager, and this image made her laugh. She was so elated she thought of her mother with resignation and forgiveness so that it seemed to her at this moment that when the bad times came again, as they surely would because they always do – and this she knew she understood so much better than the Oaklands (feeling, as she thought of this, the small, romantic body of Noah Oakland beside her) – they could never be so bad again because the good times would send forward their good influence to take away the sting of what came next.

And yet at the same time of course she didn't really believe that things could ever be so bad again, for now he took her hand in his and she thought how his had been such a sweet and reconciling prick.

'Turn over,' he said, and she did so but after a while she realised all he wanted to do was press his face against her back and fall asleep in a parody of domesticity, like a husband and wife together. She smiled slowly at the strange view of the wall opposite. She was the beautiful Mattie Oakland (née Thomas) who had just loved and been loved by a man. And she shut her eyes and saw herself and Noah in bed together as Noah himself might have photographed them: her astonished body lying long and white and slantwise across the bed and a shadowy background of cinnabar and Prussian blue which was the light slipping into the room, through the blinds and past the curtains, as dense as smoke; and next to her a second, more shadowy diagonal line which was the body of Noah depicted with butterscotch, amber, rose and indigo blue. Butterscotch was his hair. His eyes were amber-coloured, as was his skin and the complexion of his face except over his cheekbones where it darkened into rose. And indigo, of course, was the colour of the shadows on his cheeks, his chin and above his upper lip and on his body above the collarbone and under his arms and behind the knees and where the hairs were round his sleeping prick.

And Mattie thought, they have turned me into colour.

· 28 ·

The hillside was growing cold. Twilight thickened the air and a faint blue fog lay upon the grass. The dogs were subdued now. They were running close to their owners, ghosts in the twilight, loping downhill. When Hester lifted her head she could see beyond the perimeters of the park strings of light and cars flowing past along Regent's Park Road in a twinkling river of red and yellow.

At the other end of the bench Mattie's mind flipped over. In the twilight Hester heard it do a somersault, flipping as it always did from melancholy to exuberance and back to melancholy again. Now a sadder, more plaintive Mattie took its place. Hester thought that sometimes Mattie's mind was quite transparent, the thoughts quite visibly rearing themselves up in her mind in the way that Hester's child's head would one day rear up into her view like a monster rising from the deep when she is bent upon some mischief. Mattie's monstrous thoughts. This endless see-sawing. This perpetual flipping over of her nature.

She said, 'It's love that bothers me, Hester.'

'I know.'

'I don't mean Noah's love.'

'I know,' said Hester again.

'They never tell you this,' she said, 'how much you will want the love of a mother. And how far the chain of ought-ing to love extends. And who it is we can rightfully expect to love us.'

· 158 ·

'No one,' said Hester quickly. 'No one at all. Not even your parents and certainly not your siblings or your friends or the people we adopt to be our parents. There's no such thing as the right to be loved. In fact, there's probably no such thing as rights at all.'

'But I can't help it,' said Mattie. 'I keep coming back to this question, who it is that ought to love me.'

'No one,' said Hester again, sadly enough. 'People aren't bound to love us just because we love them. Otherwise where would we be, and just think of all the people we'd have to love in our lifetimes? There is no moral imperative which says they must return our love . . . '

'I'm cold,' said Mattie. 'I didn't bring my jacket. It doesn't go with these trousers.'

'Beauty before comfort.'

'Every time,' said Mattie with a flash of spirit.

'That's because you're young.'

'You're not old, Hester.'

'Thirty,' said Hester, staring into the twilight, and then she added, 'Never mind,' and even as she did she thought, how soft this baby's made me, I never used to say things like that to other women; and she felt a pang of sharp nostalgia for herself as she used to be, for Thin Shanks and Blue Stocking, her hair frizzed out in a cloud and the red gash of lipstick which was her mouth, and for her companion (take a bow) – for Frank the Piano Player, or Frank-who-should-have-been-the-father-of-her-baby-but-was-not, or Frank-who-was-so-wrongly-named, or Frank for short – a self-taught man who had educated himself by lingering in second-hand bookshops and visiting museums and who knew about nineteenth-century rockets and Aleister Crowley and the history of time travel and the futuristic skyscrapers of old Chicago and Madame Blavatsky. She had loved him for his black and curious mind. They were a terrible pair, as egocentric as hell. Nobody liked them. They were two of a kind which is no doubt why they were not still together.

Mattie knows nothing, except about love. But still, 'Never mind,' said Hester.

'You're out late, ladies,' said a man's voice, and through the darkness Hester saw the pink-and-brown man whose existence she had forgotten entirely. He must have seen her head move and her eyes open.

'Hallo,' he said, and he sat down at her feet. 'This is a lovely spot, isn't it? Is your friend all right?' (looking at the dark form of Mattie).

'I expect so,' said Hester. She thought she could hear Mattie snigger. Now she came to look she saw he wasn't at all prepossessing.

'I don't suppose the two of you would like to spend the evening with me? Maybe at a night club?' he asked. He didn't seem to have noticed how hugely pregnant they were.

'No, I don't suppose we would,' said Hester unkindly, for the thought had come to her suddenly of Frank's new girlfriend whom she had heard was a writer and how laid out before them for clever men to pick from are all kinds of sexy and interesting women, but laid out for clever women? – there is nothing.

'Ah well,' said the pink-and-brown man and he got to his feet. 'Perhaps I could give you this?' he said, and he drew a visiting card from out of a wallet and handed it over to her. She peered at it in the darkness. Lord Manchester. Malvern House. Wilts.

'My father,' said the pink-and-brown man. 'I'm the oldest son. Of course he has houses all over the country. I've been living in one lately. A delightful abode. North London. Friern Barnet. You might know it?' and with a wave of his hand he loped away in the darkness.

'God,' said Mattie, sitting up like a spirit risen from the dead.

'A large house in Friern Barnet,' said Hester. 'The mental home of course.'

· 160 ·

'Well, we all have our fantasies,' said Mattie, just as if she had never enticed him over in the first place.

They set off down the hill. After a while Mattie's mind started up again on its old obsessions.

'But even if I know that,' she said, and from her alarmed tone Hester could hear she was now being quite sincere, 'I mean, even if I know there is no moral imperative for anyone to return our love, how can I make myself believe it so I stop looking for Vanessa Oakland to love me? I do know it but it seems I don't because I keep coming back to it . . . '

'We all want mother love,' said Hester, 'but you've got to forget them,' (just as if she'd long ago forgotten her father, as if she had expected nothing from him for many years now). 'Parents don't matter. Parents are nothing. You didn't choose them. Although in this case you did. More fool you. It's friends that matter. Friends and lovers,' said Hester, thinking hopefully of the future when perhaps she would have a lover again.

'Do you think?' said Mattie. She was always looking for an answer, for the Answer to her questions.

'I know it,' said Hester. They stood by the gate to the park.

'Do you want mother love then?' asked Mattie, her face lifted up to Hester's, Mattie who is so good at hero worship, so that the terrible thought occurred to Hester that perhaps Mattie was her first baby, her practice baby.

'Of course,' replied Hester.

'Two nurses at the hospital were horrible to me,' said Mattie plaintively, and at the memory an expression of alarm slithered across her face because she was always perceptive to malice from mothers as she was perceptive to nothing else.

'Which way are you going?' asked Hester.

'That way,' said Mattie.

'I'm going that way,' (pointing towards Kentish Town). 'Maybe you should catch a taxi,' Hester added, for she saw

· 161 ·

Mattie's face had taken on a bleary, filmy look as if the hormones of late pregnancy were drowning her at last.

'I can manage,' said Mattie and she set off walking strongly but wearily, not like an African queen at all, more like an African peasant.

The lights of Regent's Park Road were twinkling prettily. The cafés were still open and bright faces were laughing in their windows. Out in the streets the big trees shifted and moved like horses in the blue darkness. Lights shone on flights of steps and stucco arches and colonnades and pilasters. In some of the houses curtains were left undrawn so that passers by could look in on Regency rooms. In one such room was a large and glossy rocking horse. Hester thought how pretty it all was – somehow Christmasy (although this was the very height of summer) and full of the promise of presents – and it was no doubt the extreme prettiness of it all that made her think of the Oaklands, giving her one of those visions to which she had become so prone.

She imagined she stood in front of the Oaklands' house and it was a Regency house with columns and porticoes and dados and all its windows lit up like an Advent calendar and Noah visible through the windows of the stairwell, taking the steps two at a time as he ran up to Mattie's bedroom. For Noah is a hedonist and takes pleasure in beauty and in pleasure, stopping in his headlong rush through life to lose himself in Mattie because of the painterly fall of the light on her limbs and then to lick and stroke and rub her into oblivion with him, because the thing about Mattie was that you could rub her out entirely and this was so pleasurable, because she would then grow back when you took your fingers away and be even more beautiful than before. Noah the hedonist took the same pleasure from sleeping with Mattie, the soft heart of the house, that he got from looking

· 162 ·

at the tallboy which Tom had designed to proportions which were pleasingly bourgeois and fat, the drawers slipping so easefully in and out, the wood a dark plum, rare, rich and solid, with a bloom on it like the fruit, and the illusion of a fuzz such as you see on Mattie's limbs. Noah took an old man's pleasure in beauty, in comfort and pleasure; but how did he know all this when he was only twenty-five? Small, thin Noah laying down his limbs so easefully on his mother's silk sheets – and what could be more beautiful and more pleasurable than sleeping with his cousin?

But in Hester's dream she was able to look through the house from fifty feet and so saw straight through to its foundations and saw that they were incestuous foundations, a chimney running up the centre of it, through the big central bedroom which is Tom and Vanessa's where Noah and Mattie like to make love whenever they can, and past where Noah's bedroom used to be on the floor above, straight over his parents' bedroom, and where Noah and Mattie still make love if the other bed is not available.

And she saw that Mattie was the heart of them, the bed at the heart of the house, and to sleep with her was to sleep with themselves, and what more could the narcissistic Oaklands want? For the Oaklands always took great pleasure in themselves, and were always, metaphorically speaking, sleeping with themselves, as well as with the tallboy, so that if Noah could fuck his mother as she stepped out of the bath because of the white light on her white flesh and if he could fuck his father because of the dark shadows on his long, patriarchal limbs – although no doubt of course, Freudian-like, he would like to kill them both – and if he could fuck his brothers when they slept together metaphorically in a puppy-like tangle, limbs tangled up and bright faces looking skywards, Aaron with his dreamy and resentful face and Jonathan with his bright, mad one, for they are not yet separated off, these boys, one from another – well then, he would, but he can't, and so instead he sleeps with Mattie, who is beauty made manifest, who is all of them made manifest, who is the Oaklands' lucky mascot, and everyone's only daughter.

'The good thing about incest,' says Hester, 'is that it does keep things in the family.'

'Incest?' say I, Hester, the storyteller, 'Don't think of it as literal, actual, physical incest. It's all in the head and looked at like that we are all of us at it. You, me, everyone is incestuous.'

'And anyway,' I say, lightheartedly, 'Oedipus, schmoedipus, what does it matter so long as he loves his mother?'

VANESSA

· 29 ·

On the day the girl came to tea Vanessa cleared the house from top to bottom. She hoovered the living room and the dining room. She loaded the washing-up machine. She cleaned the surfaces in the kitchen and carried out the rubbish and put flowers on the tables in the kitchen and the conservatory. In the study Tom and Jonathan had set up the portable television set. They were watching a Charlie Chaplin movie. Tom was a sentimental man. At weekends he liked to sit with his feet up in the darkness pouring himself wine and watching movies on the television. He had been known to weep for the little man, as pert, innocent, vulnerable, hopeful, he moved across the screen. Tom was forever saying, 'I feel this', 'I feel that', 'I feel the other', but his wife who never said what she felt only looked at him from a great distance.

Now Vanessa knew they wanted her to join them because they were laughing loudly, calling out to her and describing what was happening. But she hurried past their door with an amused and embarrassed air (for usually she considered herself way beyond clearing up for visitors) whilst she was also sending out little spurts of rage against them, because they were so masculine and so indolent, sitting there in the darkness pouring out the drinks.

When she went in to retrieve a tray of glasses which was balanced on a cushion Tom put out one arm to curl it round her waist but she dodged beyond his reach. Her love for

· 165 ·

him these days was nowhere near so pure and possessive as that which she felt for her sons. She had been married for nearly thirty years and her love for her husband which had once run along the surface of her life now ran deep underground and the channel where it had been was prettily overgrown with a pattern of need and gratitude and resentment and too much knowledge of his weaknesses. 'Sit down and have a drink with us,' he said. He was in love with her, or so he fancied today, in love with his wife, domesticity and the married state. But 'Later,' she replied, 'later.' For she still had to water the green things which were rioting and dancing in the conservatory and to take the smoked salmon and brown bread from the freezer so that she could cut the bread carefully into sandwiches, removing the crusts and cutting them on the diagonal and putting slices of lemon on top.

When she had thus reached into every corner of her house she sat down in the conservatory to smoke a cigarette and to consider the images which the girl had left behind her the first time they had met. These images were blue and white and brown and pink and blonde. They were quite different from the images which usually frequented Vanessa's head and which rose up around her like smoke from the layered house, this temple of her domesticity, from the dark, lustrous walls, the oil-paint-dark corners, the curtains so thick you could hardly draw them and so long that they sat upon the floor. But the girl worked half the year in a place called Ladakh which seemed to Vanessa to consist of nothing else but bright blue air and mountainsides with nothing on them and which soared so steeply upwards and downwards it was as if the entire country had been flipped over on its side with not one horizontal line left for miles in any direction. She ran a company, a travel agency which took city dwellers by jeep and horse into the High Himalayas. She was only twenty-three; she was young to be running a company but she had never been to university and such was her assurance she could have been anything from eighteen to thirty-five.

She had been dressed in jeans which revealed her broad bottom. Her blonde hair was scraped back from her face so that you could see her high cheekbones and her fine complexion. She hid nothing, not the good nor the bad for she was brave in this way. In her ears were stud earrings and her shoes were expensive. She kissed both Tom and Vanessa for she knew how to behave. She smiled and said hallo to everyone and especially to Jonathan, who hated to be left out, and she was even charming about his tattoo, which was more than Vanessa was able to manage, holding his wrist lightly in her tolerant, curious fingers and enquiring about the design. She stroked the black cat. She lingered to make him happy, saying as she did so how much she liked animals and that on the trek there were fifteen ponies who had to be looked after.

Brown and blonde with pearls, and pink and white.

Noah said with a blush it was her birthday and Vanessa said nothing, only smiled so brilliantly you might have thought this was the best news she had heard in years. The girl's eyes were intelligent and direct. She looked at Noah so intelligently when he talked that Vanessa who for herself liked this look very much indeed – Vanessa was afraid Noah might be alarmed by it. And yet he didn't seem to be. He had withdrawn into himself in a masculine kind of way. There was a blush on his face as he looked down at the floor but he kept looking up and sideways at her, smiling and saying her name as if he found her intelligence quite ineffably sexy.

'We're early,' said the girl. 'It took us exactly three and a half minutes to get here. Noah never went less than sixty.' 'I was trying to frighten her,' said Noah and it was true that he had hoped to make her cower in her seat if he could. But she had been in far more dangerous situations than this and so she had sat up straight as a rod and had sung out in her

· 167 ·

clear, bell-like voice, 'Macho man, macho man, don't give a damn if you don't come,' and now he was pleased – you could see this by his smile – that he hadn't succeeded. He was thinking to himself that he would like to go to Ladakh next summer and climb mountains with her to see if he could keep up.

They had sat down in the conservatory and then of course they had talked about travel and the girl had discovered that the Oaklands had only the haziest of ideas where India was and had never heard of Ladakh. So she had made Jonathan fetch his old school atlas. 'You must have an atlas,' she had said; 'No,' they had chorused, amused by their own ignorance. 'Jonathan will have one from school,' she had said and she had been right, as she usually was. So then she had pushed back the tea things and traced for them lovingly with one finger the route which her convoy took once a month until the winter snows made the route impassable. She loved maps. She had gazed at the flat pages as if she could see the mountains standing up as in a children's pop-up book. Vanessa saw this look of love and leant forward to see more closely what was going on. Vanessa thought how pretty was the pattern of the folded, wrinkled mountains on the page and how funny it was, the atlas amongst the tea cups, this intrusion of the world into her domesticity.

But the girl had been astonished to learn that the Oaklands didn't like to travel, that they went of course when business dictated it but that for pleasure and enjoyment they much preferred to spend their time at Southwold or in Italy where Vanessa still had family and which hardly seemed to them like going abroad at all. The girl had looked at them as if they were about as pretty a bunch of urbanites as it was possible to imagine and they had understood the look and it had caused them to review their own shortcomings with relish, their reddish curls and absurd profiles, their capacity to make things look so pretty, and this tiny bit of the earth from which they wouldn't move and which was so crammed with columns and vines and flights of steps and wrought-iron balconies.

'I bet you've never met people like us before,' said Jonathan complacently and the girl had answered with some asperity that yes, as it happened she had, a family in the old suburbs of a Latin American city, she couldn't remember which because she'd been to so many, but she had met this family by letter of introduction and they had been very charming and secluded and the women had had the most beautiful liquid eyes and the men hadn't been far off hoodlums and gangsters and they were very full of themselves and absolutely parochial because they never even travelled beyond their city. And at this the Oaklands had fallen about with laughter because they liked criticism when it was sharp and funny and well directed, and Noah had blushed and smiled.

'I feel intimidated,' said Vanessa afterwards in mock alarm but secretly she was pleased the girl was so clear and strong and certain.

· 30 ·

Mattie lay in bed in the empty house and waited for him to arrive. She heard his footsteps on the stairs – he was taking them two at a time as he always did. It was as if he thought that if he slowed up for one moment his cover would be blown. BANG! thought Mattie who was not at all averse to blowing up her lover, he being so stylish and self-conscious; but he looked round the door and said, 'Mattie!' in tones of amazement – he seemed always amazed – and he came and sat beside her, asking 'What are you reading, Matt? *Bleak House*? Who's that by? I bet you're a secret writer in your spare time too?' 'Charles Dickens,' she said, 'and I wouldn't tell you if I was.' 'No, you wouldn't, would you?' he said, regretfully – but he liked it best when she was sharp – and he began to take off his clothes. 'That's an amazing suit you're wearing,' she said. 'Isn't it just,' said Noah.

His clothes were a curious mixture of jumble sale and Harrods' best, bought with Vanessa's money. Wool sweaters swooned richly on the floor. Second-hand suits lay in dimpled heaps. There were clothes over the backs of his chairs and in his wardrobe and lying on the floor and swimming through the tangled air and tangled up, Oakland style, in the tangled bedclothes. When he came to her through the granular darkness, with his black-red hair and his pale skin, he was a naked body dressed in the clothes of London. He slipped into bed beside her and lay back and stretched out his arm and made room for her upon it. 'Come and lie in

· 170 ·

my arms,' he said. 'I might,' she said, for at this time she was still jaunty, it was only later that their silences wore her down.

They slept together in his lunch hour or in the evenings, or at weekends if his family was away for he kept their affair a secret. He never said it was a secret, simply assumed she knew this to be the case and she didn't mind, at least not at first. In fact she was rather pleased they shared this thing together (although she noticed that the secrecy had the effect of shrinking her world, of reducing it to the size of their various beds, to her single one, small and rather childlike, and to his double one, seven foot in one direction and six foot in the other, and the sheets and duvets tangled up with socks and shirts and underwear as well as photographs and fabric samples and glossy magazines. For the Oaklands never thought that bedrooms were only for sleeping in but liked to sit up in their beds and work and entertain in their pyjamas; and to Vanessa's with its lace and silk and satin).

And afterwards he liked to watch television or to pick quarrels with her or to teach her gambling games. He taught her poker and blackjack and pontoon. They gambled with matchsticks and one, two and ten pence pieces, and when they grew tired of betting with small change they gambled on each other's clothing and on each other's lives and on his parents' possessions, the house and the furniture and pictures, and on the cleaner and the cat and his brothers' girlfriends and their hair ('Oh yes, Aaron's hair, it's so pretty,' said Mattie – 'How pretty?' he asked – 'Pretty enough,' she said perkily), and on his mother's shoes and her beautiful painted bath. He was quite unrelenting in his desire to win. He gave no quarter and he liked it best when she gave no quarter either. He was very hard. He bruised her by his very presence but then he would reach out and touch her. 'How are you, Matt?' he would ask and really he was very tender.

He had a dapper repertoire of manners, the helpless grin, the opening of car doors for his ladies, the ushering of them

· 171 ·

ahead of him. And he was such a dandy. When he walked away from the bed dressing himself as he went in his spotted waistcoats and his black moleskin trousers, then in the electric light he cut a narrow, vivid figure. In his dandy dressing and his loyalty to his family he made her think of a gangster. And he was so small that when they slept together his feet scarcely came down to her ankles. He was so small she wanted to laugh, she pitied him for it, and yet for all that he was a man to own and be owned by. 'Let me see your palms,' she said one day. 'Why?' he asked. 'To read your future,' she said. 'Tell me,' he said at once, and he stretched them out in front of her. Nothing frightened him much except his ambitions and his fear, still secret, that the future might not fulfil them.

But she noticed that he didn't take much care of her, that he never fetched and carried for her, didn't strive to keep her, didn't seem to want to own her, seemed entirely careless as to whether or not he kept her. And he was always apparently amazed to find her waiting for him, pleased but amazed, as if he were resigned to the fact that possibly she might not be there at all. She wondered if he ever came looking for her whilst she was away at work. It piqued her that he never did anything to ensure her presence; piqued her, also, that their meetings were only a serendipity.

'Do you love me?' he had asked the first time they went to bed and Mattie had said nothing because at that moment, truthfully, she didn't feel she did love him – because he filled her up too full, because he made her feel she lacked for nothing, but was light and buoyant and not needing to love. But afterwards she felt that by not answering his question she had somehow missed an opportunity, a turning in the road, and it nagged her, this sense of a lost opportunity. She prayed the tape would be re-run, that he would ask her again, and then she could answer 'yes'. But he never did and bit by bit she came to fear that she would not have the chance again.

She would have liked to have owned him. She would have liked to have been his clothes which he took off and put on again and everywhere he went they went too. And she would have liked to have been his watch which sometimes he unstrapped and placed beside the bed before he got in. She would have liked to have been the money in his pocket and the woman on his arm and the car he drove too fast, racketing her about in it on one of their rare excursions out of bed. 'Left,' she said. 'Right,' he said. 'No, left,' she said. 'Shit,' he said as the indicators went like the clappers. 'Left, right, left, right. Call yourself a backseat driver.' He was a mystery to her. She wished she knew what was going on in his head.

'Let's play the truth game,' she said one day when they were lying in bed and he was watching the Wogan show in his usual mocking fashion. But he didn't seem to have heard. 'What are you doing, Matt? Are you watching?' he asked, for Noah liked his women to do what he was doing. She lay with her head under the duvet. 'I'm watching,' she lied and she said again, 'Let's play the truth game, Noah.' But he was wily. He wouldn't be drawn. He looked at her sadly. 'You're unhappy,' he said and he pressed his face against her. 'Blimey,' he said, 'I've never slept with anyone like you. So perfect and so unhappy. Do other men lust after you as well?'

· 31 ·

And his mother was a mysterious creature. She never talked about her feelings, not really, any more than the rest of the Oaklands did. None of them ever shouted or slammed doors or said, 'I love you,' or 'I hate you,' or 'Why have you ruined my life?', although Mattie knew for a fact they must feel these things, and she marvelled at what it must be like to be so old, to have so much of your life snaking back behind you, your own essential nature concealed by wrapping after wrapping of experience, of wit and learnt charm and affection. What must it be like to have once been a big, gauche, shy, sexy, half-Italian convent girl, to have a mind like the black vault of a church, the candles burning in clumps and in between the darkness? And what did she then turn into? – so soft and affectionate she had become and her affection keeping them all at a distance – Mattie could only describe her beauty and the effect she had on them.

It was November. The rain drummed down upon the conservatory roof. The Oaklands retreated back into the heart of the house and ate their supper round the pith stove in the dining room. Tom had injured his hand in an accident at the factory. Vanessa was feeling rather listless. Mattie thought perhaps she wasn't well or perhaps it was the discontent that seemed to have settled upon them all these days for they were eating a lot of take-aways whilst Vanessa had grown unaccountably large. She was spending money to try to shift the depression. Like Alice in Wonderland she was swelling and growing and causing the dining room to seem to shrink around her. The candles in their holders cast a curious light. They picked out the lines on Vanessa's face, gave to her a wintry look, caused her to look her age. Aaron came home from Oxford. 'Take-aways,' he said, and his was the voice of the unloved child, prophetic and unwelcome. 'Always a bad sign. Better if you warm the plates and lay the table properly, but still basically a bad sign . . . ' He had a new girlfriend, a pretty, cat-like girl by name of Bridget, two or three years old than himself, whom he brought home at weekends when he came back from Oxford; but she was tactless, terribly tactless, and Vanessa took against her.

For Bridget drank too much, and swore and, although God knows the rest of the Oaklands swore, Vanessa never did and that was the point. And Bridget, who was clever enough to know better, never emptied the overflowing ash-trays and when she did make coffee she never washed the cups; and these, although they were twenty years old and rather chipped, were of a Finnish design and beautiful, and would have been still more so if they hadn't smelt of smoke and the last person to use them. Instead Bridget liked to sit curled up in a chair talking to Vanessa very loudly – for it was sad how full of admiration Bridget was for Vanessa – about the problems she had in the office where she worked, which was for a left-wing, literary magazine. So why was it, Bridget complained, that it was always she who did the dirty work? And had Vanessa noticed that of all the sexist men it is left-wing men who are the shittiest and most sexist of all?

Vanessa listened gently but she was not really interested, as Mattie knew and Bridget ought. For Vanessa didn't think in abstract terms such as feminism. Vanessa looked at her own friends and saw that some of the men were terrible to their wives and some of the wives were terrible to their husbands. And that, it seemed to Vanessa, was the way the world worked. Vanessa was very sweet to Bridget – she

· 175 ·

would never voice a criticism, would scarcely even think it – but the sweeter Vanessa grew the more clearly she announced to Mattie that she was angry. It was by her sweetness and her temporary lack of beauty that Mattie knew it.

Vanessa was sitting at breakfast one morning, crumbling croissants between her fingers. There were brittle lines around her mouth and longer than usual pauses before she answered questions, her eyes resting broodingly, sweetly on the face of the person addressing her. She drew a plate towards herself – it was part of the litter of last night's dinner – and said, 'Oh Bridget, I wish she'd use an ashtray.' And that was all.

And another Saturday morning Mattie met Vanessa walking to Camden Town. 'Hallo, Vanessa,' she said shyly and Vanessa smiled distantly but said nothing and drew her cloak more tightly round herself and stepped out into the dirty November sky through the falling leaves. Mattie fell into step behind her. She felt the mother's mind, capricious, falling like a stone from warmth to coldness.

And then they met Bridget coming in the opposite direction. 'Hallo, ladies,' she called out. She was very cheerful. Aaron wasn't due back from Oxford until that evening but he had given her the key and she was going to let herself in. She wore jeans and a large sweater. In figure and looks she resembled Mattie a little. Perhaps she too had never had a mother? 'I love your cloak,' she said to Vanessa. 'It's a Vivienne Westwood, isn't it?' and she fingered it. She hardly looked at Mattie. She had eyes only for Vanessa, as they all did. But Vanessa said nothing and now fear touched Mattie as she realised that Vanessa's expression had grown more distant, her tone a little more brisk, her eyes no longer resting so tenderly upon Mattie.

'I love the rain,' said Mattie to Vanessa, 'Do you know what I mean?' But Vanessa said nothing. 'Where are you going?' asked Bridget. Vanessa said, 'Liberty's.'

She was absent-minded. The three of them stood together on the bridge waiting for a taxi. The copper-green rain poured down in strokes. It dimpled the surface of the canal. Along the towpath the tramps sat out as usual in poses of Christ-like resignation. At last Vanessa smiled. She knew some of the tramps by name, was fond of them because they were so scandalous and drunk; for the Oaklands, even or perhaps especially Vanessa, always preferred excess to moderation, moderation being to entirely bourgeois. Vanessa was staring at the water. Mattie thought she was looking pale and wan, as if whatever it was that kept such a big woman so sweetly strung together had given way and collapsed. She had pinned up her hair. For such a big woman she carried herself on the slenderest of ankles. Her beauty came and went. She shrank and grew and shrank again according to her moods. Or was it according to Mattie's? Mattie didn't know. Mattie thought, she's looking beautiful again. But Vanessa said joyfully, 'There's a taxi,' for she loved that moment when she put one hand on the handle of the door whilst she dropped her face to meet the taxi driver's. And taxi drivers loved her because she was so joyful when she said to them, 'Liberty's' or 'Harrods' or 'Sloane Street'. Now Vanessa stepped towards the taxi and the back of her coat swept richly across Mattie's field of vision and her pale face was set ahead as if she had forgotten Mattie's existence entirely for one moment.

Mattie would have liked to ask Noah if his mother was angry but she feared the humiliation of his bored, guileless, masculine eyes. 'What do you mean?' he would have said.

· 32 ·

'Noah?' whispered Mattie. The room was smudged with darkness. The wrought-iron legs of a table, the posts on the old iron bedstead, the lamps on the chest of drawers, all grew up like plants through the lumpy darkness. Beyond the confines of the room the Sunday rain was falling. Mattie heard it. Its sound was a grey whisper, steady and insistent. 'Noah?' she said, but he was quiet. He slept with his back to her, his body heaped up shamelessly. She could see one corner of a white ear showing from underneath the duvet. It drew her love from out of her, drew it into a peak. 'Noah?' she whispered again, and now he stirred and turned. 'Beautiful Mattie,' he said, still half asleep, and he ran his hands over the rounded limbs and pushed his fingers between her legs, those fingers which were made of honey. 'You should be on the pill,' he said, 'It would be so much easier.' She languished on the tip of his finger. He could do something with this love of hers, this body of hers, if only he would take it. But soon he fell asleep again, his face falling away from her, his body following after it; and she was left alone in the darkness where his clothes were falling steadily like the rain, and the chest of drawers grew up like a flower through the grey darkness.

He fell asleep with his profile staring at the ceiling. She saw it through the disintegrating darkness and it caused her heart to leave its socket and to lodge in her throat, so that her breath came noisily and her melancholia was exquisite.

She had noticed this before, that when he was away from her, which was often for he floated away in the darkness just as soon as he had fucked her, then her loneliness was intense, noisy with inner voices clamouring for him to return. But when he came back into her presence again she flared and flamed and wanted to lie down before him, for she had noticed this also, how her new, soft, quiet, submissive character had improved the sex no end – raising her up as it laid her low, heightening the pleasure so she sank back downwards, obediently through the mattress; and she thought how lovely was Noah's prick, which was a secret prick, causing her both to die and to rise up again. She loved him more when he moved away from her than when he stood beside her. In his company she felt only happiness, but when he took a step or two away into the world, she felt love flow after him like iron filings after a magnet.

She hoped he would want to make love to her, which he often did, he often most definitely did. 'Beautiful Mattie,' he would say with gratitude, taking off her clothes, and Mattie would think, I am still the angel of the house, the most soft and the most tender, the much loved and much fucked angel of the house.

'Noah,' she said but he was quiet again. Sometimes she felt herself quite bored by this new, soft, passive, languishing persona of hers.

· 33 ·

Mattie grew obsessed with a desire to know what the future held for her. She thought perhaps this was because of all the waiting she did in her life, the waiting for Noah's visits and the waiting for Vanessa to talk. Now she was waiting for her luck to change, for something to happen, for her life to move on. She discovered that there was no end to the ways in which you could have your fortune told. She took to hanging round newsagents at the beginning of each month, reading up her horoscope in women's magazines. She bought herself self-help books on the stars, on dice, runes, tarot, the I-Ching and other methods of divining the future. She wanted Noah but she feared that time had laid the future down already, had set it out and settled it, so that now she was looking for that crack between the present and the future, that moment which if you can finger it will divert the course of time, alter the endless flowing of the present into the future. And one morning she took thirty pounds from Vanessa's bag – because what is yours is mine, ma, and what is mine is yours – and went to Camden Town in search of a fortune teller who was reputed to work beside the bridge.

On her way she met Barry Shawcross. He was walking beside the canal. He wore that foolish grin which habitually haunted him (although it was the exact antithesis of his melancholy and judgemental nature) and she saw he was still painted up with irony from his evening with the Oaklands the night before.

He had sat beside the stove telling Vanessa stories, in his antiquarian way, about nineteenth-century Southwold, and she had sat with her head bowed down, sketching a design on the back of a telephone bill and looking up from time to time and smiling. The Oakland boys came to join her. They came swarming through the house – he saw them through the open door – like a gang of boyfriends. They made him nervous, you could see it. He was describing the pier at Southwold and how it had once been a famous dancing venue, until one night the people of the town had danced so hard they danced right through the floorboards at the very height of a storm.

'Cor blimey,' said the Oakland boys with courtesy and then Vanessa looked up and said, 'We haven't been dancing for ages,' and Aaron said, 'There's a pier at Eastbourne where the pensioners still turn out for old-time dancing and a Liberace lookalike plays the piano,' and Vanessa said, 'Oh, let's go,' and Jonathan said, 'Noah's got some Liberace waistcoats with sequins all over them,' and Noah said with dignity, 'Dear God,' and thus they slipped away from Barry. But Barry's eyes had followed after them and Mattie had seen his gaze, both stern and judgemental but also admiring because they were his Prodigal Family and he both loved and disapproved of them for their mild and sweet delinquency, his Prodigal Father and Mother and all his Prodigal Siblings. He told Vanessa some story to do with Sartre and John Huston and Vanessa gazed back at him with all her usual sweetness. 'Who's Sartre?' she said, causing him to stop and stare in astonishment. He was a lover of the past and a lover of the Oaklands but every time he went to see them they painted him up with this Oaklandish irony – Mattie had seen them do it often – and then who afterwards could take him seriously?

'Hello,' Mattie called out. She had dressed today with the utmost care even though with her feet up and flying horizontally like a Chagall lover, she was rushing towards bed. She was wearing sailcloth trousers which she had dyed with Vanessa's Indian yellow and a sweater of burnt ochre and burnt sienna; and she had painted her toenails silver and silvered the pointy tips of her black, spiky hair, and she was wearing one of Vanessa's necklaces on her elegant, jutty collarbone. She seemed to Barry to be polished up, so smooth that there was nowhere he could get a hold of her. The words rolled out of her mouth and they had the same hard smoothness. 'What are you doing here?' she asked. 'It's my birthday,' he said. 'I've taken the day off.' 'Happy birthday,' she said. 'Thank you. Actually I was thinking of visiting your cousins.' 'Oh, they're not in. No one's in today.' 'Ah . . . ' and he looked down at her feet as if to detect which way they might be going. 'Perhaps . . . ' he said, and he fell into step beside her.

'I'm going to have my fortune told,' she said. 'Really?' and he bent an uncertain smile at her and she saw that he was charmed by her unorthodoxy, but then he looked away and she saw that he didn't approve, not really, not of such soothsaying and superstition. But she liked his disapproval. She took an Oaklandish pleasure in it and, besides, as it happened it suited him, knitting him up more strongly and making him seem more significant.

'Why don't you have your fortune told as well?' she said, trying out her hand at a little light bullying, and she led him down a flight of steps which descended from the High Street, and into a yellow-lit basement where two young men this early in the morning were sweeping the floor and cleaning out the cappuccino machine. They sat down to wait. Barry was dressed as always in his careful bachelor way. He seemed ill at ease in his surroundings. A waitress stared at him and his eyes sheered away from her. 'How's Southwold?' asked Mattie.

★

He had driven her there for the day a few weekends before, had arrived outside the London house early in the morning tooting on his horn and waving from the little red sports car in which he had had most definitely the look of Noddy. Noah had seen him draw up. 'Wow,' he had said sarcastically, 'it's Nigel Mansell.' And Mattie had felt obscurely dismayed, astonished by the sports car which she'd never seen before, and cast down because it was she who'd made Barry so happy simply by consenting rather vaguely to go out with him for the day.

They had driven by way of back roads and small villages. They had stopped for morning coffee in what had once been a coaching inn. They had explored two fine examples of early Saxon church architecture. They had parked the car and looked in second-hand bookshops for histories of East Anglia. At length they'd come to Southwold.

The holidaymakers had all gone home. The cafés were shut up along the promenade, the sky overcast, the sea grey and somehow flattened, creeping up the beach with sly and silky movements. They ate lunch in the Swan. Afterwards they walked to Walberswick, taking that path which led down from the common to the marshes. She didn't know this part of Southwold. Barry walked ahead, holding the bramble stems out of her way and taking her hand in his when the land suddenly vanished and she nearly lost her footing. His fingers were dry and light and uncertain in their grasp. She thought she saw him blush.

She looked around. Below them were the marshes, a flat, roughened, grassy landscape of squared-off water meadows, mirrored dykes and patches of bullrushes. Beyond them was the village of Walberswick, a thin line upon the horizon; to their left was the sea, a bright watery line of blue, a degree more watery and more sparkling than the sky; and to their right – eight miles across the marshes – Barry pointed out the tower of Blythborough.

· 183 ·

They were looking for late blackberries. 'This way,' said Barry. 'We need to look for south-facing hedgerows.'

'Which way's south?' But he didn't laugh as the Oaklands would have done. 'That way,' he said, and patiently he pointed.

A sail seemed to jerk its way across the fields. Mattie watched.

'That boat looks as if it's sailing across the fields,' she said.

'Tacking on the river. The wind is running against it.'

'How bleak it is here in winter.'

'It's wonderful. Far better than summer. In a bad winter these fields flood and Southwold becomes an island.'

'So fish must swim across this grass? How romantic.' And Mattie stared at her toes as if she would see them now.

Barry was dipping down his head, laying his scarf across the back of his neck and straightening up to tuck its ends inside his jacket. As he did so he was marvelling that her skin could be so young and plump; it rose and fell from one edge of her face to the other, the spaces under the eyes and the cheekbones filled out with flesh, the nose pinched out from a smooth, white field.

'And in the old days,' he went on, growing more bold, 'when winters were really winters, the water would freeze over and then the people of Southwold would walk to church in Blythborough across the ice and sometimes someone would fall in and that was the end of them.'

'I like warmth and sunshine,' said Mattie. Barry didn't answer. He was crouched down, peering through the brambles. But he thought, that's because you're like Vanessa who's another warm, soft woman. Women should be warm and soft.

'You're good at finding blackberries,' said Mattie, for now he was lifting up the stems one by one and peering underneath. He would never make a personal comment like that. He handed her a blackberry, the best of the ones he had

· 184 ·

picked. She liked the way he didn't look at her. Really, his seriousness made him rather handsome.

'My father used to take me blackberrying when I was little. It's a skill, not getting pricked,' he said and Mattie remembered the poor railwayman's childhood.

'In Lincolnshire?' she asked, and she pitied him for it (although in fact it wasn't necessary, for of all the things that made him unhappy his childhood did so least).

'In Lincolnshire,' he agreed, standing up and moving along.

'I've never been there,' she said. 'Is it like this?'

'Flatter. Not so pretty. But even Lincolnshire comes to seem beautiful if you stay there long enough.'

'How long has your father been there?'

'He's dead. But he lived there all his life. Sixty-six years.'

Mattie shuddered. She thought he carried with him the taint of small towns and mild landscapes. She thought it all sounded exactly like Dunmow End.

But Barry felt her interest in him was growing and this was cheering him up. He found a blackberry and popped it into his mouth. 'Yum, yum, scrumptious,' he said, and he began to sing that song from *Winnie the Pooh* – for he had a sentimental weakness for these stories, although no one had ever read them to him when he was a child – which goes,

> Isn't it funny
> How a bear likes honey?
> Buzz, buzz, buzz,
> I wonder why he does?

And then he grinned at her and that was his mistake. For suddenly what Mattie saw was not a handsome man after all but a middle-aged man who took a sentimental interest in teddybears, and she turned away from him so he wouldn't see the cruelty of her thoughts. 'Do you like the country-side?' she asked, and she was direct, she was too direct, her astonishment was vaguely insulting. 'I like cities,' she said. 'I expect I shall retire here,' he said hopelessly.

'How's Southwold?' asked Mattie in the café. 'I'm going there again this weekend,' he said and she looked up and caught his eye, felt him yearn towards her, felt herself soothed for one moment by his decency, his seriousness, his niceness. But she knew they were impossible together, that although for one second she might lie down believing that his niceness was sufficient, she would start up again just as soon as he, seduced by her peacefulness, reached out to touch her. 'Your turn next,' she said, and getting up she hurried behind a curtain made from Indian fabric where she sat and had her fortune told.

The fortune teller was surprisingly young. An unemployed graduate, thought Mattie, and out of sheer habit she began to size him up, with a view to falling in love with him perhaps. Then she blushed and stared at him short-sightedly, for the terrible thought had occurred to her he might be the man behind the cappuccino machine, sneaked round to double up as the fortune teller. It was awful to be so short-sighted. It laid you so terribly open to the mockery of others.

He looked into the future by reading palms and laying out the tarot cards. He took her hands and laid them on the table, examining the backs and the fronts. She was embarrassed to see her fingernails, which some obscure sense of guilt had caused her to paint ironically this morning, splaying them out afterwards to examine their appalling redness and thinking as she did so, 'Oh, what a Wicked Witch of the North I am.'

His head was balding and his eyes evasive. He spoke to her in clichés. 'Your palms are hidden,' he said, 'Let me lay out the cards instead.' She wanted him to see Noah, to peer into the future and tell her what Noah would do next, but in the event he only frowned and shook his head and laid out the cards again, strong fingers spreading out at the finger tips, saying, 'I see someone small, someone very small indeed, a child perhaps.' 'You mean, I'm going to have a baby?' she asked. She was surprised. She had never thought of this before. And then he said, yes, definitely, that was what it was and this conjured up in her mind the most delightful picture of an angel-faced charmer. She wanted him to be telling her the truth. She hoped he might have a hotline to the future. She found herself looking into his eyes, which were soft and clever and sympathetic. They looked at her with a beautiful brownness. Sadness overwhelmed her and she thought perhaps she would give him another fifteen pounds and hire him for the next hour to listen to the story of her life.

'Can't you see a man at all?' she asked, and then he laid out the cards again. 'Well, yes,' he said, 'I do see someone.' Tall, dark and handsome, thought Mattie. 'Tall, dark and serious-looking,' he said, and Mattie thought, Oh god, Barry Shawcross, and she prayed he couldn't hear. 'Well, maybe that's enough,' she said, dropping her voice and standing up hastily. Outside Barry had taken out a novel and was reading it. When she saw his profile dipped down so seriously into his book she suddenly felt very cheerful again, very pleased to think how Oaklandish she really was and that it was Noah Oakland she really loved for all that he was so little, so lordly and so unregarding. 'Well, go on then,' she said to Barry, and to her surprise he rose obediently and went behind the curtain.

· 34 ·

The image of the angel-faced baby remained with her. That night Sonja Lefanu came to dinner with her little daughter Brangwen but without her husband Philip. Vanessa had brought home samples of the new range. She laid them out on the conservatory table. Their colours were Naples yellow (dark), an old, mysterious yellow, cadmium yellow, chrome yellow, and raw sienna; those of the red ochres which have a brickish, pinky tone; these colours painted over a wash of light, glazed blue so that the effect was of a shifting pattern of warmth and coldness; and touches of dark ivory and vine black for contrast. Sonja and Brangwen played together in a desultory fashion. Mattie sat in a corner. She was sitting guard over her past and her future. The Oaklands were wrapped up in themselves. They were going through the samples one by one, quarrelling and disputing over the smallest details of line and shade and form. They argued with equal passion whether the point was large or small. Meetings like this could go on for hours.

Darkness drifted down through the conservatory roof. It quietened the plants still rioting this late in the year, laid calm, grey hands upon the climbing clematis and vine and rose. When it grew too dark to see, Tom and Noah got up reluctantly and, going across to the stove, drew down the pots and pans to make a pesto. They poured red wine from a jug. Tom took a ball of winter flowers, of weeds from some roadside verge, and late flowering roses, and put them in a jug upon the table. Jonathan selected a 78 from a shelf of records and a tune began, loose and swinging and sentimental, and above it a man's voice crooning, 'How I loved you, rambling rose; always loved you, God knows.' Jonathan beat time with a fork upon the table. Tom was laughing. His white teeth flashed above the stove. In a moment the Oakland men opened their mouths and with full-throated shouts and pleasantly swinging sentimentality they all began to sing, 'How I loved you, rambling rose; always loved you, God knows.' They were partying again. They had this great talent for partying.

Mattie closed her eyes and saw the angel-faced charmer drifting downwards with the darkness, huge eyes, rosebud mouth, wavy, woolly hair, a disembodied floater. The Oaklands lit the candles on the table, leant forward their bright, disembodied faces into the candlelight and the angel-faced baby was amongst them. How pretty was the domestic litter of the Oaklands, the litter of today's breakfast and the litter of last night's dinner still amongst it, the yellow ochre serving bowls and the great plate from Persia with the opalescent strawberries painted on it. The flames stretched their long necks upwards. Darkness ebbed and flowed like a tide. The strawberries scrambled over each other to get to the heart of the plate and the Oaklands sat in brightness, the Oaklands were brightness, but the louder they talked the more silent they seemed to Mattie.

They are doing their self-deprecating thing. Jonathan has just left his girlfriend but to hear him talk you would think he had been left by her. 'I suppose I shall always love the old bag,' he says sadly and romantically, and he gives a shrug and pours himself another glass of wine. Vanessa sits and listens. How lined and worn she is, thinks Mattie; for tonight Vanessa looks her age, her face very white, her shoulders too broad, her fingernails bitten. She is not really beautiful, thinks Mattie, in fact she is not beautiful at all; and then she thinks, how small-minded I've become. If my

· 189 ·

mind shrinks any further it will vanish altogether. The Oaklands were never small-minded.

Mattie laid out her hands on the table when no one was looking and examined her palms and her secret future. She was looking for babies, for love and approval. What would the Oaklands think of a baby? Not much. They are not at all in favour of babies, those interrupters of their work who put an end to interesting talk and bring all conversations down to the boring level of nappies. But on the other hand they are very much in favour of little children, who over a certain age are promising to grow into friends and allies and outposts of the burgeoning Oakland empire.

Mattie thought how strange it was that whilst there are so many different ways of foretelling the future, not one of them would be of any interest to her extraordinary family, for the future does not lie hidden in ambush for them as it does for Mattie. Rather for them the future is something they make, painting and dying and creating it like a rich and painterly length of Oakland fabric. 'We haven't painted Mattie for ages,' says Jonathan in his swaggering, seventeen-year-old fashion and Vanessa turns her large eyes on Mattie and says, 'Mattie's a lovely model,' and Noah grins and says, 'She's our beautiful Mattie Oaklandish.' Is this forgiveness? Mattie blushes. She hopes, she fears, it is and with this thought an access, a rush of sweet, obedient daughter love flows over her which makes her feel quite faint (for Vanessa may not be perfectly beautiful and yet in her mild, large-eyed way she is beautiful enough); and the thought comes to her that, whilst she is not a creator, cannot paint or weave or work in metal or glass, but still a baby she could make and give it to her beloved family whom she both loves and hates.

Afterwards she told the women, 'I became pregnant because a fortune teller told me to.' Of course they didn't believe her.

· 35 ·

Vanessa felt herself growing old and difficult. She would be fifty-four this year and was growing both forwards and backwards in time, for old age was a lined and grey-haired child, her shoulders hunched, drawn in upon herself but peering out into the world with a bright, defiant, enigmatic and malicious look because it was not pleasant to be no longer young. It was old age which caused her sometimes of an evening to go rummaging through the cupboards in the kitchen looking for a bar of chocolate whilst her husband sat in another room and watched television. Old age brought with it a kind of physical solitude which she didn't like at all but in this matter she seemed to have no control over her own body; it shied away from Tom's embraces, preferring to be untouched so that Vanessa these days saw herself as a solitary, untouchable mountain. And when the men kept coming into the kitchen looking for this and that Vanessa met them all with her bright, defiant look because she hated to be past fifty and to see her looks were going and to know the world was leaving her behind. She was by nature powerful, she knew it, and she did it so well, and yet now her power was slipping away. And she thought of herself as a mountain down which the power was rolling like an avalanche of stones and this image made her think of the girl who was brown and blonde and pink and white, and of the mountains of Ladakh.

The girl came to see them again in January when they

were in Southwold spending a chilly week beside the sea. At last it had stopped raining. Dry winter days succeeded one another and the Oaklands sat out upon the beach in the shelter of a windbreak (for they scarcely ever left the seafront when they came to Southwold, preferring to sit and watch the life along the promenade, the striped and painted beach huts, the restless, glittering sea).

The wind blew out of the sun and coated the promenade and shingle, the sea and sky with a yellow light. There was another family playing down beside the water's edge. Just like the English they had taken off their sweaters regardless of the cold. When Vanessa half-closed her eyes she saw an abstract pattern of naked limbs flashing against the green sea, limbs which were a golden brown where they were turned away from the sun, a satiny yellow where the sunlight caught them. It soothed her thus to turn the world into an Oakland pattern.

The girl had been abroad again, this time in Latin America and she had brought back presents for them all, of herbs and spices for Tom and a human skull for Jonathan – 'Oh, my lovely, lovely friend,' he said, 'I shall sleep with him every night,' – and an Inca doll for Aaron and old jewellery for Vanessa which the girl said was endowed with magic powers. She handed it over with awe. She wasn't much given to awe. Only travel to remote places and such magic symbols as these could stir it up in her. But the Oaklands turned quite pink with pleasure for they loved presents and only when she thus arrived to take care of them did they realise how un-taken-care-of they always felt, having to sing and dance and joke for other people.

Vanessa watched the girl go down to the water's edge and Noah follow. She heard the girl say she was going swimming and Noah reply angrily, 'You must be crazy,' because he hated swimming. She was fooling around. She was dipping her toes into the water, looking out to sea with her thick brows drawn together, to where the wind was churning up the water, causing it to toss and sparkle, giving it the look of something wild but good enough to drink. The girl was laughing. She was showing him up. She was making him feel both angry and seduced. She was like one of those creamy-brown pebbles on the beach at whose heart are frozen rivers of pink. If she had been a stone the water would have sparkled on her imperviously.

Now they came wading back through the shingle towards her. It was as if an invisible rope tied them together. The girl threw herself down at Vanessa's feet, began tomboyishly piling up the pebbles into a castle. She was telling traveller's tales. She was boasting of her recklessness and courage; she didn't even pretend to modesty, and this was making Noah want to quarrel with her even more. Vanessa closed her eyes and listened to them. The girl said she was going to be an explorer. She said she could ride and dive and swim and shoot. It seemed to Vanessa, although she could not have put it into words, that in this girl who had had a happy childhood there was no distinction between what she wanted and what she did, and that it is in the griefs of our childhoods and in that gap between the wanting and the doing, that the shadows and the contours are formed. If you had drawn the girl you would have drawn her with only half-a-dozen lines, strong and simple. Vanessa wanted a cigarette. She was rummaging in her handbag when, extraordinarily, the girl said, 'Do you want a cigarette, Vanessa?' and she reached into her handbag and pulled out a whole packet and handed them over without one ounce of male reproach.

Vanessa was lonely. Time was looped. The pattern of loving in the household was that Vanessa should love the boys but that Tom should love Vanessa, or think he did, or hope he did, not all his affairs withstanding; or perhaps it was the idea of loving her he loved so much. He used to put his feet up on the table and pour another glass of wine and recount yet again the story of Vanessa's unhappy childhood, the girl sent away to convent school in England, the child

· 193 ·

abandoned by her much loved father in favour of her brother, much preferred, and sitting on the train the man who flashed at her so she crossed herself, and the more she crossed herself the more he flashed at her. *Vanessa's unhappy childhood*. It was a saying of Tom's. And Vanessa listened and smiled and believed what he said and yet didn't believe it at all, because she knew nothing of Freud, of theories of child development, of the formation of the id and its primitive impulses towards sex and love and hate and incest and death and murder, nor the formation of the ego, sad and strong – or not so strong – on top of it, and knowing none of these things she believed that her childhood, with all its money and privileges, must have been about as happy as you could imagine.

But time was looped and as she moved on through life she found her childhood in front of her as well as behind, her memories growing stronger not weaker every day; soft, marshy memories whose softness was spreading outwards to rot the experiences which lay around them, so that she was thinking more and more about her childhood, her life before Tom, her father and her mother, and inclining more and more to sadness. And yet at the same time not understanding any of this at all.

She was leaving behind her youth. She no longer carried around with her that sense of her own softness, the soft image glimpsed in the mirror as she went past, the softness in which she had for so long taken a narcissistic pleasure and by which she had made friends out of women and lovers out of men. She had run a home and a business for many years, and laid down the law, had said, 'Do this and that and the other,' and now she felt herself growing old and lonely although she lived in the very heart of a family, felt the sex drive fading, felt herself growing into a thing, an entity, even an old lady, felt a hard shell growing all over her, felt the dust settling so that nothing was left.

And things didn't seem to happen to her as they had once

done. Events took place elsewhere and friends were harder to make.

What had she once been? A half-Italian convent girl, for years remembering the teachings of the nuns, doing good with the eyes of God upon you. She had carried food into her elderly and bedridden neighbours, she had had her old nanny to stay, she had taken in girls from poor and troubled homes. But as she came into middle age she felt the spirit grown strong enough to stand alone and after that she became kind in the amoral manner of her privileged class, which is to say that, like them, she was kind to her friends, very kind indeed, and she was kind when the inclination took her, which was still very often, because it felt good to be kind and because she was by nature generous. But she no longer felt any obligation to be kind; it had become in the end only an inclination which led her thereto, and as she grew older again she noticed that this inclination came to her so much less often.

She had once thought it was kindness which gave glitter and glamour to life, and she couldn't bear life to be dusty; she was afraid of this above all else. But now the thought came to her as she sat here on the beach that cruelty might have the same effect of glamour as kindness, and this made her think again of the girl who was like herself, as she felt herself becoming, neither kind nor unkind but so altogether bold and strong that there was not much room inside her for any other quality. And Vanessa settled back upon herself, between her hunched shoulders, and looked at the girl from a great distance and gave to her her admiring look, which was a look which glittered upwards from beween her narrowed eyes and from underneath her brows. And then she thought that this girl could only breed more energy and intelligence into a family already well endowed with it. But you can never have enough, thought Vanessa, who had all sorts of theories to do with breeding and genetics about which she rarely talked. You can never have enough.

· 195 ·

The girl was turning the pages of *Harper's and Queen* and showing the dresses to Noah and Vanessa. She was growing very cheerful. She was warming up no end, and the more cheerful she became the more she played with words. 'Hey, mister,' she was saying to Jonathan, and to Noah she sang out, 'Oh, no, no, No-ah.' The years were dropping away from her so that she no longer seemed, as she often did, so much older than her age. She was thirty. She was twenty-five. She was twenty-one. She was eighteen. 'I like this one,' she was saying. 'This one's not so good. Oh, very beautiful,' she was agreeing. And she was talking also about one of the women with whom she worked, and how hopelessly inefficient she was, and at the same time she was laughing and complaining to Vanessa about herself, because it was all she could do not to shout at this woman, and Vanessa recognised that helpless, regretful sense of one's own power – because other people were so *weak* – and was liking the girl all the more for it. She said she didn't care for the company of women but nonetheless Vanessa knew the girl had a great capacity for female friendship, that she could make ties and links of warmth to the women she admired, for she had that strong, curious, enviable quality of seeming always a desirable friend to have.

It was important that your child should marry the right person. It was something you hoped and prayed for, for your own sake and for that of your child and for all those who came afterwards. Vanessa thought a great deal these days about her grandchildren, those hypothetical and not-yet-existing children. She looked forward to being a grandmother and especially to Noah's offspring, whom she was sure would be like him, with his stubbornness and his energy; and she envisaged them as chips, as sparks in the bright sky above her. And she was sure she would feel towards them only delight and not the anxiety and fear she had felt for her own children, for there is no relationship –

Vanessa knew it – more torn, troubled and traumatic than that of a mother for her child.

The girl had organised a picnic for them, had packed it and brought it all the way from London. Now she got to her feet and roused up Noah and made him help her lay out the blue-and-white tablecloth in the shelter of the windbreak where the sunlight accumulated like weak, warm water on the white shingle. The Oaklands gathered round and stretched out their feet in poses of languor and carelessness. There was Vanessa sitting amongst them with her shoulders hunched forward, glittering gently. And there was the red-haired Jonathan with his chin thrown back and his lips apart, gazing blindly forward as the girl told a joke which was making him laugh. And there was the girl with her face turned away in profile, pouring with her left hand a glass of wine for Vanessa, both blindly and assuredly, whilst Vanessa was holding forth to the table at large in her soft, amused voice. 'Oh, Barry,' she was saying, 'it's his profile, it's so pretty.' And she was standing up into the wind to illustrate his profile and how he stood, for Vanessa wouldn't give up her power so easily, and this was all striking the Oakland men as very funny.

But even as she talked Vanessa was observing subliminally the white wine pouring and was thinking, how lovely this is, and Noah, sitting a little apart, felt his mother's thought and felt relief undo his limbs and make him weak because after all his mother liked the girl, so that he reached out an arm in the golden sunlight and put it on Aaron's arm in a gesture uncharacteristic of love. And down at the water's edge the English family still playing saw this other family ducked down behind the windbreak, saw the wind and light rushing above them and fancied as they watched that this vivid family had been caught up and rendered speechless by the din of light.

· 36 ·

The night before they went away Mattie had come home late through the garden. She passed the stone bust of the lady who stared straight ahead, her broad, low forehead crowned with a circlet of flowers, her eyes wide set and benign, her nose bashed in long ago in antiquity. She saw the house ahead of her. Its lights were on and it seemed to be floating through the night with brightness at every window, like a hugely expensive, festive ship. She went in through the back door and through into the hall and found the confusion of bags all packed and ready to leave, although she hadn't even known that they were going. She heard the radio talking to itself in Aaron's bedroom. She heard Jonathan talking to the cat on the landing above. She peered short-sightedly round the dining room door and saw Vanessa on the phone talking to one of her friends. There were the sounds of jazz coming from the kitchen. There was the fullness of Vanessa's figure reclining on the couch, and her, Mattie's own pleasure in it, but it shimmered beyond her reach like a mother's; and away in the kitchen there was Tom with his broad, hard shoulders, half turned away from her, unseeing, like a father. And then Vanessa put the phone down and Mattie felt herself pressed up against the dining room wall, felt herself observing, her mind stupid and her mind's eye stretched wide open in astonishment, the look of a small child who feels she's been reproved. Confusion made her stupid, it always did; the Oaklands were never stupid.

And Vanessa came across and asked Mattie to water the plants just as if she had always been the lodger.

HISTORY LESSONS

· 37 ·

The lane climbed out of the village. It was a white, chalky road which ran between high banks and grey hedgerows, up past the gravel pit and up onto the high fields where the hedgerows fell away and the fields had a stony look about them, the sky a desolate white. Soon it became the back road, the country road which bent its way towards the smaller hamlet of Arksley Cross. Seagulls mewed above her. The sun shone in an effulgent haze, the same old sun, her mother's god, who had wheeled around the house as if he would never set. His rays were visible. They were long and straight. They resembled the petals of a daisy. Below them the sky was grey as if the past was raining downwards through the present, soaking these stony fields.

And yet the air was dry. It had a grey, subdued feeling on her skin. In London it was raining, in London it never stopped. Rain had streamed down the window panes for weeks, cars rushing past at the front, their tyres squishing softly and all their headlamps on. The water in the canal was high – sometimes she noticed it as she sat on the bed, rouging her nipples and painting her toenails – the canal boats floating level with the towpath, the water seeping up through the grass on the lawn and the air so full with water you might have thought that very soon it would rise so far they would all of them be drowned.

The light in the house was copper-green. The mirrors were spotted with silver. When she peered at her reflection

· 201 ·

she thought she had a drowned look. She watched herself as she searched through Vanessa's bed, looking for her heavy necklaces and her satiny underwear. No, really she was delectable, she was absolutely paintable, she was utterly to be desired. It was remarkable how Noah could be so late. It was one o'clock, it was two o'clock, and still he hadn't come.

She was her mother's daughter after all, that's what the mirror said; the same tall figure, the same straight nose, the same drooping mouth, the muscles on either side grown hard as granite, giving her an old-young look, old before she'd finished being young. Her mother had been the same. She'd dressed like a child, had always done so, in thin, cheap clothes, her possessions carried everywhere in a carrier bag. Her mother's childlike-ness was terrible.

Down in town the rainy trees would be blowing. It was amazing how many different things she had remembered that morning: a weedy, rainy garden, and a bed with three legs and broken springs, and packing cases to act as tables which Mattie the child drew upon with her box of chalks, and a man's voice on the radio raised up in sad ecstasy as he sang church music, and a dusty window pane through which she waved at a man whom she never saw again. It was two thirty and still Noah hadn't come. Quite soon she would get up and dress herself and take a bus down to Woburn Place and walk those streets where her mother had once walked.

Her mother hadn't always been a nutter. There had been a mother-before-madness and she hadn't lived in Essex at all but had lived in London, a young woman, a very young woman, no older than Mattie was now, a communist who had lived in London and who had attended concerts in the Wigmore Hall and who had walked down Charing Cross Road when London was still leafy, a London of cheap rents and bombsites and demonstrations and the Left Book Club; and her mother, whose mind was not yet but soon to be

· 202 ·

unhinged, soon to bang and flap fiercely like a barn door in the wind.

How wet it was. Wet clouds blowing between red-brick buildings and rainy green trees. All Saints, Margaret Street as black as thunder. Shining roads and buses skating round them and the wind buffeting against them. 'Nice Lulu's,' said a sign. A shop which sold furniture, chairs, sofas, carpets, all arranged prettily like the interiors of so many houses. Perhaps she would lay herself down out of the rain on one of nice Lulu's sofas? She had a weakness for motherly women. In a café whose windows were steaming, there was the smell of wet wool and a middle-aged woman sitting opposite, dressed in blue, her hair starting to grey, a pleasant face. Her eyes rested on Mattie, thinking of something else.

First she loved you and saw you and then she went blind and never saw you again.

Mattie was looking for her mother. These expeditions were a great comfort to her although she noticed the comfort was curiously shortlived, vanishing as soon as she left these streets and only returning when she went back again.

Noah had moved out of the house. It seemed she'd hardly noticed. He was living in a flat just round the corner. Today he was late but very cheerful. So what was wrong with him? Afterwards he went to look out of the window. Beyond him she could see the canal boats bobbing on the water. He was doing up his tie. 'Sometimes you look like your mother,' he said. Casually. As if it wasn't important. 'How do you know?' 'Oh, I remember her from when I was little' – not ceasing from his tying – 'she used to come to the house. She brought you in a carrycot. You were a baby.' To think that her mother had been in this house. To think that this cousin of hers had seen her when she was tiny. 'You never told me,' she said accusingly. How Oaklandish it was.

Sometimes she was afraid he might be a dandy and an adventurer, that he might take women in the way she had once read that the Elizabethan explorers took countries, no

· 203 ·

sooner seizing one than moving on to the next, yet always coming back to confirm that their first prizes were content and unrebellious and well governed in their absences. Liberal, lordly, high-handed and unexplaining. I hate him, thought Mattie, staring at his back and his bum and his thin legs, and yet his was a sweet and reconciling prick and when he put his fingers between her legs his fingers were made of honey.

He had put his prick inside her and stirred up all the past.

Her mother had taken up with a new lover. He had brought her here to these fields and now each time he came to visit he took something more from her, stripping her of her worldliness, her humour, her humanity, stripping her of her flesh and stripping her down to the bone. He came to her in flames and these flames burnt away her tie with the world, turning the earth to flames so that she walked three inches above it. They burnt away the love that linked her to her daughter. They burnt away her sense of time so that the years no longer unfolded. And yet she had grown unaccountably old and so terribly spiritual she would no more oppose her fate than an Indian would his caste. And when nothing else was left and they had burnt her to a frazzle then her mother was a twig, a stone, a lump of wood, and that was that, it was time to die.

The nuns came to take her mother away. They came at noon when the sun was at his highest and his whitest, wheeling round the house as if he would never set. Mattie with her remembering eye saw the small face watching from an upper window, saw the nuns' bright blue eyes and their white, floury faces lifted to observe her. They had been here before. There had been nuns for as long as Mattie could remember, their shoes stout, their habits black. They travelled in pairs, like birds. Her mother was in the bedroom mixing paints. She didn't seem afraid. Mattie thought her mother and the sun and the nuns were in collusion.

They came from the nunnery, which was a secret place on the far side of Oxley Woods. 'Why did we come to Dunmow End?' asked Mattie one day, for ideas like this floated past her in the air and she seized hold of them but then she let them go again. 'Perhaps God was here,' said her mother. They were walking to church on a Sunday morning. 'You mean in the nunnery?' said Mattie. 'What do nuns do all day?' 'They pray,' said her mother, 'and the prayers go up to heaven. But where there is so much goodness there is also the devil.' 'God or the devil?' asked Mattie. 'God and the devil,' said her mother. 'Good and evil. Opposites. They're always attracted to each other.' And Mattie drew the cosmic battle in her exercise book, angels and demons fighting over Oxley Woods and her mother partaking.

Her mother and the nuns sat talking in the living room. Mattie listened at the door. The nuns were sent by God to take her mother away. Her mother yearned to God. She wouldn't care if she left her daughter behind. When the nuns got up to go Mattie was sitting in the kitchen. She heard them carrying out her mother's spirit, although they left behind the body.

Slender ankles; suede culottes of a cloisonné blue which had once fitted Vanessa; a scarf around her neck patterned in blues and greens, like a butterfly's wing. These Oakland colours had filled the house in London but here they would bleach and fade until they became the merest scratch under this white sky. Down poured the rays of the sun, the past raining downwards through the present, soaking these stony fields.

There had been a man once, alighting at the station before they closed the line, a heavy-set and stooping man, a tanned

· 205 ·

face, a long streak of silvered hair curving like a wing. He couldn't walk; they had had to catch a taxi, old Joe the taxi man driving them back to the house. 'How very remote it is,' the man had said. 'We have to live somewhere,' Mattie's mother had said, mildly. Mattie had thought he must be God but afterwards she thought, no, perhaps he was my father. That evening she sat in the green wooden lean-to up against the house, the chipped enamel bath within, the smell of mouldering earth. 'What's his name?' she called out and her mother called back, 'Cecil.' But what could she tell from that?

And not long afterwards there came the yellow winter sun, the same colour as the ice the boys made when they peed upon the frozen ground the day before the night the nunnery burnt down and the fire engines from Colchester came racing through the village. The red flames shot out of the upper windows. The black birds flew off into the night. 'Where's the fire, mum, where's the fire?' asked Mattie, hopping up and down to make herself warm the night was so frosty, but her mother was counting stars. 'You'd think the earth was too cold to burn,' she said in such a way that Mattie knew the fire was bound to be celestial. That was what it was like, the past and present everywhere mingled together, lying up against each other as close as she and Noah.

And then she turned a corner and there it was, standing so real and solid and immediate with its pockmarked walls, its peeling windows, the tangle of grey and drying brush which filled the front garden nearly to the bedroom windows, looking so altogether real in the white sunshine she was stunned.

She went in by the back door. On the kitchen table were the remains of breakfast: a slice of unbuttered toast; a half-drunk cup of tea; a carton of milk; an open butter packet, the butter streaked with crumbs of toast and jam. Mattie stopped briefly to consider what an Oakland breakfast would look like in all its expensive litteredness. 'Mum,' she shouted, going from room to room. She felt the imprint of her mother, the suggestion of a mother's absence where a mother's presence ought to be. The toast was still warm on the table. The ancient record player was going round and round. She bent her neck short-sightedly and saw it was the Matthew Passion.

She went upstairs to the big upper room which her mother used for painting. She looked at the canvasses stacked up against the wall. Three canvasses in she stopped and blenched for there was her mother, riven down the middle from top to toe and a tree springing out of her corpse in which two angels danced in all their goodness and juggled balls triumphantly. 'Great,' said Mattie and turned her face away.

She went out into the garden. Whiteness was drifting slowly downwards to shroud the garden and give to it the look of a picture dimly printed on grey silk. There was a patina of greyness over the withered and tarnished lawn which stretched as far as the beds of turned-over earth and beyond them a veil of greyness over the rank, wild undergrowth which filled the further reaches of the garden and swamped the apple trees – grass and nettles and cow parsley and thistles, both dead and dying, veering this way and that – 'Like a Japanese print,' said Mattie sadly, 'no colour anywhere.'

Out in the fields earth and sky seemed hugely stretched from end to end and her eyes, if opened wide, could encompass, just, the fields and copses and the river plain and in some far-off field sloping down towards the road a herd of brindled cows, brown and white and very tiny from this great distance, cropping at some purple-flowering bush.

She took the path across the field. Twice she thought, she hoped, she feared she saw her mother; and once she was kneeling on the ground, an old woman – if she grew much older she would wither up and die – and once she was floating away in the sky as light and unencumbered as a Byzantine saint. But each time as she came closer Mattie saw she was mistaken. When she reached the further side of the field she turned back. Her mother was out there somewhere communing with her God. She had simply forgotten her daughter was coming.

She stood beside the garden in her fine Oakland clothing, in her cashmere sweater, her wonderful culottes, her soft suede boots, presents for her mother in her hands, and then she put these presents down on the ground and turned round and hurried back towards the village and the common. Here she stopped in momentary confusion. The big trees beside the common were flying their leaves like flags. Orangy sunlight lay upon the vivid green grass. Little boys dressed in white like angels were playing a late game of football upon the men's football pitch. It was not the Dunmow End that she remembered. Her Dunmow End had stretched one hundred miles from rim to rim and a hue of blackness had underlain its colours. But here it seemed that the past, that naked, rootless, penniless, spiritual past – it had passed in another country.

It was all our mothers' faults. They never loved us. Otherwise why else would they have died?

· 38 ·

That afternoon the girl came to tea again. Vanessa was sitting in the conservatory surrounded by smoked salmon sandwiches and musing on the girl's past when she heard the front door go and the girl's clear and bell-like voice in the front hall. Slowly and reluctantly she got to her feet. She was not yet ready, quite, to surrender all her power. And yet she felt acquiescent, pleasantly so, because it is always pleasant to let go. She went out into the hall and had a glimpse of the two of them before they saw her and in that glimpse she was now quite sure they were sleeping together. And in her stockinged feet, with her shoulders hunched, her enigmatic smile, a chocolate in one hand and her curious, diffident manner so that you might have thought she was approaching you sideways on, although of course she wasn't, she went to meet the girl whom she was sure was going to be her daughter.

The train carried Mattie back to London. She was filled with a sharp longing for the black city and its bright lights, for the beautiful materialism of the Oaklands, for that layered house so full of possessions, the pigments in their jars along the shelves, the colours for which they were so famous. The countryside was cold but the city was warm and comforting and the train was carrying her back to the wonderful world of things. For the Oaklands still had the power to comfort her, they being so worldly, so wonderfully worldly they were busy encumbering their souls as if there was no here-

· 209 ·

after. And whereas her mother by her airy godliness would float away and abandon her, the Oaklands would surround her with material possessions and so would weigh her down.

Mattie made plans. She realised now that Vanessa had grown remote, that she had become chilly, ever so slightly chilly (although when she thought of that gentle, pearly glow she thought, no, not chilly, but just as if she'd moved a step or two away, as if she were now standing on the other side of the room). And she realised also that she'd been wrong to let the situation drag on, that she should have spoken out to Vanessa earlier, should have said, look, I love you and I love your son, and it's not stealing, I'm giving, giving and I want you to accept.

She climbed into a taxi at Liverpool Street station. A thought came to her and she was filled with mortification. She remembered her mother's mortification of long ago, a Christian mortification, but hers now was a pagan remorse and she wished she had brought the Oaklands presents; she had never bought them presents before, how they would love presents of wonderful things.

She got out of the taxi outside the house. She went in by the front door, up the flight of steps, and came upon them as they all stood in the hallway saying their goodbyes. She stood on the threshold and when she saw the girl she felt astonishment, felt that there must have been some mistake, that perhaps it was her fault, that she had conjured up the girl by witchcraft because she had been thinking too much about her past, that she had somehow caught up the girl on the fringes of her jacket and carried her back from the dark lanes of Dunmow End to the bright city lights. She felt the coldness of the past lying on those country lanes, the frosty winter and the huntsmen dressed up like soldiers and the horses and their legs which were enormously long and that house with its shutters and the darkness which came down at four and the mother who inclined to fascism. For of course it was Miranda Berens.

And then as she recognised, she feared she saw recognition in Miranda's eyes. At that her childhood rose up around her like a stink, and the memory of the times they had met; and ashamed of her childhood's poverty and madnesses, Mattie thought, if she asks me where we've met before I shall deny it.

Noah and the girl were holding hands. The girl looked at her unsmilingly. She only smiled when she wanted to. But between Noah and Vanessa, those red-haired-charming-Oakland-thieves, Mattie saw a look of dawning, complicit-ous pity which they were too careless to disguise. 'Oh, it's Mattie,' cried Vanessa falsely and she crumbled away and shrank before Mattie's gaze, although even as she did Mattie saw a small piece of defiance start up inside the other woman proudly, saying, 'Don't blame me – ' because she did so hate to be blamed. And Noah said, 'Hallo, Mattie,' in his soft, nasal, cockney voice. He had come creeping into the house from the flat just round the corner, his footsteps stealthy as a burglar's on the stairs. He had been stealing and he knew it, but is it theft when these things are given to you upon a plate? And Mattie felt her nature turn over inside herself, flipping over, so that she was from this minute forth, she decided, no longer the soft, admiring, tender Mattie but something harder, more angry and obsessed. And she saw with absolute clarity the picture of Noah coming to her that night, just as soon as he was able, to put his prick inside her and make her feel better – for of course the Oaklands do not like to think of anything unpleasant – and Vanessa being kind to her, stroking her in the way that Jonathan stroked the black cat when the black cat was in a mood, with hard and rhythmic strokes until the cat began an angry purr.

· 39 ·

Barry Shawcross took a short cut through the fruit market near Camden Town. It was a cool, grey, dry evening. The lights were coming on, the market traders packing up to go home, the big trees dissolving into the twilight. Young girls walked past him in pairs. He walked slowly so that he could observe everything, savour everything that he saw. The evening was rolling over, turning in its mind to bed. The girls didn't look at him but tonight he didn't mind because for some reason he was very happy. Tonight he felt it was so gloriously sad to be himself, an observer, to feel himself such a tall, sad, romantic figure from a novel; really sometimes he could cry with pleasurable sadness for the romanticness of it all.

In his pocket he carried like a talisman an invitation to the next Oakland party. The Oaklands were the best party givers that he knew. They were always the same, these parties in the factory, the floor like golden water, the young men so louche, the guests swimming about, the staircase made of glass ascending into the dazzle of summer twilight, Vanessa sitting halfway up, so very virtuous, the provider of all this light, dressed in black velvet with a white fichu shawl around her shoulders. They were the only people he knew to lay on parties where the guests still danced on the tables and threw wine glasses at the walls. And at the very thought of their parties happiness washed sweetly up against the inside of his throat. He thought they had this talent for lapping up around him, for taking away his heaviness and sending him bobbing away.

He stopped and looked in through the window of a tapas bar. There sitting by herself sideways on beside the window he saw Vanessa's cousin Mattie. She had changed. She was so hugely pregnant now you could have rested a cup of coffee on her stomach. She was holding one hand beneath it as if to hold it up, her head drooping over it, prescribing a curve so she looked like a crushed flower. When he saw her sitting there looking so grey and weary a feeling of desolation crept into his happiness. He had noticed this before, that the sight of pregnant women didn't make him happy. It was as if there were so little feminine love to come his way that the arrival of every baby must diminish it even further. But still he was honourable and he pitied her. He shook his head to clear it of the desolation and then he stepped inside.

When she saw him her face lit up. Need jumped straight out of her. It never jumped out of Vanessa. 'So when's it due?' he asked, sitting down before her. 'Any day now.' 'Ah. Is it a boy or a girl, do you know?' 'Twins,' she said but when she saw his face she added, 'no, don't be silly, of course it's not. You don't have any children, do you?' 'No,' he said. Clever you, said her face, despairingly, and for the first time he wondered who the father was. He thought it was curious that he hadn't wondered this before. But presumably she had numerous boyfriends and one of them would be it.

'And I'm an only child,' he said easily, 'so you could say I don't know a great deal about babies,' (telling her he wanted only the easiest of godfatherly roles). 'Children are good for people,' said Mattie bleakly but he called out inside himself, I don't want that, I don't want to be done good to, my life which is so late has hardly yet begun.

He stared at her hand round the coffee cup, thought how grey and plain she had become, but full of the largeness, the largesse, the milky sadness of pregnancy for her face was blurred, her eyes distant, her body swaddled round with flesh but also with this resigned, inturned, obedient sadness; although why pregnancy should be so sad he didn't know. Pity overcame him and he smiled bravely through it although he found the feeling so uncomfortable. 'Pregnancy is very sad,' said Mattie suddenly and he jumped because it was startling to hear this observation out of her own mouth. He thought she didn't look like an Oakland any more. Once he had thought of her as very definitely an Oakland. But now for the first time he felt his happiness growing a hard shell over it which was the realisation that he preferred riches to poverty and invincibility to sadness. It was to be regretted but there you were; it was the way things were and that was that.

'Will I see you at your cousins' tonight?' he asked. 'No,' she said. 'I'm sure it will be beautiful like its mother,' he said, looking at her stomach, and her face lit up with pleasure at the compliment. But he slipped away, out through the door and, turning right, set off towards the Oaklands'.

He knocked at their door with his usual sense of delightful anticipation. Jonathan Oakland opened it and a rush of light came bursting out to meet him. The others came swanning across the hallway. They were bringing him drinks and bonhomie and stories and by the way they swarmed all over him, taking his coat and Jonathan telling him that they had decided he must be working for MI6 for what else but this could explain his cloak of extreme conventionality – 'Yes, yes,' he said, smiling with embarrassment – he knew he was more in favour now than he had ever been before.

· 40 ·

She had left Dr H. She sat in the tapas bar, drinking coffee and thinking of what she had done. For many months now she had been in a state of warmth and weakness and floating, had felt a sensation of being peeled back so that the tender, vulnerable parts were exposed. He had given her back her past – she had been a person again with a past, a present and a future – and she had felt it like a gale blowing inside her, felt herself laid bare and open for all the world to see, and blue and pink and raw and softened, but linked now to other people, even to strangers in the street, by weak, warm charges of electricity, because now she was one with them, so that she wept when she heard of murdered children and wept with relief when she heard of husbands and fathers returned from danger to their families. She had fallen in love with Dr H because he was a dismantler of her personality, a builder-up-again-of-it in a less twisted and neurotic way. And for many months now she had thought how sweet it all was, how very sweet he and she and it was altogether, and how very much she would like to retire, both she and her sadness, to some warm and windless place. My dear sadness, thought Mattie, my dear, dear sadness, where was it all to end?

But as July turned into August and she was thirty-seven, thirty-eight, thirty-nine weeks pregnant, she began to feel that Dr H had started to pass the peak of her admiration for him and had begun to slide out of grace.

Sometimes he seemed to Mattie to be a sternly old-fashioned therapist. Their relationship progressed by fits and starts. Mattie saw a book upon his shelves entitled *The Neurotic Personality* and bought a copy and took it home to read it, but what the author said both angered and alarmed her, for he spoke in weary terms of the endless difficulties of dealing with neurotics, of their insecurities and unlovedness, of their pride and ambition, of their self-hate and self-contempt. And Mattie saw that Dr H had an image in his mind of the neurotic person, and feared that it was she.

She had hoped that they might be friends. She had thought that he might become a man of wisdom in her life, but in the event he kept his distance from her, refusing to answer her questions about his personal life, parrying them and turning them back upon herself. And although this distance was a part of his professionalism Mattie took it for hostility and thought it meant he didn't like her. She would have liked to discuss all kinds of things with him. She used to say to him violently, 'You blame me too much when you should blame the world. Of course I'm depressed when everything around me is so horrible.' Thus she hoped to provoke him because he made her angry, but also to provoke him into a discussion, because quite genuinely she thought this was true, that he – like all therapists – blamed the patient too much when they ought to blame the world. But Dr H was refusing to be drawn. He fingered this statement of hers from every angle, his eyes quite black with thought, said at last like the therapist he was, 'I do not feel that blame is a very constructive way of looking at the world.' And Mattie was disappointed. She felt that his therapist's training came between them.

And she thought that Dr H exaggerated her neuroses, that he had no sense of humour, that he made no allowances for Mattie to exaggerate, to use words sometimes out of sheer, sad, sensationalist pleasure in their meanings. Mattie felt that Dr H tried to fit her into an already existing scheme. Above all, she felt that Dr H did not like her, that he saw her only as another unlovable neurotic. 'You don't even like me,' she wanted to cry out but even in this she was handicapped by the fear that her request was neurotic. And yet how could she sit here and tell Dr H all her innermost fears if she didn't believe the therapist even cared for her?

Mattie felt that the past was her own and no one else's and that like all pasts, even the most terrible, it had a certain beauty about it which arose from the fact that it was vanished and gone, although where it had gone Mattie didn't know. Sometimes she thought it still existed at the end of that railway line but at other times she knew it was gone for ever. And she thought it was a beautiful thing, this past of hers, because it was the only one she had, she could have no other; and she was handing it over to the therapist, and he was an ungrateful therapist for taking it so stolidly in both his hands and looking at it from every angle and so signally misunderstanding it.

For she had assumed he was cleverer than he was, and the discovery that, relatively speaking, he was really quite dim (relative, that is, to the cleverness which previously she had ascribed to him) had hugely disappointed her. One day she remarked to him airily – for she liked to think she was getting rather bored with all this talk about her childhood – 'Oh, it really wasn't all that bad. My childhood, I mean. My mother was very gentle. At least she never shouted at me.' Dr H's eyes were round and hard. 'Perhaps someone else did,' he said. 'Did what?' 'Shouted at you?' 'No.' Mattie was surprised. 'I only thought,' he went on with his therapist's logic, 'that you mentioned shouting because someone in your childhood had shouted at you.' 'No,' said Mattie again, both humble and stroppy, and she stared at him.

And another time she said, 'I mean, what has my mother given me? Certainly no money. Nor even any good advice. And isn't that the whole point of parents, to tell us truthfully how the world works? Sometimes, when I go out to dinner with bankers, yuppies, city whizzkids, those kind of people' – she was thinking of Barry Shawcross – 'and they ask me, what do my parents do, I say, I am an orphan because it has a nice Victorian feel to it, but inside myself I cross my fingers, really I do, and say, sorry mother, because I have denied her.' 'So you want to deny your mother?' said Dr H. Mattie looked at him in surprise. 'No,' she said. 'That's exactly the point. I don't want to deny her. I do deny her but I don't want to. I would like to acknowledge her but how can I when she's mad so that there's nothing there I can get hold of?' And Mattie looked at Dr H in bafflement. She was disappointed. She had wanted Dr H to understand everything she felt, intuitively, before she even explained it. And a great deal more besides. But he, in his therapist's fashion, had seen only the wanting to deny, and not the wanting to acknowledge.

He had misunderstood the sincerity with which she said, so insincerely, 'Oh, well, I suppose there's a certain style to having such a tragic childhood.' She was afraid he was determined to strip away at her defences, to lay bare the inadequate personality lurking within, and it did not seem to Mattie that he meant this process kindly. There was too much triumph in the way in which he picked her up on the words she used and the tone in which she used them. Once she said, 'I was very innocent.' 'Ignorant,' said Dr H. 'What?' she said. 'Not innocent,' he said, 'ignorant.' Why does he do it? she thought. What's the point? Why shouldn't I have the luxury of believing myself innocent, which I was, instead of simply ignorant? Where does it get us if I think what a horrible, ignorant person I once was?

And he was a disbelieving therapist. He liked to lean back in his chair with the tips of his fingers laced together in a masculine kind of way, looking into her eyes. He solicited her explanations but he never believed them, preferring his own every time. She wanted to talk about her feelings for Vanessa but every time she began he tried to draw a connection between these and her feelings for her mother, as if the former were only a later, neurotic, distorted version of the latter. Only, only, only, thought Mattie. What an Only Man he is, a Reducing Man, and she thought she should never have started talking to him, that she had been deceived by her desire to tell someone, anyone, the story of her life.

· 41 ·

One day they had an entirely stupid argument about the word 'black'. Mattie said to him – and she was as always both sincere and sensationalist, both melancholy and melo-dramatic – 'Sometimes I'm afraid I'm going to end up like my mother, living in some beat-up house without two pennies to rub together. I have this picture in my mind – it must be something I remember from my childhood – of a wild and weedy garden through a window and the rain pouring down even though it is high summer, and there is a bed with broken springs and one side propped up with books, and these are my school books and I am saying to my mother that I need them back because otherwise the teacher will be angry with me. Sometimes I think to myself I must be a fraud and all this which came in between,' – and she waved with one hand to indicate her fashionable clothes and the therapist with his big Victorian house and the courtyard garden with its elegant fig tree which sprang forth from the paving stones – 'all this is just a temporary aberration.' (But still she felt a tremor of pleasure for all its elegance.)

'And sometimes,' she went on, 'I think I would like to talk to the Oaklands about all this. They are my family after all. But I'll tell you what I've discovered – that the Oaklands – none of the Oaklands are really interested in the past. Do you know, they have never once asked me about my childhood, or my mother or my father? It's as if I came to them fully formed, without a past at all. And whilst I know how hard it is to understand the feel and texture of someone else's childhood – and I have never met anyone who had a childhood like my own, so naked and rootless and penniless and spiritual – I do think that if only they would mention my mother's name even, I might yet come to terms with her. Because I haven't yet, not really, have I? And this is what I blame them for, more than anything else, because they saw me as little Mattie and never asked where I came from.

'I tell myself my mother lives the way she does because it makes her happy. It's what she's chosen. But of course I don't believe it. Did I tell you she used to try to kill herself every autumn? Before they put her on permanent medication? Now the drugs have blown her up so she looks like a balloon. When I think about my mother's life I picture it as black, completely black from end to end. It is terrible to have a tragic mother. I feel as if her sadness follows me everywhere, dooming me to blackness also, and the blackness of it all makes me feel terrible.'

Dr H looked up sharply. 'So why do you think of it as black?' he asked.

'Because it was so unhappy.'

'Yes, but why black? I don't understand why it seems to you to be black.'

'Because it was unhappy.'

'Yes, but why black?' he persisted.

Mattie went back to chewing her nails. How angry his obtuseness made her. Her mind flew up against his but his was hard and plain and he had no faith in the glittering surfaces of things. He always cast around for a deeper meaning and yet, she thought, he wasn't as clever as he liked to think, his mind not even redeemed by intelligence. At length she said, 'We don't talk much about my father, do we?' It was the first time the idea had occurred to her and she was interested despite herself. She thought Dr H looked interested also, hopeful almost, she thought; so she clamped her mouth tight shut to serve him right.

'I wanted him to like me,' said Mattie to Hester afterwards. 'In fact, I wanted him to love me. But he was stern and cold and he picked away at my personality as if it were an academic exercise. And yet he wasn't even clever. He didn't even get it right.'

'Love,' said Mattie to Dr H, 'that's the point. Who is it that we can rightfully expect to love us?' and she looked at Dr H to see if he had got her message. 'And blame,' she said, 'don't forget blame. Personally I blame Vanessa, and hold her responsible for everything that happened.' Dr H shook his head. 'Blame, blame,' he said, 'maybe we should get away from blame and look for truth instead.' And his black eyes settled on her broodingly. 'I don't agree,' said Mattie violently – her head was buzzing, the words sounded hollow in her ears – 'I don't agree. I think even before you get to the truth you need justice and how can you have justice until you apportion the blame?'

There was silence. 'But I don't know,' said Mattie, anger flowing, mouth smiling dangerously, eyes pert and bold and sad and brutal, 'I think you are a fraud, I mean you, Dr H, because you peddle the belief that by self-knowledge we will be saved, because that's the root of therapy, isn't it? And yet I know what I know, and I don't feel any better, I don't feel better at all.'

'I think you are confused,' was all the therapist replied. 'I was,' said Mattie, 'I was, but I am not any longer.'

· 42 ·

One morning she woke up and knew she didn't intend to go back to the therapist. She rang up Dr H's secretary and said that she was ill. That night she sat down and wrote a letter to him, saying she would not be attending any more sessions of his therapy. But Dr H was surprisingly persistent. On the morning he received her letter he rang her up three times. Mattie was out but Katherine the cleaning lady took the messages and Mattie came home to find them placed in a row upon the kitchen table. She snatched them up, went straight into the living room, dialled his number and lowering her voice – for the Oaklands had the sharpest of ears, and especially for gossip – she said straight out, 'Look, I won't be coming back.' 'I think we should talk about this in my office,' he said; for he wanted to see her one more time, wanted to say to her, look, this is the pattern of your life, first love, then anger, then rejection. But she didn't want to hear. 'No,' she said, and she added, 'listen, I don't want to.' Which was unarguable with. So that was that.

She went with Hester that afternoon to the Catholic church in Camden Town because she wanted to light a candle and to make a wish for herself and for her unborn baby and because she liked to feast her eyes on the painterly extravagance of its walls and ceilings and to marvel at the Immaculate Conception and at how very maculate her own conception had been.

She had been tired of Hester that day. She felt that Hester

was too old for her, because she wasn't old like Hester was, and Hester made her tired with her small, cramped, domestic, thirtyish considerations. Hester put ten pence in the prayer box. 'What are you wishing for, Hester?' asked Mattie, that eccentric Madonna. 'It's not a wish, it's a prayer,' said Hester, who gave away nothing. 'Same thing,' said Mattie. 'Same thing,' Hester agreed. 'What are *you* wishing for?' asked Hester. 'For love,' said Mattie, who gave away everything, and the church received her words in silence.

They sat down on a pew. Mattie was peering past her huge stomach as if still trying to see the past beyond it.

'How do you think Leonie got pregnant?' she asked.

'I don't know,' said Hester. 'The same way that everyone else does, I suppose. Some things are private. Not everyone is as indiscreet as you and me.'

'Don't you sometimes think how peculiar it is that the act itself is so small and the consequences so big?'

'All the time,' said Hester.

'So how did you come to get pregnant?' asked Mattie, and her voice was loud to shock the praying people.

'Exactly that. It was no big deal. It was nothing much at all. Not when you consider what's come out of it.'

'I made holes in my cap with a pair of scissors. Five holes. One. Two. Three. Four. Five. And then I waited for the middle of the month and wanted very hard for it to happen.'

'Wanting's got nothing to do with it.'

'And the sex was so sexy, Hester. That's adultery for you. Miranda wasn't sexy. Miranda was rich but she was never sexy.'

'Sez who?' said Hester. But Mattie went on regardless, 'No wonder I got pregnant the first month that I tried.'

'And sexiness's got nothing to do with it either. Orgasms don't make the sperm run any quicker.'

'How do you know?' said Mattie. 'I think they do. If sex is theft then adultery is even more so. Lovely, soft, sneaky theft when the flesh comes together. Why didn't you have an abortion, Hester?'

'I didn't want one.'

'Nor did I. But I thought you were a feminist. I didn't think you defined yourself by babies.'

Hester shrugged.

Mattie put her hands together. She looked as if she were praying.

'I didn't really make holes in my cap, Hester,' she said. 'That wasn't true. It was a mistake. It happened one afternoon last October. We were drinking whisky. Whisky always makes me brave, very brave. We got drunk together. When I looked at myself in the mirror I was so pretty and so healthy-looking and he was so thin and pale and little I thought I'd got it wrong and it was me who was so strong and him who was so weak. I wish I could feel like that for ever. He was so pretty I wanted to eat him up. I didn't think you could get pregnant through just one mistake.'

'Dear God, Mattie,' said Hester, and now she spoke so loudly Mattie thought she saw a praying person jump. 'Dear God, Mattie,' said Hester, 'don't you know anything?'

But Mattie was insulted by what she took to be Hester's criticism. They parted rather coolly by the tube station and Mattie went to the tapas bar and ordered herself as usual a cup of coffee. When she stood up to pay she felt a trickle running down her leg. She thought her bladder had given way. She pulled in her muscles tightly. The trickle didn't stop. She smiled with embarrassment. She said to herself, 'Yes, quite definitely, my bladder has stopped functioning.' She was like a character in a comedy whose trousers have fallen down. A look of dismay passed across her face. She even made a gesture as if to pull them up. 'But this is amazing,' she murmured aloud, and the man behind the bar looked up at her sharply; she smiled at him, vague, childlike, embarrassed, for the trickle was turning into a rush and now without doubt she knew her waters had broken.

· 225 ·

HESTER

· 43 ·

On my second night they brought the women in and my ward, which hitherto had been inhabited only by myself and my newborn baby, a strange and alien creature, was now filled with the shrill cries of newborn infants, by gowned figures moving beyond the curtains in the half-light, by the wheeling in of the beds and the drugged and plaintive voices of the women.

They had been brought down from the labour ward on the floor above. From the outside there was only one entrance to this ward, a tiny door like the postern of a castle which at night a sleepy-looking woman unlocked to usher us in. But after the babies were born they wheeled us down by means of internal lifts, along corridors where there was no true darkness even in the dead of night but rather a yellow half-light from dimly lit bulbs, and through the windows the city spread out below us – for this hospital was built on a hillside – and the yellow city sky was full of lights.

They were nights for UFOs.

The women woke me from a light and troubled sleep. They were complaining quietly. One of the voices seemed familiar. Some of the women knew each other already from an antenatal class. Two had given birth to babies with large heads. I heard them saying, 'His head was stuck. They had to use forceps. It was agony. They never told me it would hurt so much.' And yet all the while they were talking to their babies with soft and soothing murmurs. Even by day pain hung around us like a nimbus. It was all pain and pleasure in this maternity ward.

The first night I slept the sleep of the astonished or the dead. But when day came I got up and explored my surroundings. I found they consisted of four corridors arranged in a square with the rooms leading off. At one end was the nursery where during the day they taught us how to feed and change and clean our babies, and where at night nurses of quite extraordinary ferocity might take your baby but only until she cried, whereupon they gave her back at once. At another corner were the swing doors through which you could reach the lifts, and by means of these the rest of the building. But only in theory, for it was forbidden to go out of earshot of your baby. One day one of the women in my ward went downstairs to the cafeteria. Her baby began to cry and by the time she was found and brought back he was screaming lustily. They rebuked her roundly. I wanted to go outside and sit in the sunshine. I wanted to drink a cup of coffee in the patisserie opposite. But they told me they had no insurance to look after the baby if I left her and she was too young for me to take her with me. I was trapped. I thought I saw triumph in their eyes. They wanted me to undergo a rite of passage. They thought I was a baby but now I had a baby they were determined I would become a mother.

The nurses were brusque and unmotherly. Each morning they inspected our bodies. One morning a nurse marched in, tweaked each of my nipples hard, loudly pronounced, 'No milk,' and left as abruptly as she had come. All day long they pursued me with instructions. 'Bring your baby to the nursery, Mrs Croxthorpe. Have you topped and tailed your baby? When did you last feed her? Where are your slippers, Mrs Croxthorpe?' and so on. The women in my ward submitted to all this with a childlike docility – they had given up their bodies to the system nine months ago – but each morning I dressed myself in proper clothes and

· 228 ·

then the nurses frowned, for I was having trouble with my milk and they thought the baby would feed more readily from my breasts if I lay down quietly and submitted like a mother. The others were wearing nightgowns. Our silhouettes were still those of slow and heavy pregnancy.

The women in my ward cried a lot. It was the lack of sleep, the shock of having a baby, the milk which painfully engorged us, the babies – a remarkable number of them – who unnaturally, it seemed to us, fought our breasts with the flat of their hands. At night the nurses wheeled round the painkiller trolley. The woman in the bed next to me was weeping softly. They enquired if she would like a painkiller. 'No,' she said. 'Are you all right?' they asked. 'Yes,' she said. 'Then why are you crying?' they asked her, both loudly and nastily. Lack of sleep was making me hallucinatory. At night I dreamt they kept me here for ever, behind these hermetically sealed windows, breeding babies one after another. I was reminded of a cowshed where I had once seen cows munching hay to the sounds of Radio Two. It was a vision of my future as a cow and I found it both sweet and repugnant.

I disliked the days but liked the nights. My baby woke me every hour. Her cry was shrill. One cry set off another and soon the ward was filled with the plaintive wails of babies and the sounds of mothers stumbling out of bed. At night my baby lay in her plastic crib with her face turned towards the window as if she thought she were still on another planet. Her forehead was high and domed. She looked like a pretty Martian. Her hands were clasped together like a monk. When I picked her up I felt what I had never felt before, pity, quite distinct, who is first cousin to love, a trickle, hot and sweet, threading its way inside me. I sat with her on my lap and stared at her and dreamt my dreams of heroism, of saving and protecting her. I was overcome by the purity of my intentions towards her. I was a pale, thin Saint George looking for a dragon. And as I sat there on the second night I heard that familiar voice again, the brisk voices of the nurses and the voice sleepily responding, the thin wail of a newborn baby – very young – beside her, and realised it was Mattie.

I dreamt a great deal during those Martian nights. I dreamt that time, which previously had seemed to wamble, backwards and forwards and round and round, now moved more straightly, more inevitably towards its close; moved from the past to the future and bypassed the Oaklands altogether.

And I dreamt that Vanessa Oakland was a small, middle-aged woman dressed up in a suit, her reddish hair tied in a bun, the sensitive lines around her mouth and her manner which was proud, efficient, bourgeois, a businesswoman. She sat beside our beds, not looking at the babies but at us, and her eyes were despairing because we were so messy and emotional and this was how we had rewarded her for all her generosity; and I felt my story slip away, become a mere neurotic construct, a fabrication of my brain, a projection of my own, Hester's, motherless needs, a so-my-mother-never-loved-me wail of sorrow, a so-you-have-so-much-and-I-have-so-little wail against the universe. But through my distress I felt a stab of interest, of curiosity and pleasure because I realised that on Vanessa's fatness, her opulence, her large space in the universe, my entire story had been predicated.

I woke up. Through the yellow darkness I heard a baby cry, footsteps skating across the floor, a voice which whispered 'Hester?' and there stood Mattie with the baby in her arms – they had brought her in from another ward, her baby was twenty-four hours older than mine. 'Hester?' she whispered again, and she sat down smiling. For that one moment I loved her. 'Look at that sky,' she said. 'I can see a flying saucer.' 'Is Vanessa large or small?' I asked her, the dream still fresh in my mind, but she was busy examining her daughter's feet and she didn't even hear me.

For Mattie had undergone a curious transformation. I saw

· 230 ·

that at once and knew the same transformation had overtaken me. Her expression had lost all malice, all sharpness, all cynicism. Her cheeks were full, her eyes glowed, her mouth curved upwards in a perpetual smile, her head bent down towards the baby in an attitude of adoration. She sat like a mother, heavy and complacent, her feet four-square upon the ground, her legs parted a little to take the baby's weight, as if it were heavy with importance. She was crooning and smiling and stroking and laughing and touching the vulnerable parts where the skull bones were not yet knitted together. She smiled with lordly pleasure to see my baby – but then so did I at hers – because each of us was thinking the other's was nowhere near so beautiful, so exceptional as our own. She'd had a little girl after all, a tiny creature whom she called Stella, with a fuzz of blackish hair and a rosebud mouth. 'My daughter,' said Mattie, 'my daughter,' and I saw that she was marvelling at this love and how it replenished itself, the love spent only to renew itself once more; and we who hitherto had been capable of only the smallest and meanest of loves! 'Who does she look like?' I asked. 'Like my mother,' said Mattie and she drew back the blanket from her baby's face and said, 'Look, how sweet – those ears – the eyes – how lovely.'

And then another night I dreamt I had invented Mattie or she invented me, because we were after all only versions of each other, I of her and she of me, and Aaron Oakland was another, being all three of us motherless children. And I also dreamt a dream which I never afterwards discovered was real or not – for once the babies were born we did not discuss the past again for many years – but in that Martian night I saw Aaron Oakland go down to the water's edge in South-wold, where the waves burst and then receded and left behind a thin, transparent undertow to run across the shining pebbles. I saw him take a step into the water. A wave broke against his legs and soaked his trousers. The water was as cold as ice but it anaesthetised him pleasantly. The high wind blew out of the sky and blew straight down his throat, blowing the words straight back where they had come, and the water sparkled and tossed. He took another step and the shingle fell away and now he was in up to his waist. He was wearing a woollen sweater. He hadn't realised wool could be so heavy when it was wet.

Jonathan was the first to see him go. He saw the funny side of it, the broad shoulders and the head of curly red hair with the morning sun on it, the figure fully clothed wading into the sunlit sea. 'Oh look at Aaron,' he said, smiling at me and pointing, and the rest of them looked up and slow, stupid alarm registered on their faces for he was in up to his shoulders now, the head nothing but a black dot, appearing and disappearing in the heaving water. 'Aaron,' shouted Tom and he and Noah ran down to the water's edge. They went in after him but they weren't as heavily built as Aaron, they were smaller and slighter and they couldn't make head-way against the thundering surf. Twice Noah went under and came up gasping and spluttering. Vanessa stood on the beach. Her head was high, her eyes were sightless, her red dress flapped around her legs. The years which she had held at bay for all this time were gathering in her face. She was an old woman. She opened her mouth and let out a wail like a cat for her child.

But out to sea Aaron was thinking with astonishment that his mind would not let go, that it gasped and panicked and strove to keep afloat and yet the sparkling water was overwhelming him, the body searing with pain, the mind panicking and shouting, don't panic, don't panic, just try to keep afloat. But his clothes were heavy and his years were heavy and he felt the weight of all his learning, his Os and his As and his Oxford degree, and he felt himself cold as we were cold, and heavy with resentment as we were too, the weight of his passions pulling him down and the sparkling water filling our mouths.

On the beach people stopped and stared. They were drawn

· 232 ·

by Vanessa's screams. Two more men went in but they were half-hearted. They were frightened of the towering waves. They slipped and slid and clung on to each other. Up on the promenade a woman broke the glass on the emergency telephone. She rang first of all for the coastguards' helicopter which was sited on the beach at Aldeburgh fourteen miles distant, and then for the local lifeboat. A flare went up in the town and I who stood on the beach knew that they had launched the lifeboat from the river mouth. It came bouncing across the surface of the foaming waves. The helicopter overtook it, the pilot coming in low, the crew scanning the waves, looking for a body.

They found him at last. He had floated further down the coast with the tide than they had realised. They tried to winch him into the helicopter but the winch wouldn't hold so instead they pulled him into the boat and turned the boat to land. Tom and Noah were still in up to their waists. They were shouting to the boat, 'Is he still alive?' but the wind was blowing so hard they couldn't hear the answer. Two men brought him ashore. 'He's still alive,' they muttered to Vanessa but they didn't stop. They were rushing him across the sand to where the helicopter was landing.

They passed within yards of me and I saw the leg dangling down, the shoe come off, the foot swollen with water, all its angular lines of bone obliterated, the skin puffed and swollen to the softness of my baby's feet, for Aaron was my baby and my baby was myself and I am Hester-Mattie.

'Vanessa's coming today,' said Mattie to me in the hospital. 'I've just phoned her,' said Mattie in whom the love slops over in all directions; it is her best quality.

She told me about Dr H. 'I should never have started talking to him, Hester,' she said. 'I was deceived by my desire to tell someone, anyone, the story of my life.'

But I, Hester, listened and thought that there is no revelation that lasts, that truth comes and goes, peeks upwards out of the water, and then slides underneath again. And that mostly she fell out of love with him because he didn't love the Oaklands as he ought to have done. 'Look,' said Mattie, unfolding her baby's fingers one by one, 'like the petals of a flower. I'd like to read her palms but she won't undo her fingers. I want to know her future.'

There were other visitors: Henry, embarrassed and confused, sitting beside my bed, and Leonie and Lindie and Caroline and Barbara all come to see us, and Judith, our antenatal teacher, plump and distraught, picking up our babies with a distracted, professional interest for she was, after all, many years away from young motherhood. I had heard rumours on the grapevine that one of her children was sick. She brought intimations if we cared to see them of how sad it is to have a baby, to feel the heart drawn out of the chest, the centre removed, the mind bound like a serf to another creature's well-being, intimations of how badly the future would press down on us, of how very quickly we would grow sick with fear and anxiety for everything it might bring – death, disaster, tears, tragedy, theft, leukaemia – for our babies. We had no idea how the future would grind us down just as once the past had harried us. In our ignorance we knew nothing but the present moment drawing itself out, the baby lying in my arms and how innocently she drew the soul out of my body and left me without a centre.

That morning a joke came to me, the most enormous joke of all, and immediately I forgot it, but when I remembered it again it went like this: that although I do not know anyone who believes their mother loves them, so it is also true that amongst all those women on that ward there was not one who in her panic-struck, astonished way did not love her baby. And when I thought of this I laughed and laughed and laughed.